SEE-THROUGH

Moist after being spanked by the help, and at the additional prospect of being taken on the stairs, her sex allowed Frank to slide inside her effortlessly when he pushed forward.

'Harder, Frank. I want it hard.'

'Not yet,' he said. 'Not until you tell me why.'

'Bastard. Why I need to be fucked like this? Why I have to have this all the time and why one man is never enough? Mmm? You want to torture yourself with that, Frank?'

'To have me to yourself, you just have to take me and show me why I should be yours. Go on, Frank. Take me. I know you can. I've always known it was you. Knew it the first day I saw you.'

And the few remaining restraints and fears and doubts and inhibitions were gone. Looking down at that long and supple body – the legs splayed, stockings creased, one high heel dislodged, breasts swinging free, smudged mouth open, blonde hair fanned across the stairs, he thrust harder than he ever thought possible.

'That hard enough?' he said, breathless, angry, excited. 'Is this what the performance was for? So I could take you like a slut in a stairwell?'

SEE-THROUGH

Lindsay Gordon

This book is a work of fiction.
In real life, make sure you practise safe sex.

First published in 2001 by
Nexus
Thames Wharf Studios
Rainville Road
London W6 9HA

www.nexus-books.co.uk

Typeset by TW Typesetting, Plymouth, Devon

Printed and bound by Clays Ltd, St Ives PLC

ISBN 0 352 33656 0

For Hershey Simmons

Prologue

During the early 1970s, the US military invested vast sums of money into a secret military project dedicated to enhancing the extra-sensory perceptions (ESP or clairvoyance) of its service men and women. It was envisaged that these psychic capabilities, if cultivated, had enormous potential for the military. Locating downed aircraft, finding hostages, prisoners of war or missing soldiers, and spying inside military installations belonging to hostile foreign states were envisaged as its primary functions.

Individuals displaying psychic abilities, who were recruited and trained by the operation, were called remote viewers. It is claimed some viewers harnessed the ability to receive visual and emotional impressions from targets situated at either great distances or as far away as the next room.

One

As Lucretia walks into the bedroom, she is nervous. Afraid, too, but it is the exhilarating fright of the rollercoaster ride or cliff climb. With each step of her spike heels across the red rug, she is watched by two men. One of the men is dangerous and hides somewhere inside the room she enters. His name is Eldrin Crow. The second man sits in a leather chair, four floors down. His name is Frank and he watches her without the aid of a hidden camera. His eyes are closed.

Working undercover as a front-of-house concierge, in this exclusive apartment building in the west of the city, Frank nearly breaks from his remote viewing when the tension Lucretia experiences upstairs becomes almost unbearable inside him downstairs. Her inner life has become his inner reality.

Deepening his concentration, he returns his vision to the place that is between relaxation and sleep. Keeping his eyes closed, he fights off mental distraction. The desire to think and articulate an understanding is the death of any psychic, or remote viewing. He knows this; his experience as a remote viewer is considerable. His ability to receive multi-sensory visions from a distant location is among the best the military has ever produced. Frank continues to watch Lucretia and to share her feelings.

Fear is not the only emotion she experiences. Curiosity and a playful desire to wound is at work inside her, too. This ambiguity challenges and fascinates Frank, just as it preoccupies the other man inside the bedroom: the dark Crow who Frank is unable to see.

As Frank watches her move through the room, lit only by two bedside lamps with the red shades, his skin prickles in sympathy with her skin. A crackle of electricity runs up his spine. It makes him feel cold for a moment. The shudder is followed by a snap of static in his teeth. So much emotion it becomes physical in her and Frank – the target and the voyeur.

Further and further, she gives her long body to the bloodied half-light in that room. A place where everything looks back at her. Mirrors are fixed above the headboard of the bed, attached to all the walls and to the doors of the closet space. It is a large room and the curtains are never opened. In fact, through the power and clarity of his insight and intuition, Frank becomes certain this room is always sealed from natural light. Unusual things happen here. No one is supposed to look in.

To Lucretia and the dark man it is a sacred place – a place of ritual and worship and confirmation. To the others who are taken there it offers the intensity of pleasure found in any paradise. Only they never suspect these same joys will develop into the longings of those trapped in hell.

And in that room, the old, black soul of Crow becomes agitated. He waits for what Lucretia brings with her. Yes! This place is always full of expectation, too. And mixed with the excitement and hunger for whatever it is she is supposed to bring, is a jealousy that singes the air. In here, Frank knows she will feel fire.

But on this day – the first day of Frank's investigation – she has returned to the apartment building alone and not bearing a gift, because she knows she will be punished. Moments before Frank began the viewing, she had walked through the front door of the building and teetered to the elevator with her face veiled and lowered. She'd not even acknowledged Frank, the new concierge on the front desk. So had she tried hard enough to find what her dark man wanted? She would be asked this question. And she knows she did not try hard enough to bring him what he wanted because she wants to be punished; because there is no such thing as free will and a deeper part of her was determined to fail anyway.

Conflict is passion to them and their passion is something she thrives on.

Intrigued, Frank feels his objective distance threatened. He has been briefed by his superiors to stay away from her. To do nothing but observe her. But these feelings of hers arouse him. He is suddenly overwhelmed. In an instant, he wants her and he wants to punish her for wanting such things – such terrible things from men. The first hint of her desires again threatens to shake him from the viewing.

Now that she is in the bedroom, she stands at the foot of the bed and removes the black fur from around her shoulders. Milk-white flesh. Lightly freckled on the shoulder bone. Perfumed and soft. The hat stays on and her face continues to half-exist behind the veil. She has full lips, thickened by crimson gloss, a thin nose and dark eyes beneath unclipped brows. Are her eyes genuinely so black, Frank wonders, or is it the weak light in that room that makes them appear so? And could any woman's lashes be so long as to always give her eyes a suggestion of sadness and prettiness that is hypnotic? In the vision, he loses

4

himself in those eyes of hers by trying to fathom them out, when he knows the search for such fine detail is distracting. And as he does this he fails to see Crow make his move – her keeper, jailer, teacher, master and lover.

From where did he come? Until he appears from out of the shadows, most of what Frank senses of Crow is jealousy. But at least it is some preparation for the rage and passion that will follow. Lucretia is immediately thrust into discomfort when one of her wrists is seized and tugged behind her back. Mouth open, she gasps and then begins to breathe quickly. Marched across the rugs by this brute, she stumbles in her heels and pencil skirt. She tries to explain. But her cries are not entertained and she is cast down to the bed. Her free hand swipes out to break her fall but is snatched from the air and pulled to the small of her back, where it is decisively cuffed to the other gloved hand. Face first into the covers she falls. One shoe dislodges. The bracelet of her wristwatch snaps.

Uncomfortable in his seat, Frank feels compelled to remain within the vision. 'You must prepare for unpleasant insights,' the agency told him. 'You will witness an unconventional relationship between two traitors, two dangerous conspirators, a couple of degenerates and enemies of the state and its security. It's like nothing you've seen before. And we are counting on you to watch and to record your every impression before we go in.'

No sweat, he thought, during the short briefing. With his remote viewing he enjoys an 80 per cent success rate in finding downed aircraft. Bodies he has seen aplenty. Tortured statements of people in plane seats strewn through trees. Lives suddenly put out by collisions with mountains clouded in mist, or dives into deep seas, or emergency landings in jungles so thick the wreckage is covered after a week of rain and steam. But he has found the crash sites and then led others to recover the hands severed from arms, the feet without shoes and the pinky-white-yellow lumps that go inside ziplock bags. And in terrorist hideouts he has watched hostages with heads inside mail sacks awaiting a bullet from their captors, who, in turn, await their demands to be met or their lives to end when men in black jump suits drop down from nowhere, announced by a shower of glass. Deep beneath the desert sands, in concrete bunkers, he has also seen invisible weapons sprayed on visible targets who jerk and choke inside cells made from reinforced steel and glass. 'No sweat,' he told the agency, 'I have seen it all in vision and dream.'

But had he?

Knocked from her head, Lucretia's hat rolls across the bed and her blonde hair fans across the black sheets. Ruffling up her back, the bolero jacket reveals a white blouse. Crumpling over her thin waist and delicate spine, the blouse gives way to pure skin about to be lined pink with an evil stick. Broken or yanked to the end of its runner, the zipper of her skirt is opened next. Fisting the hem of the skirt, Crow then tugs it down her thighs. Her helpless body is lifted from the bed and then dropped down as the skirt is torn down her legs. The remaining shoe is pulled from its host. The patent high heel bounces on the floor, down there in the silent darkness beside the bed. Black and seamed, her stockings are long and glassy-sheer and imprinted with a tiny white script on the welt that grips her inner thighs. Dark and gauzy, her panties fit like tight shorts. Through them, her small bottom looks eerily pale, like a lily under cloudy water. It is these buttocks Crow wants to reach with the cruel rod.

Flashes of white pain strobe from her into Frank. Caned buttock-red and back-sore, her mouth bites the bedlinen and her lipstick smudges. As the ebony crop in the assailant's hand falls, Frank flinches. Horrified, he shifts in his chair to accommodate the swollen cock in his lap. Hating himself, he wants to shout 'Yes! Yes! Yes!' as she is caned. He wants that stick to keep on falling. There are tears in his eyes. Did he feel what Crow feels? Was he communing with Crow's madness? Or did Frank foresee his future undoing and despair in this beautiful woman's hands and want her beaten in advance? Was he already acknowledging the end of himself in that room, in the shape of a blonde executioner who wears spike heels and paints her lips as blood-red as his future wounds, and whose eyes are black enough to absorb his misery and then twinkle with glee? Frank shudders in the shackles of the vision and never allows himself to know.

Crow is so enraged, Frank fears he will harm Lucretia. And of him, Frank only catches impressions. He wears a black gown. Possibly made from silk with a red pattern of a Japanese dragon on the front. Or is it a rose with falling petals? His skin is pale, too, but rigid and corded with knots of muscle and bluey vein. Blond hair shakes across his face, when a moment before it was immaculately styled like the hair of the American air force officer who trained Frank in Groom Lake, Nevada. But, above all, with those spiky movements and dark apparel, Crow resembles a large spider, or a bat, falling upon its prey.

Kneeling beside her, Crow's gown falls open. Something long and thick and white sticks up between his thighs. Lucretia sees it and her mouth opens. Still clutching the crop, Crow speaks to her.

7

Frank cannot hear what is said, but receives her impression of how the punisher feels: although she is stripped white and striped red, it is he who suffers. And it is he who is contained and imprisoned in the luxurious dark of their apartment, not her.

Strung out? He must be a junkie, Frank guesses. She has failed to score. Expecting to medicate and now disappointed, he expresses his frustration with the crop and cock.

Smiling through her tears with her face turned away from him, a sigh of contentment escapes from between her smudgy lips. And Frank looks long at that half of a face no longer smoky behind a veil; it holds an expression he will not forget. But does his blind, groping and instant need for her prevent him from seeing the cruelty in that heavenly face before she presses it deeper into the bed, so it is hidden from both men. Was that a warning? Will he ever know before it's too late?

Why does she make Crow suffer, then? So she can be beaten when he is on edge, craving the nourishment she fails to bring? And why has she filled herself with the drug that was promised him? Yes! In the most vivid psi viewing Frank has ever experienced, he senses something moving through her arteries and veins – something foreign that is now being absorbed into the purple of her velvety insides.

There is no time for him to reason when *under* – that is, when viewing the target from a secondary location – because the thin wood is soon whipping through the air again and Lucretia's long body is jolting from its shock treatment. From her stomach come grunts. It feels like Crow is inside her and she is moaning at the end of his every thrust. Smarting but aroused, she writhes and twists her captive body in the silky sheets. Sliding her slippery legs against

him and clenching her painted toes, she is lost to a
pleasure that thrills but also sickens Frank. The scene
inside his head dims and then flashes to a white-out,
like the power between them has become irregular
and threatens to short. This, too, he has never
experienced before, and Frank is struck by a fear he
can smell rising from his damp armpits. Being so
attuned to them could fuck his subconscious, but he
keeps looking. She has him hooked, like she has
Crow hooked, like she will have so many strung out
when she breaks Frank's heart loving them right
before his closed eyes.

After throwing the crop across the room, Crow
then slips a hand between her legs and his fingers
creep inside her. They return wet and are held up for
closer inspection before his eyes, and then for further
analysis under his nose. He places one finger on the
tip of his tongue. She smiles when he tastes her
betrayal.

Suddenly, Frank's head seems to weigh nothing at
all. This is too much. If his impressions are correct,
then she has not only denied Crow's desperate need
for what he presumes is a drug, but she has also given
herself away. Recently, she has been with another.
Frank tries to swallow but fails.

An exquisite stretching discomfort, when Crow's
cock enters her sex, clears the fog of Frank's ecstasy
and confusion; he is forced to watch the angelic body
of this devil working itself up and down her back.
Face down, open and spread, Lucretia is defenceless
and intruded with a hard thing that Crow works
furiously to round the right angles of his inner ache.
Under her hip bones he digs his fingers – piano
fingers. Against his hard stomach she is pressed,
ground into and finally shaken like a white rabbit in
a wolf's mouth. With her face buried in the bedlinen,

she will reveal nothing to either her betrayed lover or her spy.

And then Crow's mouth opens wide and he lowers his face to her shoulder. There is a flash of his black eyes and Frank is hit by an impression of a terrible feral appetite. His inner world turns red. The only thing missing is a snarl. Is he . . . Is he going to . . .

Suddenly, like a firecracker has exploded under Frank's chair, a terrible noise snaps him out of the remote viewing and he is fully conscious.

Where he sits, on the ground floor of the building, someone demands his attention. There is an alarm behind the desk to alert a concierge whenever the front doorbell of the building is depressed. Somewhere in the distance, he can also hear the palm of a hand banging the glass panels of the door.

Frank's eyes open. He looks up. His neck is stiff and the sudden explosion of electric light on to his face makes him wince. He gasps and is left with only a trace of his targets upstairs; together on that bed, still at last.

At the front door of the apartment building, a woman demands Frank's attention. Wrapped up in a long black coat, she has just disembarked from a cab and is standing outside in the cold. There are four shopping bags leaning against the sides of her legs. She wears knee-length boots. Each bag has a string handle and the plastic is brightly coloured. Two bags are pink, one blue and another turquoise. He guesses they are full of clothes from boutiques. He has seen other wealthy women carrying them through this part of town.

A little unsteady on his feet, he rises from the chair and straightens his tie. Quickly, he walks through the reception to the front door where the female resident waits. Although he is capable of opening the door from a switch on the console behind his desk, because of the delay he assumes it best to deal with her in person. Dizzy and still profoundly affected by the vision, he stumbles before reaching the door. And it is only the fury on the woman's face that finally clears him from the residue of the psi-vision.

'Are you the new concierge?' she says, when he opens the door and feels the cold air gust through from the grey street.

'Yes, Ma'am.'

'The last one was idle and a drunk.'

'Yes, Ma'am.'

'Are there not a number of surveillance screens behind your desk?'

Frank nods.

'Well, in future, young man, I do not expect to be left outside in the cold. If you were paying attention you would have seen my taxi pull up outside.' She walks into the reception. Perfume swamps him. He guesses she is in her 40s. Affluent and unpressed by the gravity of anything but the intrigues of her social circuit, she has remained handsome but childish, well preserved but brittle. 'Take the bags to number thirty. That's my apartment. I am Mrs Barnes-Dubois.'

'Yes, Ma'am.'

She marches to the elevator as Franks bends down to retrieve the string handles of her bags. Anger invades him. Not just at the way he has been spoken to – and as an ex-intelligence officer it is not a tone he is accustomed to – but because she disturbed his viewing. Perhaps he should have objected, to set a precedent with this residential bully before she interferes further with his operation, but he is still gripped by the last he saw of his targets upstairs. It has left him scared.

Had he remained in the remote viewing a moment longer, Frank is sure he would have awoken anyway, only with a cry like he was emerging from a vivid nightmare. Before the door buzzer smacked him back into full consciousness, in that red room upstairs he had seen the back of Crow's head pressing his mouth into the soft part of Lucretia's neck. On the nape where it joins the shoulders. She was penetrated in the neck and in the sex.

Two

Like a sensitive schoolboy, Frank suffered a shyness so acute his head burned. Larynx shrivelling, he cleared his throat before he spoke. 'Let me help you, Miss.' Lucretia's perfume had gotten inside his head, confusing him, though not in an unpleasant way.

'Will you? So kind.' Standing beside her black Mercedes in the basement garage, she had taken a number of packages from the boot of her car and placed them around her feet.

Upstairs, Frank had just admitted her to the garage with the flick of a switch on the control console: a panel behind the reception desk that operated the doors into the building as well as monitoring the fire and intruder alarm systems. Then, on one of the black and white monitors fixed into the wall above his desk, corresponding to the security camera in the subterranean car park, he watched her alight from the driver's seat and open the boot of her car. Immediately, he took the stairs down to the garage; it was the concierge's job to assist residents with their baggage.

Bent over and fumbling with the straps of the carrier bags at her feet, he collected himself. But she was watching; looking into him from above. Frank could feel her stare. Never having been so close to a target before, her scrutiny made him anxious. It had always been his role to observe from afar, never to investigate within the immediate locale. Active roles he had always craved and now he had a chance he harboured doubts about himself. He was too nervous. It all felt unnatural. Stage fright. Frank went for small talk. 'Number forty, Miss?'

'You're new?'

'Yes,' he said, still bent over, momentarily hypnotised by the gloss of her shoes. Patent leather formed a tight, elegant case around her long feet. Spike heels elevated them like priceless sculptures mounted on pedestals. A golden ankle chain was visible beneath her nylons; at rest above her ankle bone and near the bruise at the bottom of her calf. And, yes, on her other leg there was a dark circlet of marked skin, too. Frank swallowed.

She left her feet where they were, planted on the concrete, as if unashamed of these signs of Crow's passion she knew Frank had seen while admiring her legs. He felt angry at himself for this indiscretion, but aroused by the presence of these marks. Abuse of women he found loathsome, but this was different: the way they suggested something of *her* desires affected him.

'You know where I live and yet we have not been introduced. No?' she said, the voice subdued, but the tone made stern with serious inquiry.

Frank straightened, two bags in either hand. 'Oh, I . . . Because I saw . . .' In an attempt to break the awkward silence with his moron jabber and in an impetuous attempt to steal a moment of conversation with her, he had raised her suspicion. Hot and uncomfortable inside his suit, Frank attempted to meet her eye. And failed. One glance at that beautiful face and his stomach turned over. He looked down.

Amused at his confusion, a faint smile appeared at one side of her mouth. 'What?' she said. Rich girl humours idiot.

'What, Ma'am?' His voice was the voice of a guilty boy too frightened to defend himself before age and authority.

'You began to say something,' she prompted, her voice gentle, intelligent, a trace of a European accent. German, perhaps. And how old was she? He couldn't work it out. She looked about ten years younger than Frank, and he was three years past 30, but something about her manner and voice suggested a maturity far beyond her years. And if she had been older than him, then this sense of wisdom, this weariness that was also sensual, would have suited her, and only because experience had informed her that younger men were generally up to no good but were disarmed by a handsome face and an understanding tone of voice. Tempted to be offended, as if she had condescended, he hesitated.

'Yes,' he said, fighting a stammer. 'You asked how I know you live in forty? Well –'

Frowning, she said, 'You're mistaken. I never spoke.'

Sweat poured. Damn it; he heard her ask him how he knew she lived in 40. He heard her voice like it was behind him. Was he reading her mind? But that came in the form of feelings and impressions, rarely language. Maybe in his excitement he'd imagined the voice. Only later did he recall how the experience resembled the received messages from only the most advanced psionics. Like those two Russians he trained with, who were able to ask their targets questions over vast distances. Frank was dumbstruck.

She eyed the perspiration on his brow and emasculated him by reaching out to take one of the bags.

'Let me take one. It's the bottles that make them heavy.'

'No. No. I'm all right.' He backed away from her, clutching those bags like they belonged to him and she was about to trick him and steal. But not before her fingers grazed the back of his hand. She was wearing tight leather gloves that matched the black leather of her suit. All the hairs on the hand she touched stood upright. Sweat dried to a shiver all over his body.

She caught his eye and held it. He could not look away. She smiled like he was an earnest but foolish child. 'The parking space I use belongs to number forty. That's how you know where I live.'

Frank breathed out, relieved. 'Yes.'

'So observant. Perfect for security. An occasion when a man's eyes don't make women uncomfortable. It's good to know a man with keen eyes is looking after me. No?'

A compliment? If so, he wanted to bask in it.

But her eyes still searched his face like she was looking for something else. Then she laughed. At him? A young woman's laugh after a mature woman's words. And had she just complimented him or belittled him?

Confused, he was left holding the bags as she walked away. Was she taunting, or was there even a chance she was flirting? Or was he so damn nervous he'd imagined it all? Hating himself, he kept his eyes on her, watching her buttocks in the tight leather skirt and her long legs in flesh nylons until she disappeared into the elevator. Between the click-clack-click-clackerty-scrack noises of her heels, as she moved across the concrete, he'd heard a hiss. It came from between her thighs.

It was only when she had gone that he relaxed; his body made rigid by an exhausting cocktail of anxiety and desire and a longing to please. He wasn't even supposed to speak with her unless absolutely necessary; that was the brief. Having planned to be stony-faced and casually indifferent to her if their paths crossed in the building – acknowledging her with nothing more than a nod or polite smile – he'd fallen to pieces on a first meeting. Her first impression of him? Weak, ineffectual, socially defective and emotionally immature. Self-loathing filled Frank. He wanted to run after her and tell her he was not a loser, which would have made him the biggest loser in the world.

Most perplexing of all, he realised too much blood had flooded his groin. Everything felt heavy and tender down there. Only in retrospect did he understand the impact of that first meeting. It was the reaction of a man hopelessly infatuated with a stranger.

In a stairwell, Frank hurriedly searched her bags. It was his first assignment for the agency, following a transfer from air force intelligence to something much bigger. Opportunities in the agency come solely by invitation and, as he was due to meet the operation's supervising agent that night, he wanted to show them he was thorough and that they had chosen well. But his strongest motive for rifling her possessions ran much deeper: he couldn't help himself.

Too long with the bags, though, and the target might suspect he was up to no good. Only a quick look was possible and he made sure not to disturb the surface contents. One bag was full of candy – chocolate and sweets – supporting the theory that her sadistic lover was a junkie. Another contained prepared food – pasta, sauces, meats, sushi and so forth from a delicatessen. The third was full of alcohol –

good wine, scotch and gin. The last had make-up and clothes inside. Expensive clothes. Looking deep inside those bags he realised the garments would soon be next to her skin. His gut lurched. There were two brassières in there. Transparent, black bras. Stockings, too – real nylons with seams and big price tags. And something shiny and made from PVC or leather with suspender straps dangling from it. Just the sight of all this poled his cock up and made him sick with himself. He forgave himself. From his training and quick debriefing with the agency in Nevada, he was flown straight to New York. As a result he hadn't been with a woman in six months. And there was so much lingerie in the one bag it gave Frank a vicarious thrill, reminding him of the time he snooped in the overnight bag of his sister's school friend during a sleep-over, way back when he still lived at home. Always looking where he shouldn't until it became a profession. But in his defence, he'd not been through a woman's bag or top drawer since the time his sister's friend caught him. She'd made him undress under the threat of parental exposure. Protestant guilt reflex: probably why this felt so good.

He'd itemise what he saw and enter it in a report after the shift. He could file it that night before his rendezvous with the supervising agent. Already a profile was forming: foreign girl becomes a drugs mule who also turns tricks to support dangerously unpredictable boyfriend's habit. He then beats her for screwing the men who paid for his fix. Fuck pad, sicko, junkie schlock. Job for the police, unless Crow had secrets or illegal arms to sell. Why else would the agency be interested? They told Frank his targets were conspirators, but little else. It was bad practice to suggest too much to remote viewers; otherwise they struggled to differentiate between fact and implied thought. Primarily, his role was observation. Detection would be a bonus, but he couldn't prevent himself from wondering who they were. Little did he know, but Frank would soon be wondering what they were.

When he arrived on the fourth floor, the door to her apartment was open. He rang the bell, too self-conscious to yell, 'Yoo hoo!' No answer. Poking his head inside, he saw a black marble corridor run the length of a big penthouse. Mirrors both sides; oil paintings; two busts and some plumed plants in heavy vases. Taste and wealth. All the money in the world to buy smack. Did she charge the Johns a grand an hour or was his call girl theory dog shit?

But Frank could smell her in there and, not for the first time that day, he allowed his thoughts to wander. Or rather, the overwhelming effect of her presence left him with no choice. Ignorant as to where they originated, Frank experienced a series of quick psi-impressions. Some say these flashes are glimpses of future events, others see them as symbols of what occurs in a particular locale – a visual metaphor capturing the spirit of a place. His viewing the previous day was only received after lengthy preparation – it had required discipline and time to facilitate himself as a receiver – but these images came thick and fast when he was unprepared.

First, he saw her strutting down the same marble concourse in front of him, only it was lit up by candles. She was dressed in something black and shiny, complemented by long boots and gloves. She was laughing and her eyes were glassy. Around her mouth and smeared down her chin was something dark. Frank shook his head to get it out.

It was replaced. Maybe it was wishful thinking, but then he saw her taking it like a dog on a rug. Orange light from an open fire illuminated her. He was mesmerised by the way her lower back dipped and how her breasts shook from the force of the thrusts. Her head was thrown back and she panted encouragement to whoever slammed himself into her from behind. And she looked up and smiled when the next man kneeled down before her face to stuff his sex in her mouth.

Next he saw her white body strapped in tight leather. And she was blindfolded while a group of men were using her, moving like busy predators feeding on their catch. But the smile on her face told Frank she was not the prey.

Out of his depth; aroused but scared at what was suggested. These images seemed incongruous to the kindly face she had shown him downstairs. Aircraft wreckage strewn through fields suddenly seemed simpler to deal with.

'Come on in,' she called out and broke the spell.

Frank looked up and saw her at the far end of the corridor. Standing in the doorway of the kitchen, she held a drink. The thick crystal looked outsized and heavy in the hand that probably still smelled of those leather gloves. 'Bring them in.'

Walking to her, he kept his face lowered. Feeling the scrutiny of those dark eyes again, he became heavy with guilt and could not resist thinking of himself rifling through her bags on the stairwell.

'In here,' she said, and moved her head slightly in the direction of the kitchen. Not making any attempt to move aside for him, Frank moved sidewards through the door. There was a moment when their faces were level. She looked at him over the rim of her glass. There was a strange half-smile on her face again. It seemed to be challenging him. 'Don't be frightened of the rich,' she said. 'They want to be seen.'

20

This made him start and he knew his face had tightened to a giveaway.

'Downstairs all day, at the desk, you must be curious about what is on the other side of these doors.' She turned away from Frank and walked across to the kitchen counter beside a gleaming oven. It was an elegant room. Just what he expected to see in one of these places after skimming through glossy magazines like *Tatler* and *Vogue* in doctors' surgeries, but it seemed too empty or too clean to have ever been used for anything but show. Maybe they had a maid.

When he put the bags on the counter beside the spotless utensil rack, he was so tense speech was not an option. She lit a cigarette and looked him over. 'Are you ever tempted to sit in the cars down there? I know you have keys. Or to look in the *bags* residents bring home from all the fancy stores?'

Playing games. 'No, Miss,' he said, and tried to snigger his way out of breaking down. All he made was a hateful snorting sound that produced a bubble at the entrance of one nostril.

She blew smoke at the ceiling. 'What is your name?'

'Frank.'

'Frank.' She said his name slowly and, for a moment, he swore he could taste her lipstick. 'If you like, you may look around. Get it out of your system.'

He cleared his throat. 'No. No thanks, Miss.'

'Always be frank with me, Frank.' She laughed, but it was forced. She stopped laughing. 'Don't be frightened.' Smoke drifted across her face.

Uncomfortable in his skin and not just the suit, he made for the kitchen door, catching a swipe of her mocking smile as he passed. He sensed he was in the presence of someone far cleverer than himself.

'These two bags go in the bedroom.' She wasn't smiling when he turned in the doorway. Moving past him, she beckoned with one hand for him to follow. A gesture at odds with her youth; a senior Bette Davis in possession of a twenty-something's body. Annoyed that he'd dismissed himself, perhaps, or not quite bored with the help yet, she had a point to make. Spooked but excited, Frank collected the remaining bags and followed her to the bedroom.

'Put them on the bed.'

He avoided looking in the mirrors. In every one he seemed hunched and ungainly, she beautiful and icy. The thought of what he'd seen happen in here suddenly overwhelmed him. Her clothes had been ripped from her body and she had been punished. She had taken a stick in here across her back and buttocks. And if his intuition served him correctly, she had not only enjoyed it, but manipulated the whole scene to get it. Frank felt light-headed; it was too great a moment of intimacy.

'On the other side of the bed. Near the closet would make sense.' Her voice seemed sharp, accusing even. After executing the task, Frank stood up with his back too straight. Injured by her sarcastic tone, he marched from the room.

'Frank,' she called out, when he reached the front door. 'Wait.'

He stood still. She caught up with him. In one hand she held the drink, in the other her purse. It was black with a gold chain hanging from the top. He'd sooner have been strangled with the chain than have her open the purse. She stretched a hand out. 'Here.' Dark red fingernails pinched a twenty. 'For your trouble.'

It could have injured his pride no more if she had rolled it up and then shoved it in his ass. He shook his head. 'No, thank you, Ma'am. It's quite all right.'

'Take it.' If he wasn't mistaken, she now genuinely wanted him to like her, as if a test had been passed. But he didn't want to be seen as some kind of gimp. Not by her. Not like that.

'No, Miss.'

Now she looked wounded. She lowered her face. There was a long pause before she said, 'I didn't mean to offend you.'

'This is your home, Miss. I don't expect a tip for carrying your bags. It's all part of the service.'

She looked at her feet, embarrassed. 'This place is too elegant for me,' she whispered. 'I'm sorry, Frank. I never know if I'm saying or doing the right thing. You're a proud man. I'm not always like this, only . . .' She looked over her shoulder and into the dark behind her.

Maybe she was just lonely and vulnerable. Mistreatment could do that. Loving Crow was taking its toll. And drinking so early in the day? All she wanted was a friend in this big mausoleum. That bastard down there in the dark place beat her and she was only toying with the concierge to get company.

'No, Miss. You haven't insulted me. And it was a pleasure to meet you. Have a good day now.'

When she smiled his guts liquefied.

What did she mean with all that about him snooping? There was no way she could have seen him look in her bags. Anxiety was circling and tightening inside. He'd begun to agonise about the connotations of her every word. Small talk, compliments, innocent suggestions or ill-thought-out remarks from a distracted woman: what was what? What exactly was she trying to say to him?

In so many ways it had all begun – his total involvement. Maybe if he had run right then at the

23

beginning of the assignment and told the agency their work wasn't for him, he would have been saved. But to run from her, knowing what he was? Never. And they knew it. Damn it, the agency knew it. They only employed him to exploit his weakness and disgrace.

His disgrace . . .

And it was early in the evening, following that first meeting with the target, when Frank began to feel restless again. It was coming – a clairvoyant moment of extraordinary power. Sitting in his chair with all those thoughts and questions, he began to wonder if he'd unravelled himself, just plain thought too much. But then the viewing hit Frank as if he were sitting in a draught. It was like a sudden chill. Thinning blood and spine shivers led to disorientation, until all he needed to do was close his eyes and see.

She was getting ready for something. It all seemed like a ritual that involved a special costume and mental preparation as severe as the garments. The way she sat on that bed so alert and serious-faced, he knew her thoughts were uncompromising. Something had to be done to someone upstairs. Could it have been a request she was to fulfil, or could it have been part of a game?

Clairvoyant episodes are rarely so defined or charged. He usually only received impressions of a target person's surroundings and mood after a lengthy period of concentration on a photo of them, or while holding a piece of their clothing. But images of Lucretia flooded him, fooling him into thinking the empathy was so strong between them, and the synchronicity so great, they were like twins separated at birth.

She was in that room again – the one with the mirrors – sitting on the end of the bed. A dark bathrobe lay beside her as if she'd just showered.

Fresh make-up had been applied heavily and that naturally beautiful face had not only been made more beautiful but also wanton. Yes, with the thickened lips that looked wet, the dark eyeliner, cheekbones purpled, hair pulled back into a bun, she was demanding attention by becoming a doll. A doll you wouldn't know where to start with, so you ended up just staring for a long time without breathing.

And the underwear complemented her face. Shiny and black, the corset pushed her breasts up and together. Suspender straps swayed over her thighs like thin serpents eager to clamp their tiny jaws on something soft and defenceless. While she dexterously tugged at the zipper behind her back to seal her torso in rubber, he almost heard her squeak.

Up her legs she then rolled the stockings, seams straight, heel and toe fitted, until the tops could be stretched right up and into the summit of her thighs and then clasped in place, framing the triangle of golden hair around her sex. Over the smooth nylon, tight rubber boots were then zipped thigh-high so only the welts of her stockings and a horizontal band of the lighter coloured and sheerer fabric could be seen. Elevated to her toes, the spike heels then made her body shimmy as she walked across to a wardrobe. Long rubber gloves were pulled up her arms to the shoulder. A choker slipped around her throat, pushing her chin upward. Over the ensemble she wore a black rubber dress with a high collar; concealing the revealing. Ready. She closed her eyes and smiled. It unnerved Frank.

Where was he? That bastard, Eldrin.

A buzzing from the front door.

Jolted awake, Frank stood up, dizzy. Then angry that she should be taken away from him because of some ... some idiot who refused to remember the security code to get into the building. Peering down at the glass panels of the front door, he expected to see Mrs Barnes-Dubois with a face like a spree killing.

Who the hell . . .?

Benjamin Stratton was the name of the slender-faced youth and he had come to see the lady in apartment 40. Three times he checked his watch as Frank wrote his details and the time of his arrival in the guest book. Agitated, the man couldn't keep still and began to pace through the lobby when Frank reached for the house phone to call Lucretia. He hesitated to clear his throat before picking up the receiver – just the thought of speaking with her again filled Frank with a kind of nervous reaction that infuriated him.

But she anticipated him. He jumped and said, 'Shit,' when the phone beneath his hand began to ring. On the switchboard the red light beside 40 lit up. 'Hello. Front desk. Frank speaking.'

'Send him up,' she said. 'Send them all up.'

And she hung up before he could say, 'Yes, Miss.'

Her voice had changed. It sounded strange. Thick like a woman's can be after eating chocolate, or when husky with excitement. It made Frank hard.

The guest found his way to the elevator. He was soon followed by another two men who arrived moments later. Young, handsome, tall; as if tailor-made to a specific requirement or taste. They all arrived by cab, were all immaculately dressed for dinner and all displayed the same signs of anxiety. Number two – the man who called himself Bradden Ford – leaned against the wall beside the elevator as if to support himself. Number three, the blond man, Edgar Lawrence, had mopped his brow with a silk handkerchief and then sniffed something from a silver inhaler to gather himself.

Up they went and into the next remote viewing Frank sank.

Statuesque, she moved between them, handing out drinks and smiles like a hostess among the mob in Vegas. Each of them sat in a chair in the living room before an open fire. Subdued light emitted from the walls kept the floor in shadow. Flickering light from the fire illuminated the staring eyes in their pale faces: transfixed, anxious, anticipating. All restraining something inside themselves she wanted to be even stronger. That's why she unzipped the dress and let it drop to the floor before she gave them the cigars.

Every pair of eyes was directed up her rubber-booted thighs to her naked sex. And when she refilled their tumblers with scotch, she made sure everyone was offered a closer glimpse into her pale cleavage. Unable to hold back any longer, one man reached out to touch her leg. She moved away and deliberately lavished her attentions on his closest neighbour. And when he, in turn, dared to stroke at a thigh, she moved away from him to entertain the third guest with whispers and deep stares, her face an inch from his nose. Her perfume filled their heads with madness.

Ties were loosened, watches removed, cigars stubbed out in heavy ashtrays.

Stretched out on the thick rug before the visitors, using nothing but her eyes, she beckoned the first man to come to her.

And those beautiful dark eyes flashed wide when he stood above her, naked. With one hand holding his heavy girth at her eye level, he issued a command. The first of many the young men would give her that evening. And the other two, still dressed and tense in their chairs, gripped the upholstery with whitening fingertips when she tilted her head back, parted her glossy lips and accepted the thick head of the purple organ inside her mouth.

With his hands cradling her head – fingers spread through her immaculate hair – he flexed his knees and began to push his cock deeper and more forcefully inside her head. Eyes closed, she seemed to tremble, as if from fear of suffocation or lockjaw. But his rhythm was soon accommodated lovingly and she gripped his shaft, the skin now stained with the burgundy of her lips. Beating it through her long fingers and painted nails, she seemed eager to mass-age the milk from the muscle – as if she would starve without it, as if she deserved the tightening grip of his fingers on her skull and the increasingly brutish thrusts of his sex inside her whole head, which was tugged back and forth from the force of his lunges. And when she was pushed on to her back, and he kneeled beside her, she moved the tip of his cock an inch from her shiny lips and vigorously pumped it through her hand. He was panting hard and unable to turn his eyes from her face. She taunted him with language so sluttish and foul he was not long in coming.

They all saw it. Five clots of thick, whitish stuff were shot quickly between her parted lips. And she swallowed it all and then sucked the strawberry thickness of his cock-head clean before pushing him away with one gloved hand. Reclining backwards, she then opened her long, rubber-coated thighs that glistened like oil, and flashed a salacious look at the other two men, now straining forwards in their seats to see her at play.

It did not take them long to undress and then address her needs.

Feeding with their faces sunk between her thighs and buried in her corseted breasts, she began to make animal noises to encourage their devouring of her long and shapely whiteness. But soon, so eager for a ruthless and consistent penetration, she clutched at their cocks to stroke them up so they would be hard enough to be painful when they went in her. But they made her wait. Knowing they were lost to her, they wanted her beaten for their loss of control, and for her appetite that no single one of them could fulfil.

One man spanked her until she panted, leaving her buttocks an inflamed pink and his arm tired. And as she was flogged by this hand, that so deftly wielded a squash racket in an exclusive fitness club three times a week, another of her lovers tried to masturbate over her face. Pummelling his sex at a furious pace with one hand, he stood before her until she reached out, seized him and then stuffed his rigidity inside her mouth.

Gulping him down, too, she felt herself mounted and penetrated from behind. Releasing the spent cock from her mouth, she dropped her head, bent her elbows and fell into rhythm of the rear onslaught. Only when Frank received a strong image of her face, the features screwed up in a writhing discomfort of exquisite and liberating pain, did he realise the man had entered her anus. And any woman who wanted such an intrusion, suddenly and deeply and barbarically, was intent on going somewhere most women would only dare dream of.

And then her first lover began to handle her breasts and, in co-operation with the man who plundered her rear, they placed her on her side. In this position she was squashed between two hard male bodies and filled to the back of both womb and rectum with solid male flesh. Squashing their faces into her hair and the cheeks of her face, they must have muttered to her, and to each other, that they were going to come inside her, because she suddenly began to cry out and jerk her body between them as if to increase the heat and depth of their joining.

At the end, their thrusts were so fast and vengeful, those arms of hers, shining in tight PVC, fell limp and her uppermost leg draped itself lazily over the thigh of the man facing her. It was as if some goal had been achieved and now she could give herself completely and without taunts or prompts to whatever vicious and desperate acts the three young men could conceive.

Their lean and naked bodies shining with sweat, they pushed themselves deep inside her, to the top of her most private canals, and then released a lava flow of youthful seed to scorch and wet and drip from her innards. Their eyes glassy, their bodies spent when the last weakening stream of fluid was released from their red, rubbed cocks, her two lovers pressed the sides of their faces into her back and breasts. Through the dishevelled hair that had fallen across her face, she looked up in the air and smiled, right at Frank.

Subdued by them and subjected to them, but curiously in control of every single moment and somehow influencing every decision and offering every choice, she was led from that lounge on her hands and knees by the first of her lovers to recover from such a powerful expenditure. A collar and leash had been attached to her neck.

In this second bedroom that Frank had not seen before, she had laid out her props – the devices they were to use on her. And it was between the two wooden uprights that she was hung, tied at ankle and wrist, in order to receive wet 'placking' slaps from a flail that looked like a horse's tail. And then over the leather-covered bench she was bent to have her buttocks lined with a cane that whined through the air only to make a dull fleshy sound that was soon drowned out by her whimpers. And if a moment of mercy was shown, where a stroke was pulled short or delivered soft, she turned a tear-strewn face towards her tormentor and cursed him.

Still clad in her corset, gloves, boots and stockings, she was taken from the apparatus and then laid on a thin mattress. And it was here, against the gloom of those dark sheets, that all three men swarmed over her, relieved of any awkwardness or reticence at being so close to each other's naked bodies. Filling their mouths with breast flesh – warmly popped from the tight cups of a rubbery corset – licking spiked boot heels and capped toes, sucking at her hot and smeared mouth, they went at her.

Laughing, she lay open to them, accommodating the hands that turned her from side to side, or arranged her on all fours, or raised her legs and placed her ankles on brawny shoulders. Complying with her search for this most extraordinary craving for sensation, the men came twice each, both inside her and over her.

But where was he; that bastard who put her through this ritual, the pale-faced man who arranged this orgy, that surely she only complied with because of her self-destructive love for him? Not once did the viewing reveal Crow to Frank. But he sensed him up there. Somewhere behind a wall the spidery thing was crouched over, taut and knotted inside with rage and jealousy, and yet insanely exalted by her betrayal at the same time. Electrified by the sweet shocks of her wantonness, his black mouth cursed her and promised greater and more unacceptable tests of faith.

Eventually, when the three men were spent and half-sleepy from their intoxication with her, Frank viewed the fragments of her final act. It seemed as if her wide mouth were moving from one throat to another, and then from one softening penis to the next. Dipping, then fastening, perhaps, and finally smearing itself on these parts of their bodies, the contact of her face on their flesh seemed to absorb the last of their strength and consciousness. When she appeared sated, each of their bodies was limp.

And as she too fell into a fatigue that was also euphoric, absolving her from care, the remote viewing dimmed to an end. The last Frank experienced of her were the sensations of her body: the marks on her skin, salted and still pleasing with their sting; her sex and anus stretched and still holding the impression of the hard meats that had been applied through them; the taste of something thick and salty in her mouth and the odour of a rustiness in her nose she found delightful. She drifted to sleep and Frank awoke, face down, shirt wet, mouth open, like some drunk lecher found in an alley behind a peep show.

But Frank's night did not end there. An hour after the remote view concluded, the house phone rang. Once again it was number 40 lit up in red on the switchboard. 'Frank. Frank. Is that you?' Her speech was slurred. He sensed she was swaying on her heels at the other end of the phone line.

Hurt by what he knew she had done, but curiously emotional and ecstatic because she had phoned him, as if she were his lover who had gone astray but still cared, he swallowed before answering, 'Yes. It's Frank.'

'Frank. I need a favour.'

For a few seconds he was sure his heart had stopped beating. 'Anything.'

'Call a cab for me. My friends have ...' She laughed. 'They have indulged themselves.'

'Yes, Miss.'

'Call a cab, then help them down. Do it now.'

'Sure,' he said, but trembled from the injury of her sexual waywardness. And when she laughed, she turned something in the wound. Never had he felt so excluded from a place and from a person he so desperately wanted for himself. And the thought of only seeing the inside of her world and receiving her attention as a servant, who would clean up her mess, shattered him.

She hung up.

When Frank stepped out of the elevator on the fourth floor, the door to her apartment was open. He rang the bell and poked his head inside. Out of the dark she came; heels striking the black marble like firing pins on live rounds. Smiling, her mouth was stained . . . Yes, he had seen this before. This he had predicted. Like the other scenes he had endured this night – when she was mounted like an animal on the fur rug, and then tied up in leather – he had foreseen it.

But no, as she neared him, she was not wearing the shiny black underclothes, or even the long dress that covered her from neck to toe, but a floor-length nightgown instead. Her hair was perfect too and her mouth was a bright crimson in colour because of the fresh lipstick she must have recently applied. And there were no candles lining the corridor.

'Frank,' she said. 'They are in the living room. I thank you for this.'

He nodded.

'Can I tell you a secret?' She put her cold white hands on either side of his face. 'Can this be between us?'

Frank swallowed. The groan that dislodged itself from his throat she interpreted as a 'yes'.

33

'Don't disapprove of me. I want us to be friends.'

'Sure, Miss. Whatever you say.' And as she looked into him, he forgave her, and at that moment he would have done anything to help her, despite the lies she told.

From the darkened living room, where the fire had burned down to red coals and ash, Frank found the guests. One seemed to be asleep. The other two were awake, but barely. They didn't seem to know where they were. Each gave the impression he had been dressed by someone else. One by one, Frank took them down in the elevator to the waiting cab.

The muttering gibberish to themselves, or just stared into inner space. Frank searched them in the elevator. And he handled them roughly, angered by the fact that their hands had touched her and their bodies had been next to her own. He then shoved them inside the cab and gave the driver the addresses he had found when rifling through their wallets. Unable to restrain himself, Frank then wandered back up to her apartment to see if there was anything else he could do for her. But as he walked out of the elevator and stared at the open doorway of her apartment, he heard a man crying. And interspersed with these sounds of his grief, he could also hear her laughing.

'All of them. They all had me!' he heard her say from somewhere far off inside the apartment.

'What about me? You never think of me. You know I need it, too.'

'You only have yourself to blame.'

'Why do I?' he shrieked. 'You know I cannot leave. They're all over me. They watch me constantly. You must help me instead of just gorging yourself.'

And just as Frank leaned forwards to catch more of this exchange, the door of their apartment slammed shut and nearly stopped his heart with a bang.

Three

She took Frank by surprise with her pretty, freckled face dominated by large green eyes. Her red hair was shiny and cut short in a style that suggested efficiency and professionalism without sacrificing a natural though introverted glamour. Elegance and simplicity she commanded with a chic, black, two-piece suit and sling-back heels. Good breasts pushed themselves out from beneath the white, ribbed T-shirt she wore under her jacket. Pleasingly curved in the tight skirt and rustly slip, her buttocks would have made any man's hand move of its own volition when in the vicinity. And this patter-cake-magnet tapered into the sturdy legs of a girl who worked out. Not at all what he expected a supervising agent to look like. For a start, agent Ally Kram was a young woman, and on a case of such a sensitive nature he'd assumed a man would have been assigned as his partner. He had much to learn.

Suddenly, he felt humiliated by the state of his tenement apartment, acquired by the agency for the duration of the investigation. Some laundry hung to dry before the window that opened on to the fire escape. The rooms were smitten with a gloom unrelieved by even the most powerful lighting. Every wall was stained with damp, his bed remained unmade, and the garbage still needed taking out, of which there was a great deal as he'd eaten take-outs for two weeks solid. But worst of all, it smelled of an estuary at low tide. The deprivation in the neighbourhood and the squalor in this building had already taken his heart out of keeping it clean. And besides, he felt compelled to spend as much time as possible at work, watching Lucretia.

'Was this the best the agency could do?' he asked, by way of apology, and waved a hand about above his head.

'What else could a concierge afford?' she said, and pulled a chair out from beneath the kitchen table. The moment she was seated she crossed her legs. Just before she smoothed her skirt across her thighs, Frank instinctively looked down. She saw him glance at her legs and her face regressed from cold to mean. But, for a glorious moment, as he tried for a teeny peep of her white cotton panties – agency issue, if there was such a thing – he looked up a skirt-corridor of flesh-coloured silkiness, that stretched along one of her thighs and ended in a red gusset. Great legs. He began to look forward to Agent Kram swinging by to pick up his reports on a regular basis. Maybe it would help distract him from his fixation with Lucretia. Already, the first signs of wretchedness were in place.

Ally Kram lit a cigarette without asking permission or offering Frank one. 'People in this neighbourhood would kill for an apartment this size,' she said, without appearing to have any interest in these people or the apartment they coveted.

'You know, that's what worries me,' he replied, smiling. But her face never moved. Over by the sink, he finished preparing the coffee, in silence.

'So, what have you got for me?' She raised her brows over those arresting eyes – so clear and sparkly-clever – and then blew a long plume of smoke towards him as he joined her at the table.

'Some great material,' he said, excited. 'It's the weirdest thing I've ever been asked to do.' He placed a cup of coffee before her. She never looked at it, but continued to stare at Frank with what he interpreted as disdain. Besides her beauty, and the fact he felt uncomfortable revealing such a shitty apartment to a senior ranking agent, he found her gaze unnerving. Both his enthusiasm and insides suddenly cooled when he realised she didn't approve of him. There were so many myths about the agency he heard serving in the intelligence corps of the forces, and he wondered if she was a killer like the others.

'It's . . . It's kind of delicate. You know, it's . . .' he grinned stupidly and then coloured. Frank pushed the report across the table towards her.

'They fuck,' she said, almost spitting the word out. 'You see them fuck a lot. So what? Let's get one thing straight, Frank. I want it all. I want to hear and read about every time she goes down on him, or anyone else she entertains. I want to know if she takes it in the ass, too. And if she does, how hard does she get it? And I especially want to know if she likes rough trade and whether she prefers a cane to a whip to a good old-fashioned hand. You hear me? And if he likes to be pissed on from a great height, or likes to lie under a table with a glass top when she takes a crap, I need to know. Do I sound like a woman who needs protecting? I want names, times, places, every visitor, every fuck, every number plate. You tell me everything and don't spare my delicate female ears anything. Do you understand?'

From cold and jumpy, Frank felt hot and shouty. She'd sauntered into his apartment and refused his proffered hand. No smile, nothing. So he tried to make her feel welcome, because he presumed they were going to work closely together, and he tried to use a little tact to prepare her for the information collected on the targets, and all he got in return was attitude. She waited for him to open up and then shot him down. This is how it would be. This was not the first misgiving he'd harboured about his new employers, either, but after his discharge from the air force, it was the only way he could stay in psionics outside of a fairground tent or spiritualist church. No thanks.

'Are we clear on that?' she pushed, neither her tone nor expression lightening.

Frank nodded.

'Good. Now what do you –'

'It's all in there,' he said, snapping at her, and flicked the report in a manner that suited his sullen mood. Months of ball-breaking from other agents during the induction in Nevada and now this. Once the agency's equivalent of basic training was over, he'd hoped to be on more familiar terms with staff whenever he met them in the field. Kram was spoiling the ideal.

'Perhaps I should be straight from the start.' She had lowered her voice to a confessional tone, which made her all the more odious, but Frank still looked up quickly, eager to forgive and start over. 'Fraternisation with other agents can lead to an over-familiarity. In my experience, I find it distracting.'

So, as a pretty girl, men make passes. And she's a professional and demands respect. Fair enough. But even though he'd been caught looking at her legs, he felt insulted she had to issue a warning. But more than that, he'd begun to feel as if her attitude was just a prelude to something she was about to say that would hurt and humiliate.

38

'It's rare any of us work in direct collaboration with other agents,' she continued, and it was an effort for her to temper her aggressive stance. 'So keep your distance and don't get any ideas of me being a friend. It'll never be like that. Ever.'

Bitch. 'If I need back-up, will you consider fraternising enough to maybe save my life,' Frank said, his face and voice puffed with anger.

This stalled her. But then her face went all kind of pinched and pale. Her voice came at him in a whisper. 'What do you think this is? The fucking police department? You go down, you go down alone and you have nothing to say to anyone with your dying breath. That's how we work. Everything is need to know. This isn't the air force. Don't go expecting a Labor Day barbecue.'

Frank held his hands and closed his eyes, too choked to retaliate. Fuck her beautiful eyes and breasts and legs, he hated her. She'd get exactly what she wanted – typed reports and no civility. 'OK. OK,' he said, now unable to look at her. 'We don't even need to talk. I'll just drop my reports through the open window of your car or something. We can come to an arrangement.'

When she laughed, he wanted to smack her. 'The girls don't play fair any more, do they, Frank?' What was she getting at? He looked at her and swallowed the lump in his throat. 'I looked at your profile, Frank. And you're a creep. Is it any surprise a woman would be wary of you. After developing and mastering the greatest gift a human mind is capable of – the ability to see inside other minds and to look through walls, or even into other countries from the comfort of your own chair – what do you do? Huh?'

'Get out,' he said, in the tone of voice that suggested his stack was about to blow.

She snorted, stuffed the file in her bag and then stood up. 'I'll let you know when I'll be dropping in again. And if I think you're taking an uninvited peek into my head or hotel room, I'll kill you.' Her cigarette butt fizzed in the coffee cup.

'Go,' he said.

'If you haven't worked it out yet, Frank, I want you to know why the agency hired you for this job: it takes a degenerate to understand a degenerate.'

'Out! Goddamn you!'

When the door to the apartment closed, he started to shake. Frank put his face in his hands and knew with these people he would never escape the past. Why had he kidded himself?

His disgrace. What he was. Dishonourable discharge; peeping Tom; worrier of women; snooper of military personnel; a remote viewer who couldn't look at nerve gas laboratories in the Middle East any more, and who just couldn't face another crash site or hostage scenario. A man who let himself get distracted by the secret and private lives that women lead. Important women.

He could still see them all, vividly: Major Anne Gillingham; Flight Lieutenant Stacy Allen; Captain Barbara Skinner; Medical Officer Helen Roberts; at least one dozen female naval officers; an air force chaplain the Navy Seals called 'hooters'; two female astronauts in training for a shuttle mission; three wives of high-ranking officers; six federal agents, and at least fifteen random encounters with the wives and girlfriends of servicemen on a base in New Mexico. But it was his insights into the nocturnal habits of the vice president's wife that sank his ship. All were the subjects of his roaming remote views.

And if you're going to peep where you shouldn't, make sure you don't keep a journal, even if it is standard practice for remote viewers to write down every dream and subconscious impression. A lesson he'd learned the hard way. Back in the air force, the transcripts of his illicit visions were read by a female colleague who became suspicious of his long silences, lengthy absences from the psi-facility, and exhaustion caused by excessive self-pleasure. They had seen it happen before and knew how to spot the tell-tale signs of 'rogue viewing'. He'd turned his 'gift' to other purposes and was declared unfit for active duty. It seemed not even the thoughts of a psionic were private any more.

Declared a pervert by those who trusted and developed him on some of the most sensitive military projects of the late twentieth century, he felt colossal shame. Of equal magnitude was his desire to vanish into a new life, new job and new name. The desire was granted when the agency stepped up to the plate. An agency who could use a man of his abilities and interests. An agency untroubled by morals. An agency 40 levels above top secret.

And he had nowhere left to go. People who had seen all he had seen and compromised others the way he did were lucky to be living outside of a military stockade, if at all. There were still moments of self-pity, but Frank comforted himself with the assumption that any man with the ability to read other people's minds and see through walls, would have done the same.

If others had seen the crash wreckage of recovered alien craft in US hands, and were certain they knew what happened with JFK (and both of those viewings took time to perfect), what any sane mind would be tempted to do, as when faced with any of the bigger questions, was to earth itself or lose itself. Frank chose the former option and suddenly took more of an interest in what was actually around him. The military stifled his sexuality, but enriched his God-given clairvoyance. He'd needed relief.

Naturally, he began to think of the women he'd seen around the bases; to really think, to concentrate hard, go to sleep with them on his mind, and meditate on how they struck him as interesting. And before long he was getting glimpses, receiving impressions, having unnaturally vivid dreams and enjoying syn-chronised feelings – he would know when his targets were horny. Ultimately, he was able to share their sex lives.

Once he'd seen two female naval officers, wearing the full whites of dress uniform, making love to each other in quarters, his life in the services was forever altered.

They were as tall as beach volleyball pros, with indifferent catwalk-faces he never underestimated as being incapable of displaying real passion. Frank became curious about their relationship the first time he saw them walking through the base where he was stationed in northern California, to work on locating a missing sub, devastating in their pressed and spotless attire. He picked up on the little whispers and quick, intense glances they exchanged. And some time later, at the far side of the running track, when they were certain they were not under observation from anything but the bright sun, he saw a look of mutual longing pass between these girls and knew he had to experience their *association* under the scrutiny of a remote viewing.

Never expected it to be so rough, though.

It was the broader girl who dominated affairs. She got jealous. And the first time Frank watched them from the comfort of his own cot, on the other side of the base, this dominant athletic vixen (who he named

42

Tough Girl) was so in love with her more submissive girlfriend (who he dubbed Sweety) that she decided to make a statement of devotion.

On the night he selected to first make contact with the targets, his preparations for the viewing delivered him to Tough Girl's room – containing an immaculate desk and single bed surrounded by spotless, undecorated white walls – where some kind of interrogation was already underway. The host, Tough Girl, wanted to know why Sweety, who had just slowly undressed, was wearing butt-riding panties, a lacy garter belt, white stockings instead of military pantyhose, and a satin brassière under her dress uniform.

Of course, Sweety had slipped her long and toned body into all that slippery loveliness to please her lover, but Tough Girl thought it too good to be true. Fisting her hand into Sweety's hair, she upset all of the pins holding that stylish arrangement together and forced her head down, waist-height. Sweety was crying. Tough Girl started sniffing too, but still managed enough composure to shout her mouth off about Sweety making goo-goo eyes at some civilian in the typing pool on base, and about some liaison that she really wanted to occur but couldn't deal with.

On her hands and knees in virginal-white lingerie, Sweety started to redden in the face. She stopped crying. And out came a surprise attack that put Tough Girl right in the middle of an emotional Pearl Harbor. Angry at the injustice of her lover's accusations, Sweety then confessed to an anger-inspired, fictional infidelity.

She was dragged by her hair to the cot in the corner and then thrown on to the tight white sheets and taut cream blanket. Her body bounced off the mattress and Frank almost heard the springs scream in the cast-iron bedframe.

Belly down, red face squashed sideways, arms pinned uselessly at her sides, silky panties uppermost, Sweety was soon at Tough Girl's mercy. But Tough Girl didn't have any mercy after hearing Sweety's confession. She slapped her pink from just above her knees up to her waist, and slung the occasional open-handed jab at Sweety's face.

Worn out, Tough Girl finally stood back, breathing hard, with her raven hair hanging in streaks across her pointy cheekbones and nose. And her eyes were all vacant looking when she unthreaded a belt from the pair of jeans that hung over the back of a chair.

Hard to say if Tough Girl was in control of herself at all when she went at Sweety with that belt. It made Frank wince. But under the flurry of leathery blows that engaged with Sweety's already blushing skin, he noticed Sweety had slipped a hand beneath her tummy and down to her sex. And the elbow attached to that hand was rotating between lashes. Did Tough Girl notice? He was never sure; she had the faraway look of the fanatic, the possessed and the dispossessed all at once.

She then ripped her own pantyhose down her legs and pushed the odiferous crotch into Sweety's tear-stained face. The long and empty legs of the hose were then used to tie Sweety's ankles to her wrists. With her legs bent, the little pinky heels of Sweety's stocking-clad feet nearly touched her buttocks. Using the panties, tugged fresh from her sex, Tough Girl then fashioned a gag in Sweety's mouth that pulled her lips back at the sides until she was smiling like The Joker from *Batman*.

Don't mess with the big girls was, quite plainly, the moral of this story – and one Frank simply refused to learn.

44

Tough Girl wiped her hair back from her face. She closed the khaki-coloured curtains, turned on a bedside lamp, and then opened the doors to her wardrobe. After rummaging around in the bottom, she pulled something out that looked like a squid at first glance; a collection of leathery tentacles hanging from a thick-headed shaft. She then placed the squid-thing on the pillow, beside Sweety's gagged mouth, so she could look into the future and know its dimensions – the space it would require, and the time it would take to complete its journey, fuelled by lesbian hate-lust. Tough Girl followed this threatening action with the removal of the rest of her uniform and underwear until she stood at a magnificent, naked six foot before her vanquished lover. But at this point, Sweety was no lover, she was the 'bitch'.

With slow-moving fingers, Tough Girl attached the squid-like apparatus around her waist, and then stroked her hand along the new length that hung between her legs. In profile, in the gloom of that cell, Tough Girl resembled a beautiful hermaphrodite creature with a large erection and breasts. Of course, it was not a squid at all but a sex aid of considerable girth and weight. Sweety's buttocks tensed.

First, Sweety was made to taste it; to take it inside her lips so wet with pink lipstick and to suck it. The order was given; the order was obeyed. And while it was mauled by Sweety's mouth, Tough Girl caressed her own nipples – brown and firm between her square-ended fingers.

After being made to suck the false idol, Sweety was turned on her side so her appealing torso faced Tough Girl. With one hand between Sweety's thighs and another at work on Sweety's bigger and pinker nipples, Tough Girl put her lips close to Sweety's, without kissing her, and asked pertinent questions to extract what Frank imagined to be a full and detailed confession of the submissive girl's infidelity.

After the intelligence was gathered, Tough Girl's face was a fright to behold. It seemed that Sweety had touched every raw nerve connected to Tough Girl's dysfunction-nucleus with a convincing account of what Tough Girl had suspected all along.

Oddly, she caressed the tousle out of Sweety's silky hair, and then untied the pantyhose hobble. Forgiveness? Frank thought with dismay. But what he then witnessed made his eyes water.

Face down again, and making absolutely no attempt to escape or plead or struggle, Sweety allowed her assertive girlfriend to seize her hips and pull her buttocks up and into position, so she was somewhere between lying prostrate and kneeling on all fours; a languid and subdued spectacle of a beautiful long-boned woman, resigned to penetration from the rear.

Rag-dollish, she was jerked back and forth and rooted deeply by Tough Girl, first in her sex until she threw her head back and bit at one of her own hands, and then in her anus which took the strength from all of her limbs. When she was finished, Tough Girl slapped Sweety up and off her bed, threw her uniform into her arms and then expelled her from the room.

Three days later, Frank observed Sweety with a bespectacled civilian from the typing pool, in a motel room downtown – a notorious flophouse for the third sex. And then again, two days later, in the rear of a family station wagon, out of town. On each occasion they never undressed, but hiked their skirts up and spent over an hour with their pretty faces between each other's thighs.

That was only one of the many shocking, refreshing and educating relationships on military bases Frank was able to view with his psionic skill. With most of the others, he recorded the real names of the targets in his journal, which fell into the shapely hands of the director of the psionic unit. A 53-year-old woman with a lifelong affectation for young cowboys. The time he saw her ridden front and back in a pick up truck, by two youths smelling of beer, was almost worth the dishonourable discharge that soon ended his career. And there was no doubt in his mind, during this stage of the investigation into Lucretia and Eldrin Crow, that supervising agent Ally Kram knew of every discretion between military personnel that he pursued, observed and delighted in. Hence her disgust.

Out of defiance, professional pride, and a confrontational streak, Frank decided after that spiky first meeting with Kram, that he would not hold back on anything, right down to every clinical detail, nor would he make excuses for how and when and where he conducted the remote views into Lucretia's life.

Agent Ally Kram, prepare to degenerate.

Four

Red lips slide down the length of his cock. Smudges of ruby are left around the pale skin with the greenish tint of vein beneath. All of his solid arousal goes into her mouth until she can feel the hair at the base of his erection. It tickles her nose and top lip. She withdraws the mouth back to the lollipop of his phallus. She sucks at the hole in the top, a tiny red mouth in a blind worm, and makes a little noise at the back of her throat as she consumes the greyish juice that has seeped out; melted butter promising the full-bodied draught that soon will rise to fill her mouth and throat and tummy.

Dipping that beautiful face deep into his lap in the back seat of the Mercedes, she goes up and down, up and down, up and down with her eyes closed. Moving his spine up the seat so the leather upholstery groans, momentarily obscuring the sound of his whimpers, the young man keeps his eyes open. Then his sweet potato balls, with the halo of golden fuzz attached to the ruffled skin, go into the crimson smear of her mouth too. Baubles of seed ready to discharge on the gums of a queen.

His eyes are wide. At seventeen, he had begun to think he would never see this: a female face in his lap. His cock – his actual cock – is inside a woman's mouth! All of it.

And she's making that noise like it tastes delicious. Does it? He thinks. And when his balls go inside too, a brief fear of castration gives way to the pleasing sensation created by the presence of her lips where his sac joins his trunk. Initially, the pressure of her tongue on his balls is almost painful. Feels like a faint bruising. But then this ache and his anxiety give way to a feeling of immense comfort as his balls float inside the warm and caressing envelope of female mouth. He exhales.

When his balls slip off her bottom lip, she looks up at him and smiles. 'Mmmm.' With her hand, still tight in a leather glove, she holds his cock and begins a slow rub. A lazy rub-a-dub-dub: the beginning of a languorous wank. 'You like?'

'Yes, Ma'am,' he whispers.

She giggles and sounds very European. 'Lucretia is good, no? Better when you do it?'

'No. It's great. You're . . .' He wants to say she's a dream come true, but it's too hard to talk and concentrate on her at the same time. And it would sound silly to say something so clichéd, even though it was true. He gets muddled and just stares at the full lips and the mesmerising blue of her eyes. Never seen such a blue. Indian jewellery has that colour. Comes from a shell. Comes out of the sea.

She smiles. 'Has a girl had this pretty cock? Your girlfriend maybe?'

He doesn't know what to say. Should he lie to appear experienced? Act like he knows what he's doing? He hesitates.

She winks. 'Ahh. First time.' Slowly, she moves her tongue over her teeth while staring deep into his eyes. Long eyelashes beat once. His heartbeat pauses. 'Then I must be good for you. Make it special.'

He swallows. For a moment he thinks he could faint.

Outside the car, in the alley where the limo is parked between two tenement buildings, a bum shuffles up to the vehicle in shoes made from cardboard. A damaged face is pressed against the side window. He tries to see inside, but the glass is one-way.

The youth stiffens. Lucretia says, 'He can see nothing. Relax.' The bum shambles off to slump under the fire escape attached to the tenement. The masonry is red and slick like fresh meat.

'Take these off,' she whispers into his ear, and tugs at his jacket and shirt. She follows the gentle command with a kiss on his cheek. 'I want to see your body.'

He complies, but his nakedness in the back of this strange car with Lucretia, who he has known for less than an hour, makes him feel vulnerable. It's like his limbs have suddenly wasted to an impossible skinniness. It adds to the sense of utter insignificance he feels, like the enormity of the impending adult world is too much for him.

'So smooth,' she says, and then purrs before her lips attach themselves to a nipple. When her lips touch him here, he shivers more than when her mouth was on his cock. Her leather fingers go inside the waistband of his jeans and shorts. He raises his backside. As he moves, his naked back sticks to the leather seat. She slides his jeans down to his knees. He leans forward and his spine peels off the upholstery with a ripping sound – *shlik*. He helps her disentangle the jeans from his feet. As he fumbles to untie the laces of his boots, one of them begins to knot. He is suddenly engulfed with a wave of impotent anger. He wants to cry out with frustration. Some crazy notion tells him that if he delays with undressing the world might end and he'll never know what it would be like to have sex with this woman. The boots finally come off. Droplets of perspiration cool on his forehead.

When he leans back he sees she has unbelted her jacket. It is a dress but also a coat and has an expensive leathery smell. Something the size of a golf ball blocks his throat. His face feels hot.

Under the dress-coat she is wearing black panties. They are see-through and are cut like men's boxer shorts. Only these are tighter on her body and look much better. French knickers; he's seen them in his mother's catalogue, but not the transparent type. Under the panties, garter straps line her thighs. They attach to her stockings with clasps made from gold. White flesh, gold jewellery, black nylon; it radiates something profoundly feminine to him. Makes his stomach seize up. Her breasts are also screened behind a thin layer of silkiness that is transparent. The gauzy material of the brassière is black, but is so fine he can make out the pink of her nipples. His mouth fills with saliva. A strange sound comes from the top of his nose that embarrasses him. He swallows and cannot stop staring at her all-over loveliness: skin so white and unblemished; legs stretching down into the shiny blackness of her knee-boots, which in turn descend into the darkness of the footwell; long fingers still hugged by leather; blonde hair pinned into a coil on top of her head; one strand has fallen down but does not quite touch her collarbone. Where do you start?

'Let me lie down,' she says.

He moves off the back seat and crouches beside her. Under his bare feet he can feel his rumpled clothes. The car is warm. His armpits are wet with sweat. He can smell the leather of the seats, the musk of her scent, the brine of sex and a trace of cigar smoke that reminds him of his grandfather's study.

'Fuck my mouth? Or fuck my breasts? Which would you like?'

He can't believe she said that word. His jaw starts to shake and he is almost afraid to touch her in case she vanishes.

'Come,' she says, smiling. Touching his face with her fingers, she guides him over her, closer to her. Around his buttocks, her fingers slide. He places one hand on the carpeted parcel-shelf. With his other hand, he grips the armrest of the passenger door. She opens her mouth and stares up at him adoringly. Between those unnaturally long and white teeth, he slips his cock. Her mouth closes and she tilts her head back. Slippery lips form a seal. The heels of her boots bang against a window. Rubbing her thighs together makes her stockings hiss. She makes an 'nnnnn' noise with the bones at the front of her face. He feels it vibrate in his stomach.

After six or seven long strokes between those thick lips, his world turns to red. 'Coming.' His voice sounds strangely childish as he cries out.

'Mmmm,' she moans. Pulling his cock from her mouth, she giggles and beats it through her hand while rotating his phallus over her nose and parted lips.

It just keeps spilling out; hot wax from the liquid centre of a fat candle. One strand hits her chin – it looks like white silly-string launched on to a teenager's face at a birthday party. A second goes clear but glossy on her cheek. The third, fourth and fifth she takes inside her mouth. He completes his ejaculation, she then sucks hard on the head of his cock. Through his dispersing vision, with a galaxy of pinhead flashes falling across it, he can see her wet face and sucked in cheeks. For that moment, he has never been so excited.

And it is not long before he is hard again. She is pleased to see this.

After clambering on her hands and knees, she pushes her buttocks into the air. Kneeling on the seat behind her, the boy can see the cream of her buttocks and the pinky sucker-mouth of her anus through the sheer panties. Wet and stuck to the fabric, he can see part of her sex too. Brownish folds of skin seem ominous and incongruous to her immaculate face and body. Nature intruding on aesthetics. But the sight, and even the faint scent of her sex, adds an urgency to his desire to penetrate her. 'Like this?' she says, smiling over her shoulder.

There are two slits in her knickers: a long one in the crotch of her knickers and a smaller slit above her anus. He pushes at the long vent stuck to her sex, hoping his cock will rifle through those furrowed lips and just go inside her. But she has to put her own hand between her legs because his attempts at making an entrance are clumsy. Smiling, she gently fingers his cock and slips the tip of his phallus through her panties. When it touches the mouth of her sex, she hisses. Then she bares her teeth in a grimace. That surprises him, but excites him more than he can comprehend. 'Now,' she says.

So tight. Resisted, it feels like her sex is pushing back at his cock. She grimaces. 'Slow. You are big. Slow at first. That is it. Oh. Oh, that is good.' The ring of tightness passes halfway down his shaft and then disappears, like a tight band of elastic wound around his cock had snapped. Only softness remains.

Red-faced, he trembles all over with eagerness and delight. He slips out three times. The first two times, she slots him back inside her sex. The third time he pushes into her without any help. His cock had gone a little soft from embarrassment and fear of failure, but now feels and looks thicker and harder than ever before. And it's as if it's the thickest and hardest thing she has ever felt inside her. Lucretia bites the side of one hand. White teeth sink into black leather. She makes a snarling noise. Then begins to punch her body back at him. As his cock goes through her, she cries out as if in pain. He seizes her garter belt and then her buttocks. Steadying himself, he begins to thrust harder and deeper until she falls face first into the seat cushions. Sounds like she's weeping. Blonde hair comes loose from the grips and spills across the seat. He thrusts at her for a long time. At times his cock feels curiously numb. Then the sensation returns and he has to squeeze all the muscles inside to stop himself from shooting inside her. Condom, he thinks. Never even thought of a condom. 'Fuck me,' she says. And that's the last time he thinks about birth control.

Falling across her back, he squashes her long body into the seat. Wildly, he kisses and licks the side of her face. Her eyes are closed and she's making girlish noises of distress. Biting her shoulders, he loses all sense of self. As he bangs his crotch against her, they make the sound of raw meat slapped down on a kitchen counter. Her forehead creases into frown lines. 'In my mouth again,' she says. 'Fuck my mouth.'

'Now,' he tells her and then pulls out, quick as he can. His cock pulses.

So fast, the way she moves. Rolls on to her back; pulls herself down between his legs; gets the first bolt of come in her hair; whimpers up to him like a baby creature in a nest wanting to be fed; then rotates her wide-open mouth beneath his pumping cock. Thick syrup chugs into her mouth for a second time.

Vatican roulette, he thinks. That's what it is. Why she made me pull out. But some of it still went inside her. I felt it come out.

Collapsed together, they lie on the back seat in silence for a while. From her handbag, she produces white Swiss chocolate. Eating the chocolate bar, he whispers how good it was with her. His articulation and confidence has finally grown, and she knows the only comparison to her he possesses is a fantasy, and that pleases her. The fire-glow dims in his cheeks, but inside he's never felt so complete. In his mind, the vastness of life and experience no longer seems so daunting and his future is full of possibility and opportunity. Then she rides him.

With one hand over his mouth, she finishes the milking. Making the abducted teenager taste leather, she bucks and grinds and rubs herself on the pelvic bones of his slender boy-body. Filling her womb with inflexible cock meat, she uses gravity to force it deeper inside, craving every fraction of penetration. Head back, mouth uttering strange curses in a Slavic language, while his fingers work on her breasts under satin-with-stretch, she takes her pleasure and his youth. Innocence shot into a stranger's womb. Back seat of a limo. His first time. No one would believe him. Not ever.

Only Frank. He saw it happen. And will see it for ever when he replays his memories to make himself burn for her. Who will believe Frank?

So young; she'd even take them that young. Barely seventeen he was, this youth Frank watched her collect on one of her shopping excursions. But in truth, her prowls through department stores for designer labels were really hunts. And she, the huntress, chose carrier bags from boutiques and platinum credit cards as her camouflage. It also indicated that she was loaded. So that really torpedoed Frank's theory of her turning tricks as a call girl to support a boyfriend's expensive habits. But where the inexhaustible credit line came from was still a mystery. The prostitution angle was wishful thinking. Maybe then he would have a motive for her behaviour. In the early days it was just too hard for Frank to believe the real reason behind her appetite for flesh. Fresh flesh. Young flesh.

There was something in the young ones she craved (yes, there were others too); something they had in surplus. Vitality that would renew itself so soon after being depleted by her mouth and sex. Exuberance she could tutor. Dexterity allowing them to support her weight, waist-high, so they could work between her suspended legs, or to bend and entwine their bodies into shapes that would allow them to reach inside with their cocks and touch her at depth. Innocence, too, and it was this she desired most. Perhaps innocence had its own flavour that she craved, because she feasted on those young fools like a glutton. Like some deranged schoolmistress or governess draped in black, whose passions had enough hysteria woven through them to make her students and wards accessories to her corruption. She went after them, took them, and then left part of herself behind to haunt their memories and dreams.

Yes, there was an edge to her cravings when she captured the younger ones; something ravenous. Though a young woman herself, when she surveyed their supple limbs and tight physiques, it was as if the expression on her face betrayed an adoration of something she had lost and needed to be reminded of. She appraised them like an older woman, matured and wise but not bereft of the strong desires and needs she'd once experienced as a young and beautiful woman. It was hard for Frank to understand; this sense of experience in her, this contradiction. Something so far beyond her years coveted these yearlings to the extent that he felt she was trying to absorb them; to take from them what they would only possess at that very moment of their lives. Faces of boys with the desires of men; a turning point before youth, beauty and innocence becomes something spoilt, handsome and often disappointing. Catch it, her eagerness suggested, before the vulnerability and tenderness goes from these boy-men.

At first Frank could not believe what came through the viewings in the weeks following her party with the three society bucks – that was inadequate preparation for what was to follow. They came to her home, nervous but desperate to mistreat and be mistreated. But the boy who followed her through the department store was still a high-school virgin.

Chauffeur driven to six floors of retail luxury, Lucretia needed to recover from a particularly bad row with Eldrin that Frank witnessed the previous evening – one that left her laughing and him in tears. And on that day, as Lucretia walked into the department store, she turned every straight man's head and scorched the guts of most women with a green flame. Indifferent to the attentions of others, she smiled at this staring teenager as he stood mumbling before the perfume counter on the ground floor. On a mission for some sweetheart, he had gone to that store to buy a romantic gift, but his world stopped turning when Lucretia came through the polished lobby, intent on giving him a present he would jealously guard in secret for the rest of his life. An experience with a goddess; someone perfumed and dressed and painted like the creatures with the unreal beauty displayed in the magazines he kept at the back of his art folder. Deities he worshipped long before his most recent birthday. But this one was real

– he could see her with his own eyes and smell her fine scent too. And she had smiled at him. He'd looked away, his face hot, his collar suddenly too tight. But when he peeked again, she turned and took a second look at him too. And she smiled.

When they look back, that means they like you. That's what his older sister said. But no. Not this one. She was at least ten years older than him and too pretty to be interested. It just couldn't be true, he thought to himself with eyes as big as a raccoon's in a torch beam.

Sweetheart forgotten, he turned and followed her, spellbound by the rhythm of those long stilettos on the marble floor of the store, and enchanted by the invisible gas of scent, wafting from her pale throat to engulf his head in magic mist. Behind her on the escalator, this blond boy could not tear his gaze from her body. Long in leather of pale blue, her curves moved carefully, slowly, patiently, which made her figure all the more sensual under the dress-coat, belted tight in the middle, as if she were some delicate cargo, strapped in place and then painstakingly transported on heels of an unreasonable height. Meticulously piled beneath her little cap, her blonde hair was kept from obscuring her lovely face. But the top half of those divine features were screened by a veil, as if ruin would come to any man who saw her eyes in full.

Never had Frank seen her so beautifully prepared and never had he felt a viewing so tainted by the lust of the scores who passed her, or stopped to follow her with their eyes. But they knew they were not for her; that it would be pointless to pursue and banter and pester. They could sense that she had already made a selection. And who could ever predict where a woman's affections will be placed?

Burning from the inability (or refusal) to blink in case he missed the briefest moment of her, the boy's stare was then transfixed by the seams on the back of her calves, like they were the puppeteer's strings that manipulated his drifting legs. And to the store where they sold the most finely crafted shoes for women, he followed her.

Standing outside the shop, staring through the window displays, he wanted to kill and then replace the young female assistant who touched her legs and cradled her ankles as ten pairs of shoes were tried and nine discarded. And this tall woman who pulled him inside out, did she then notice him on the way out of the shoe store? Did she see him? He'd looked away too quickly, unable to meet her eye. But yes, when he peeked back again, unable to restrain himself, he caught her profile and the corner of a smile as she turned away and continued her journey around the first floor.

To another three boutiques he followed her and watched her buy silk scarves, a leather suit, flimsy black things that you could see right through, like tiny bats' wings fluttering across a bright and full moon, and then jewellery, until she was laden down with her purchases. Should he? Should he go to her and offer assistance? No, she had seen him downstairs and then again on the first floor. She would know he had followed her.

Then he lost sight of her behind a fountain. How could that be? She had walked from the jewellers, moved behind the spray of water that looked gold with the yellow lights shining through, and then she had vanished. Damn it! He ran around the fountain, bumping against two people in his haste to find her. Someone dropped an ice cream. Unable to apologise, he became frantic. Not like him at all. Always so quiet, so diffident, so self-deprecating, so shy. It had taken so much preparation to build the confidence to even speak to the woman behind the perfume counter so he could buy his sweetheart a present. And now look at him: girlfriend forgotten as he followed a stranger. He felt sick with himself, disgusted, concerned for this part of himself that, in the past, had been guilty of nothing more than staring for too long at his French teacher or at one of his mother's divorced friends. Desperation from too much repression.

But what was that smell? Her perfume!

Suddenly, he turned. He started, stepped back, opened his mouth.

'Surely I am not so ugly.' Her voice was somewhere between the purr of a jungle cat and the whisper of a smoker.

He swallowed. His voice failed.

A smile spread slowly across her mouth and around her eyes. 'I am sorry. I startled you.'

He grinned. His surroundings became semi-real. Yellow light shone through the sudden silence.

She raised her eyebrow. 'Am I mistaken, or are you following me?'

He shook his head, furiously, but had given himself away by colouring so deeply and by denying the accusation too quickly and too emphatically. If he had been innocent, he knew his reaction would have been different.

'I am so sure I saw you downstairs. You were staring. And then again upstairs. Am I right? Yes?'

He nodded, but it was an effort. Dizzy spell. He should run. He imagined the police arriving and then the phone call he would make to his parents from the precinct. 'Mom, you know that call you're allowed? Well, this is it. I've been arrested for stalking a

60

woman through a department store.' The shame. The disappointment on his mother's face.

'I thought so,' Lucretia said, with satisfaction creeping into her tone. 'But you are so young. Do you not have a sweetheart, a pretty boy like you? Come with me, help me with my bags and we shall find something for her.'

And off they went. Still mute, he carried her bags. His sly eyes looked at her legs, her breasts, and then her eyes. When you do that, you're finished.

She did the talking. 'Do not worry. It was I who looked first. You reminded me of someone I once knew. The likeness is uncanny. But for this indiscretion we are both guilty, and we will make amends. Each to the other.'

It had been some time since she had taken a lover. Following the night when she gave herself to the three men, Eldrin had kept her close, suffocating her with his accusations and red eyes and long speeches and reprimands until she had finally flown, petulant and driven to this. Choosing her moment, she fled to the place that eases a woman's pain, to do the thing that takes away the true impossibility of men for a while – shopping. Only now her appetite dictated what she would take home. Her hunger was terrible. Frank could sense it. After so bitter a fast, Lucretia secured this youth inside her Mercedes within 45 minutes of sighting him, gawping by the Estée Lauder display.

Under the dim white illumination of the back-seat lights, her mouth worked around him as he slept in post-coital bliss. At the time, it looked like she was giving him a long, last kiss between his legs while he lay there, grinning but too tired to continue. And as her blonde head nuzzled near his balls, Frank suffered interference with the viewing. Like the time she moved among the exhausted bodies of the three men she entertained at home, his vision broke up. The dream was over and he woke. He lost the limo, the youth and Lucretia. All gone.

Curiously weakened when he awoke from the coma of the deepest sleep, the boy was finally relocated by Frank after several failed attempts to reconnect with either of the targets. Anaemic-pale, he was slumped on a bench in a park when Frank found him. Around his unlaced boots, red and brown leaves blew across grass that looked black, like the water between icebergs. The immediacy of his short-term memory was gone and he sat alone, mystified by both the taste of lipstick in his mouth and by the sore patch under his balls that he would need a mirror to look at.

Semen and blood. Shot full of it. Frank imagined her lounging in the car, smiling all the way home. And if he had been on duty that evening, and if he had met her outside the front entrance, to carry her purchases up to her apartment, Frank knew her speech would have been slurred.

What was she?

Five

This man's feelings for her were so passionate, his cravings so perverse, his stare so intense, maybe she sensed him? Sensed his attentions or even smelled his excitement and fear. Predators can do that.

Down in the bar of the hotel, a strong woman like that must have intuited the presence of a man so weak with his particular weakness. How else could this guy explain it? Women like her never looked at men like him, not in that way and not unless he was paying them by the hour.

And he'd never seen a pair of boots like that either. Beautifully cut from the best leather, treated to a patent finish, and then fashioned with a skintight fit over her feet, ankles and calves. Cruel heels would have made walking difficult for her; he could see that too. Spikes more than heels, if he were to be precise, while he watched her front foot snake around the legs of her stool.

Attempting to view another of Lucretia's excursions outside of the building, Frank's remote viewing carried him to the perspective of an ordinary middle-aged man in a suit. He was sipping a cocktail in the bar of a good hotel, yearning to get on his knees before Lucretia as she sat on a barstool, further along from his lonely and nervous vigil. Sometimes, while trying to reach a target and intuit their state of mind, Frank's psychic ability latched on to the point of view of someone near Lucretia, who felt strongly for her. Someone, like this guy, who wanted those silver-tipped stilettos on his body with her weight behind them. Wanted her spit on his face, her leathered knuckles beating his body, her . . .

Stop it, the guy in the good suit told himself; it was never going to happen. And soon he'd start to think he'd been missing out his whole life and would go to bed drunk and depressed.

But it was no good. Subconsciously and then consciously, his thoughts turned to her again. This woman, three stools down, drinking alone with that severe look on her exquisite face, was the kind of woman he worshipped: the length of her body (a veritable giantess), the arch of her eyebrows, the black leather suit and fur coat, the leather gloves, the boots . . . those boots. Damn it, he couldn't stop looking at those boots and imagining them doing damage to his body. Punishing him for being wealthy and influential and out of shape and comfortable with a big colonial house, a wife and three kids. But she wouldn't care. She'd grind him into the carpet of his hotel room, call him vile names, clean out his wallet and leave him choking on her underwear. If only.

Shaking his head, he looked into his drink. Another one finished. Just melting ice cubes and sour water left. Why did he have to see her? What was she doing here? This was the preserve of a travelling businessman like himself, looking to put another day out of its misery on a barstool. There was no date and she wasn't looking for company; he'd seen her shoot four guys down already. And she was only drinking mineral water. It seemed odd, but he still felt she had come to this bar for something specific. Something that was about to happen. Yes, it was imminent, he could see that. Maybe she was a high-class hooker waiting to go upstairs when the client was ready. He'd seen that look before; a hard focus before committing an illicit though necessary deed.

Sighing, he took his eyes off her and looked down at his hands on the bar. So now, he'd have an image of her trapped inside his head for weeks, months, years, maybe for ever. He had most of what a man of his age wanted and worked for, but still found himself looking forward to nothing and craving her, and if not her, the idea of her. Why couldn't he be satisfied with what he had? He didn't deserve his lot in life because he still wanted her – a woman like that – to break him.

He supposed he could call an escort agency; he often did on the road. But it would never be as good with a hired mistress as it would be with a woman who was naturally sadistic; a young and beautiful woman who would get off on his discomfort and pain and humiliation; a woman who would only let him lick those boots to further his debasement and her pleasure; *the* woman he had always wanted to meet. Maybe he would hire a call girl after all, just to pretend it was the girl in black, six stools down.

But wait. She was coming over. Not smiling; no, that wouldn't suit her. But definitely looking at him for the first time that evening, as she elegantly untangled herself from her seat and then strode towards him.

'Let's go,' she whispered into his ear, once she stood close to him. He smiled up at her. She looked away, like he was despicable or just not worth it. And she was in a hurry. 'Your room,' she said.

Short of breath because of this sudden tightness in his chest, the man grabbed at his jacket and followed her, too afraid to blink in case she were nothing more than a sour-mash-mirage.

Ten minutes later, he found himself naked and trussed in his hotel room with this mad Russian, or whatever she was. Perched on the bed with her legs crossed, she looked down to where he lay on the rug, a few feet from her heels. Smoking a cigarette, the only expression on her face was displeasure.

Except the two lamps on the bedside tables, all of the other lights had been doused by her swift, leather-clad fingers. She'd then used the curtain sash for securing his ankles and the cord of his robe to bind his wrists. And they were tied tight; his skin started to itch where it touched the restraints.

'You make me angry,' she said, in the tone of voice he guessed she would use to ask a waiter to take food back to the kitchen. It pleased him. She continued: 'Perhaps I should have warned you before I came here that I will be severe with you. And in no way can I respect you. Know that.'

He nodded. It was as it should be. Inside, he felt good. 'Yes.'

Angrily, she stubbed her cigarette out on his thousand-dollar suit, draped over the bed, near to where she was perched. 'It speaks. But does it think I care what it has to say?'

'No.'

'That's right. So it won't mind if I gag it.'

'Well –'

'Shut your fucking mouth,' she said, without even looking at him.

He swallowed. His eyes watered when she unzipped her skirt. 'Did I say you could look?' she asked, meeting his eye and momentarily pausing when her skirt had been pushed down to her hips.

Down on the rug, the perspiring man shook his head.

'Then don't.' He turned his face away, but heard the sound of soft leather moving across nylon. Genuinely wary of her temper but exhilarated by the potential for its fullest expression, and desperate to see her long legs disappearing into those cruel boots, he turned his head and risked a peek. Seamed nylons coated her legs – essential in his experience for a woman to reach the height of her powers. They were attached to the leather corset that kept her slender body so firm beneath the suit and flimsy blouse.

One quick step and she was by his side. The toe of her boot was jammed between his teeth. Decisively, she turned his face away and then placed the tip of a heel on the crown of his balding head. 'Did I say you could watch?' She raised her voice to repeat the question.

He shook his head.

'Then would it be unreasonable of me not to correct your bad manners?' Her voice had adopted a sarcastic tone.

'No, Miss.'

'And that's the last of your pitiful voice I ever want to hear. The very last. We do this my way.' Between his lips he felt the salty fabric of her panties. With a gloved finger, she stuffed the whole garment inside his mouth until he nearly gagged. Breathing through his nose, he felt his cock stiffen against the carpet.

She walked away and opened a drawer of the bedside cabinet. He guessed she wasn't reaching for the *Gideon Bible* either. When she returned, a sleeping mask was pulled over his eyes. From the end of its range, the elasticated band was then allowed to snap against the back of his head, which produced a muffled yelp from behind his gag. His world was dark now.

Her voice came from above. 'The next thing you will see, if you're lucky, is the face of the maid who will find you tomorrow at noon. She will be the first, but I hope not the last, to see what a piece of shit you truly are.'

He had business meetings the next morning. No! Instinctively, he tried to cry out and discharge the obstruction from his mouth, but succeeded only in chewing satin; the panties were crammed in too tight. And what about another woman seeing his disgrace; one dressed in the pink uniform of the hotel's cleaning staff that he had admired earlier? That was too much. Too good to be true. Clenching the muscles in his groin, he struggled to collect and pace himself.

'While I work on you, I only want to see the marks I make. The only interesting thing about you is your suffering.'

At last, he thought. At last. And in his darkness and within his bonds, she took him to his limit like she was in tune with his inner life.

Rolling him over and over with the sole and the sharp heel of her boots, she forced him towards the bed. 'On your knees,' she said. 'Bend over the bed. Face down.' The first two times he struggled into position she flattened him back down to the carpet with the sole of her boot against the side of his head, and then repeated her command. After the third instruction, she allowed him to rise from the floor and then flop his torso and head against the duvet. He felt like a long, blind, wormy creature with no limbs. The nerve endings on his back began to prickle. He knew what to expect; this girl liked to tenderise her meat. And when she flexed and snapped his leather belt through the air close to his tailbone, it made the sound of wet towels in changing rooms.

For the next 30 minutes, she slowly basted him red with his own belt. First his thighs, then his naked buttocks, then his back; the strokes being hard and continuous. And to complement the deep, refreshing discomfort and the idea of his abject debasement at the hands of this young and lithe creature, he entertained an image of her in his mind, dressed in the leather corset he had glimpsed, the seamed stockings and the boots. Even without the use of his eyes, he somehow knew that while she worked him over, not a single hair on her head would budge, and that the stiff look of contempt on her face never eased. Nothing of Lucretia changed besides a delightful flush of passion on her cheeks and the evidence of a new wildness in her eyes.

Only when her shoulder began to ache did she throw the belt aside and catch her breath. On the bed, her worm had stopped moving. That is, until she clenched one gloved hand in the hair at the back of his head and seized his wrists with the other hand before moving him back to the floor. Eyes watering, he found himself face down on the rug again.

But for a while she did nothing; did not even move out there in the darkness. And it was tortuous waiting for the next sensation. She could have been robbing him, or even photographing him; he was entirely at her mercy, as it had to be. But when he finally felt the tip of her boot heel at the base of his back, he knew she was ready to start walking again.

Pressed down by the weight of her beautiful body, her spike heels moved between muscle and bone, preceded by the flat, heavy oval of her leather soles. From his waist, over his ribs and on to his shoulders she moved, and then turned, making him scream into the gag before retracing her spiky steps down to his buttocks, still acutely sensitive from the lashing.

Rolling him on to his back with short but swift kicks against his ribs, she then removed his blindfold.

Now he could see the length of leg towering above him, the leather tight on the curve of her calf muscles – a line only the most skilled artist could replicate. And he stared at her knees and thighs, still glassy in nylon despite only a dim illumination from the bedside lamps. And the sight of her unclothed sex with the hair trimmed right down so her puckered lips were pronounced, and her breasts compacted in leather cups of her corset, he wanted to believe this gift of sight was a reward for his unconditional trust and surrender. But it was doubtful; he sensed little compassion in Lucretia. His desire to submit fuelled her craving to bully and dominate; that was the only certainty. So why did she remove the blindfold? Perhaps to watch the look in his eyes during the ultimate debasement.

Crouching, with her ankles gripping his ears, her sex hovered a few inches above his mouth. Drenching his face, filling his nose and throat, her sour-salty smell made his sex strain upward. 'You want to taste me?' she whispered, her voice soft.

He groaned over his gag.

'You want my sweet pussy in your mouth?'

The man tried to nod. She pulled the gag from his mouth. But before he could speak, she reached over her thighs, hooked her fingers into his cheeks and pulled his lips wide apart. She laughed at the sight of him and then said, 'Well I don't care what you want. This is about me. Keep your mouth open, or I'll fucking destroy you.' Slowly, she removed her leather fingers from his saliva-filled mouth.

Gripping the hair at the side of his head, Lucretia then pulled his face up towards her sex until his nose was tickled by her floss. She widened her knees, too. And at that range, when she allowed the clear, hot urine to flow from out of her, he caught most of it in

70

his mouth. Any that missed dripped off his chin and ran in stinging, spicy rivulets over his cheeks and down his neck.

'Now stick your tongue out and keep it firm.'

Spluttering a little, and still reeling with shock, he managed to comply with the next of her wishes. Tilting her head back with her eyes closed, she lowered his head back down to the floor and her body with it. Balancing on her feet, still in a crouch, her sex met the tip of his tongue. Placing a hand on each of her shiny knees, she moved her body in a tiny rotation as he kept his tongue upright and still. All the muscles in his mouth began to ache. 'Good,' she murmured, and brushed her lips up and down, so his tongue furrowed within them. 'Mmm. Now close your mouth and grit your teeth.' He obeyed. Moaning, she began to gently rub her sex over his chin and lips and nose. Using one of her own fingers, she pressed and then rubbed at her clit. 'I'm going to come on your face,' she said, in a louder more triumphant voice. And while he lay still, she used his face for her own pleasure. Pressing down hard and grinding herself on the bones of his sticky features, her movements eventually became jerky and she uttered a series of short coughing sounds without even opening her mouth.

Holding her head and smiling to herself, she stood up and began to walk around the room, lighting a cigarette with her back turned to him. He extended his tongue and licked the salty brine from around his mouth.

Casually, she returned to his prostrate shape and gave it an idle kick. 'You have a not displeasing cock,' she said. Immediately, he began to shiver. He was still erect. In fact, he could not remember the last time he had sustained such a continual state of

71

arousal. She had flogged him, trampled him, showered him with piss and then used his face as a sex aid: she was good. And now she might even let him fuck her. But the moment he had that thought, uncannily, he seemed to share it with her.

'Shame you're not going to use it,' she said derisively. 'Just not worthy. And I like them bigger, to be honest. Wimps don't fuck me. I prefer to fuck them over. But, my little doggy, I have another use for that tongue.' Without another word, she untied his hands, but not his ankles.

Sitting on the bed, she stretched out a leg. 'Take my boots off. My feet hurt. But if you touch my legs, I'll make you wish you'd never been born. Understand?'

He nodded and then lowered his eyes. After crawling across to her, the man pulled himself on to his knees. She watched him closely. Cradling the heel of her boot in his lap, beside his hard and veiny shaft, he pinched the zipper of her boot and slowly drew it down her leg as if he were defusing a bomb. Agonising though it was, he never once allowed his shaky fingers to stray against the warm nylon on her lower leg, ankle or foot. Once the boot was removed, she stretched her toes back. At the end of her long and supple feet, her toenails were painted the colour of polished fire engines. 'Now the other,' she said, after exhaling a plume of smoke. Her eyes were half-lidded. After repeating the same delicate manoeuvre, he sat back on his bound ankles and awaited his next instruction. But down in his lap, her hot and tired feet began to rotate and brush against the now straining muscles in his sex. Spreading her toes, she pushed his shaft against his abdomen and then rubbed the foot up and down. Swallowing, the man gritted his teeth and felt his eyes water from the exquisite touch of her foot. The end of his phallus became shiny with pre-come.

'My feet ache. Lie on your back and face the ceiling with your head between my ankles.' Executing the instruction without delay, the man eagerly awaited her next move. And though to many it may have seemed ridiculous, or perhaps mysterious, Lucretia's plaything experienced all the joys of orgasm without ejaculating when she pushed the soles of her tired feet on to his face. Massaging the hot underside of her long toes and heels and gently rippled instep against the contours of his bone structure, she closed her eyes and smoked another cigarette down to the filter. He could not breathe when she ground her pads against his nostrils and filled his mouth with her shiny toes. But he risked suffocation just for the honour of having a young, bad-tempered, demanding and spoiled bitch's feet trampling his face and identity into that of a nameless object: naked inconsequential foot furniture.

When her feet were sufficiently revitalised, she peeled her stockings off her legs, right above his wide and now protruding eyes. Pulling him on to the bed, she punched and slapped his body straight and then pulled his arms wide apart before tying them off to the bedposts with her hosiery. Untying his feet, she then used the old restraints to tie his ankles to the bottom legs of the bed so his body formed a star-shape. 'Is that too tight?' she said. 'Maybe a little uncomfortable?'

The plaything nodded, daring to smile. She slapped it from his face with a leathery backhand and said, 'Good.'

Straddling him, she unlaced her corset. For a few minutes he stared at her breasts, and could see the faint lines left behind by the edges of her underwired foundation wear. But soon the sight of them and her naked body and cold face were lost to him, and he would never see them again. After pulling a pillow from its sleeve, she hooded him with the pillowcase and tucked it under his chin. It seemed Lucretia was ready to pleasure herself again.

Gripping his ribs with her knees, she held his erection at the base and eased her body down and over it. When his entire manhood had been swallowed by her sex, she built up her rhythm until the entire bed shuddered and squealed under her bouncing, pumping, extracting onslaught. And as she rode him and ground herself against his pelvic bones, she lashed out with her leather fists and indented not only the pillowcase but the sweating and grateful face beneath.

He managed to hold back until he heard the sounds of her pleasure, but as he came with considerable force and volume, he felt her teeth sink into his flesh, below the left nipple. And then Lucretia and the hooded plaything were lost to Frank.

When Frank awoke from the viewing, he realised that although she enjoyed the thrill of the hunt, she liked to shoot fish in a barrel as well. And the next time he saw her, Frank learned she could also be the bait to get her fix.

Six

Indoors, she still kept the sunglasses on. Slicked back from her face, her blonde hair looked dark, like the leather suit she wore; jacket and knee-length skirt both catching the electric wall lights in the hotel corridor. Beneath the jacket – open to her breastbone – her blouse was made from white silk. Heels were thin and high. Hosiery was nude and seam-free. Rouge bruised her cheeks, the lipstick a wet red against the pallor of her throat. A leopardskin coat completed her ensemble. Permissible provocation.

When she stood before the chosen door, she brought her gloved hands together in front of her stomach. Looped across her curled fingers was the strap of the attaché case she carried. Although her face was impassive, Frank could sense the excitement inside her. She was thrilled by something that was about to happen. And this anticipation excited the hunger Frank had come to identify as a prelude to her illicit behaviour. Five days had passed since she left that man in the hotel room, which was about as long as she could possibly go without sex and the curious biting ritual that always followed intimacy.

The door opened and she was admitted to a large hotel suite. It had a living room with furniture: a sofa, two easy chairs, a coffee table with the debris from a recent room-service order on top, and against one wall there was a black cabinet. Fixed into the cabinet was a large television set. On the television red flowers protruded from a vase. On a silver trolley there was a stainless-steel coffee pot, a dish of mints and some menus. Hotel crap.

There were three men in the room. Two dressed in dark, formal suits, and then a third, wearing a bath-robe, appeared in the doorway of the adjoining bedroom. The hairs on the back of Frank's arms stood up in sympathy with Lucretia's identification of a threat. The man in the gown appeared to be the leader of the group. His face was scarred in places and he had different coloured eyes. When he smiled at Lucretia, her stomach tightened.

The two suits searched her. Seemingly indifferent to their touch, she stood with her feet planted apart. The heels of her slingbacks sunk into the thick carpet. It was the colour of oatmeal. One of the suits stood behind her and patted his hands up her arms to the shoulder. Then he checked under her arms and down her back to her waist, where he gently squeezed her. Over her stomach his broad hands then moved upwards, tracing the contours of her ribcage. Briefly, he cupped her breasts in his hands and the rough pads of his thumbs brushed over her nipples. It made her shiver but she kept her face straight.

On his knees before her, the second suit massaged his fingers up the outside of her skirt – knee to thigh to buttocks – and he was in no hurry to complete the search. When he felt the impression of her garters beneath her skirt, his hands became hesitant and his touch lighter. Before his arms fell back at his sides, they smoothed down the teardrop curves of her calves. Nylon swished against her waxed skin. He stood up, glanced at the opaque lenses of her glasses and then turned around. He nodded to the man in the robe. When Robe smiled, the men in suits relaxed their shoulders.

Lucretia moved further into the room. Robe walked towards her, his face creased with pleasure, both hands outstretched in greeting. Ignoring his welcome, Lucretia sat down on the sofa. Shrugging off the dismissal like he enjoyed it, the scarred man offered her a variety of beverages while the suits took up positions beside the hospitality cabinet. Lucretia accepted water from a bottle. The air in the suite was too hot, or was she cleaning her palette? Beneath the leather suit her skin dampened. Frank's perceptions were vivid. It was like he was in that room with them.

On the glass top of the table she placed the attaché case. She worked the combination and then unclasped the brass fastenings. Finally, she pushed her glasses into her hair. Then she slid the case across the table towards the couch where Robe sat.

Packages the size of bricks were removed from the case by Robe. There were six parcels. Each was wrapped in white tissue paper. Around the outside of the paper was an unbroken seal; the kind seen in bank vaults. The actual contents Frank never saw, but felt their lure and the evil they inspired.

Grinning, Robe loaded the packages back inside the case. Rubbing his hands and grinning, he spoke to the guards. They collected the case from the table and took it to the bedroom. Slouching on the sofa, Robe smiled at Lucretia. His gown slipped off one knee. He patted the seat next to him with one hand. The fingers of his other hand played with the tassels on the fringe of a cushion. Payment was somehow incomplete. She raised her chin. Frank felt the growl inside her, but Robe did not.

Lucretia stood, walked around the table and sat beside Robe. Knees together, she stared straight ahead while he whispered in her ear. Gently, the fingers of his left hand brushed her shiny and exposed knees. Leaning across her, the man then began to fondle her breasts. She did not resist; she did not even move.

Then he pinched a nipple, and she gasped and writhed in her seat. Clattering with gold bracelets and a watch, one of her arms swung around like the boom across the deck of a laser yacht. The blow connected. Robe caught her wrist on the rebound from his cheek and then seized her other hand too. Squeezing, he hurt her wrists. His eyes glinted with a sadistic delight and he grinned at her. She tried to pull away, but he held her fast. Spiking his naked ankle with the heel of her shoe, she made him yelp and he released her hands. But before she could rise from the sofa and escape, he recovered enough to slap her face, hard.

Shocked, Lucretia touched her glowing cheek. Inside, where only Frank could go, she relaxed and warmed. Between her legs a reaction began that ended in a shiver on the nape of her neck.

Both bodyguards appeared beside the sofa and began to dither. Robe was smiling again. He issued an order to his henchmen. Lucretia raised her chin and issued a silent challenge. The guards exchanged glances and then looked back at their leader for confirmation. His smile disappeared when he repeated the command.

Lucretia was helped to her feet by the guards, who took an arm each. Gently they led her to the adjoining bedroom. Pulling her elbows free of their loose fingers, she walked the remainder of the distance unassisted before coming to a standstill on the white rug at the base of the large bed. Robe followed them into the room.

In here, the doors of the walk-in closet space were mirrored. Without looking at Lucretia, Robe opened one of the wardrobe doors. He removed a digital camera, tripod and black case. He closed the door. The case was placed on the bed; the camera set up by the open door of the bedroom. Robe's cheeks turned ruddy and he wiped his fringe from out of his eyes. One guard rubbed his shaven jaw; the other removed his watch.

Her face adopted a sly expression; half smile, half contempt. She removed her leopardskin coat and tossed it at the guard with the blond crew cut. He caught the coat and held it reluctantly in the crook of his arm, like a man with a baby at a christening. Lucretia pinched her earrings from her ears and stepped out of her skirt.

White panty girdle, no panties, stockings, heels, white silk blouse: all three men paused to take in the vision. They were amazed at the compliance this go-between exhibited; they thought it was going to be difficult to have their way with the delivery girl. Excitement grew among them. Silence added to the anticipatory ecstasy. The guards stopped dithering. They went to her. Tilting her head back, she closed her eyes and let them cover her face, neck and shoulders with kisses and bites. As they hurriedly undressed, they became ungainly and tugged her about before pressing her back towards the bed. Falling on the mattress, she then used her spike heels to push herself into the middle. They pursued her. One still wore his socks, the other his white T-shirt.

After checking the camera angle, Robe hurriedly opened the black case he had removed from the closet. Carefully, he extracted a short baton. Pointing it at the floor, he unwrapped the long leather braids from around the handle.

79

Holding her shoulders, Socks pushed Lucretia's body face down in the bedclothes. T-shirt grasped her ankles and placed them between his knees. They pushed her body towards each other, and she was forced to all fours like a concertina. Her slick hair became disordered and fell across her cheeks in spikes.

Robe began by trailing the strands of leather across her thighs and backside. As he did this, he taunted her; told her what it was she craved, and just how her reaction on the sofa was evidence of that. Frank experienced an impression Robe was reminding her of the last time she delivered a package. His words made her smoulder with shame, anger and an over-whelming desire for revenge. They also made her crave a debasement, abuse and a handling like the last time she and Robe met.

It was then Frank received a snapshot of her memory at work: superimposed over the scene in the hotel room, he saw her pressed against the brick walls of an alleyway as three men took turns holding her in place before furiously throwing themselves inside her. And from the long shadows their heaving bodies cast up the alley, Frank knew Eldrin watched with satisfaction. What was it she sought in these bad men?

When Frank's viewing refocused on the hotel room, he intuited the potency of her growing passions and the foul things that would spill from her mouth as the evening matured. Robe thought he understood her. He did, but only in part. She looked forward to surprising Robe with the depths of where her noctur-nal adventures would soon plummet – the part of her he underestimated.

Robe lashed her, counted to four, and lashed her again. She whimpered. The guards with the long erections watched her. Through their hands they felt her softness tremble. Through their knees they felt the vibrations of her grunts, expelled by the impact of the thin leather tails, beaded at the end. When she cried out 'Bastard' they renewed and tightened their grips on her shoulders and ankles, anticipating a struggle. It never came. Robe continued to lash her until she fell silent and her pubic hair was plastered to the lips of her sex.

He threw the flail down and moved back behind his camera. Pale-faced, he swallowed and seemed to be shaking like a man no longer in control of himself. One of his eyelids began to twitch; it annoyed him but there was nothing he could do to stop it. Unable to look her in the eye, he muttered something and the guards became active.

T-shirt gently turned her over. He brushed the wet hair off her forehead and then kissed her nose. Lucretia gulped at the air. Not fooled by this show of tenderness, she prepared for something ruthless. Socks sunk his face between her thighs. Stroking her legs with his unnecessarily hairy hands, the attentions of his lips and then his tongue were surprisingly skilled and drew a reaction from Lucretia. Although appearing to resist, she turned her face to one side and her red lips parted against the duvet cover. T-shirt began to stroke his hand along the length of his cock, about a foot from her exposed cheek. Lucretia turned her face and stared at an incredible girth.

To Frank's horror, she wet her lips in readiness. There was no resistance as it was pushed between her bright teeth. In fact, her face emitted an expression of adoration. The cock stretched her mouth wide and she swallowed three quarters of its length. She felt pleasure. He intuited this and also sensed her helplessness. The two merged and became indistinguishable.

Around the bed, Robe strolled. Most of his face was concealed behind the camera. After seeing his partner's cock greedily eaten, Socks removed his wet mouth from between Lucretia's thighs, sat up and began to rub the tip of his phallus through the folds of her sex. Her buttocks began to gyrate in readiness.

Frank lost sense of her specific thoughts; the calculations and manipulations vanished and she became an entity that existed for sensation and for the sense of what it was to be assertively handled and thoroughly used. Everything was cast off; this was what she had come here to feel. She could not free herself of these needs. And no drinks or drugs were required to remove her inhibitions. Those chains within had been broken the moment she began dressing at home. And the fact that she could do this sober, with those she felt nothing for, sent a shudder through Frank.

Perturbed by the unfathomable, he anticipated a sudden counter-attack from her. He saw the men in that room as being temporarily useful to her, like the diminutive mates of a black widow spider. Robe never did; he couldn't see much further than the end of his zoom lens. Socks and T-shirt resorted to that tired male response of 'slut', unaware that there was no such thing, that there would always be a deeper, more complex motive to a woman's surrender. And when faced with her compliance, their first climaxes were not long in coming. Lucretia's mouth was filled first.

Holding her own legs under the knee, she widened herself and closed her eyes to enjoy the penetration between her legs when the stranger in socks began to hit the right spot. Her cries of passion induced a harder response from Socks. Hammering himself between her legs, he moved her body right up the bed until she had to fend the wall away with the palms of both hands, her nails becoming drops of blood on the smooth white decor. Pulling out at the final moment, he massaged long ropes of cream on to her breasts, staring all the time in mute disbelief at what he was doing to her.

And so it continued and the bodyguards exhausted themselves by failing to exhaust her. Swapping positions, they took her mouth and sex one more time each. T-shirt again came first and lay back to watch his colleague enter her tight backside while her high heels locked behind the back of his head. And when he came for the third and final time, not a drop was spilled on to the crumpled bedsheets.

Her make-up washed away by sweat and tears and lips, her stockings twisted, and her hair flattened, Lucretia still managed to elegantly remove herself from the bed and to kick off her shoes. Without a word, her face inscrutable again, she then disappeared into the bathroom to shower and repair herself, leading Socks by the hand behind her. What affection could she possibly feel for this brute? Watching her walk to the bathroom with him in tow was the greatest horror of all for Frank.

Robe turned the camera off and nodded in salute to the exhausted and sleepy T-shirt, who lit a cigarette to stay awake.

Again Frank's viewing began to break up. Always at this point, after the sex. Prepared, like he'd planned to be the next time a psi-episode was threatened by this fragmentation or fade, he managed to hold on to something. Continuity was not constant – there was no smooth narrative of events unfolding in real time. Instead, he received a series of snapshots

83

or polaroids like his very first attempts at synchronised dreaming so many years before. But the psychic debris that flashed and then faded in his mind, like sixteen-millimetre film exposed to dust and sunlight, would never be forgotten.

Gagged by her panties and hog-tied at ankle and wrist by knotted nylons, Socks stared up at Lucretia from the tiled floor of the bathroom. Steam clouds from the blasting shower spray misted his nakedness. Through the fog of vapour, Frank caught sight of a suggestion of something crimson on the tiles. In Socks' eyes was a frozen look of horror. And before the bloodied mirror, screwed to the wall above the sink, Lucretia reapplied her lipstick.

By the time she opened the bathroom door, Robe and T-shirt were drinking Red Label High Balls in the living room.

Darkness.

Long white fingers with immaculate red nails stroked the leather of a shoulder holster.

Another break in transmission.

Muzzle flashes came out of the picture break-up. One, two, three, four.

Blood on a white robe.

Muzzle flashes. Five, six, seven, eight. And a body fell through the top of a glass table.

Job done, but four more muzzle flashes just for fun.

Another break in transmission. Frank grasped and swiped at every recollection he possessed of Lucretia, trying to get back to that hotel room, so that he would know what she had done.

Into his head came an image he struggled to accept: the picture of a naked woman on all fours. Head dipped, tongue out, Lucretia lapped at something that had been spilt on the carpet, like she was a cat who had secured the Sunday joint in her jaws and taken it down to the kitchen floor to feed upon.

Frank awoke with a jolt; his shirt like a rag at a car wash. Then he slumped back to the nightmare place. Or rather, was dragged to it, like it was she that now insisted he see more.

Stumbling down a hotel corridor in her slingbacks, smiling to herself, Lucretia left the way she came, only this time she carried a small tape from a digital camera, along with the attaché case in her hands. And this time she could not walk in a straight line.

Seven

Ran until he could taste blood in his mouth. Ran through a storm where the wind blew the rain, with the merciless cold bite of sleet, into the side of his head. Kicking up the leaves in the park and slapping across wet tarmac and sidewalk, his feet propelled him until his heart began to stutter and the pain in his lungs was a scream for him to stop. Frank ran because he had to.

First day away from the building for a whole week and he was compelled to seek exhaustion to obliterate emotion. And although he was some distance from his place of work, Lucretia was still with him; always with him now, awake or asleep. Desire clashed with horror. Fear clashed with obsession. Sympathy clashed with repulsion. Images of her haunted him: cocks in her mouth; cocks in her sex; cocks in her hands; cocks in her ass; red stripes on her back; hands with white knuckles restraining her wrists; wilfully submitting on all fours or dominating in high heels, she possessed Frank. Anonymous faces under her feet, or between her legs, or those he'd seen staring into her eyes, appeared in his daydreams or broke his feeble concentration on other matters, or crashed into his attempts at meditating towards emptiness. Gun flashes in an uptown hotel room. Blood on the tiles and blood on the mirror and blood on the carpet. Couldn't let go of it. All kept coming back – motives and scenes he couldn't synthesise or understand. Exercise was the only respite from his thoughts of her; pursuing distraction through fatigue. Extreme behaviour for extreme times.

Lucretia was smart and beautiful and elegant and educated, so why did she do these things? Why was she mixed up with that pasty fuck Eldrin? Why swoop on a high-school kid in the department store? And what made her go at the guy from the bar so savagely? Did she really whack those guys in the hotel room? And why did he always lose the viewing during those crucial moments after her encounters had been consummated? Was his scrutiny becoming tainted by infatuation to the extent that he imagined these half-glimpses of her biting her lovers? The remote viewings were more vivid and multi-sensory than anything he'd ever experienced. Which even raised his doubts as to their validity. Was it humanly possible, even in the too untested realms of ESP, and even for a man like himself, no matter how sensitive or well trained he was, to actually see, feel, intuit and sometimes hear so much about this woman from a remote location?

And there was another reason why he was running so hard: Frank had broken his brief. Nothing in what he was receiving from the remote viewings made sufficient sense now, especially when compared to what she had told him herself. *What she had told him herself.*

Running all morning, trying to pound the residue of these visions and fresh anxieties out of his system with every heavy footfall on the sidewalk brought only a temporary relief. Because after he climbed the stairs to his tenement apartment, gasping all the way like a goldfish on a hearth rug, he found the front door open. And then he smelled cigarette smoke.

On the kitchen table, three spent butts were stinking out his favourite coffee mug. Ally Kram lit another cigarette when he appeared in the doorway. It was a 100 which made the body of the cigarette look especially long between her thin fingers. Through the first exhalation of bluey smoke she looked him over. 'I have a problem with these.' With a red fingernail she tapped the three reports she had taken from the desk in the living room and placed on the kitchen table before her. They detailed the last three viewings he'd undertaken. The folders were open and the paper clips had been removed.

Frank glared at her. 'And I have a problem with you helping yourself. How the fuck did you get in here?'

She held up a key and then dropped it back in the pocket of her suit jacket. 'You take issue with invasion of privacy? Surely not.' She smiled, but not in a way to bring pleasure to the recipient.

After kicking the front door shut, Frank bent over and put his hands on his knees. Sweat had begun to dry cold on his spine.

Kram spoke to the top of his head. 'Hit the shower, Frank. You're starting to smell. And I can't deal with you in this mood. This is twice you've been rude to me. Not at all professional.'

'Fuck you and fuck professional,' he muttered and left the kitchen, seeking sanctuary in the bathroom that smelled of black mushrooms that grew under people's stairs in boxes filled with soil. Ripping the dressing off his neck made him wince; but the flesh no longer looked angry. The red puckered skin had become purple, barely perceptible – a scratch, a love bite. There was no cold water again. Just a scalding spray of sticky piss from the shower head. 'And get me a fucking plumber!'

When he came out the bathroom – two layers of skin lighter and looking as pink as a King Prawn – Agent Kram sat in the same chair in the same position, her long legs crossed at the knee, the front foot bouncing with impatience. She drew hard on the cigarette. The filter was stained plum from where it touched her lips. 'The high-school kid I don't have a problem with. The gimp from the bar is believable also. But this thing in the hotel room? No. Definitely not good. We would have heard about that. And while you were out running, I made some calls to make sure. It never happened. No shootings in hotels in the period you mention, or at all for over a month now. Which makes me think your visions have been tainted.'

There had been nothing about the demise of Robe, Socks or T-shirt in the papers. Frank had checked. He guessed it was something the cops or the Bureau were keeping from the press. They did that sometimes, and what he'd seen in that room had been extraordinarily clear, at least at the start. And wasn't this what he was looking for: criminal activity? 'She greased them. All three. One in the bathroom who she tied up. The other two in the living room. She emptied the fucking magazine. The maid or someone would have found them. The next morning at the latest.'

Agent Kram exhaled. The plume of smoke came right at him. She shook her head. Her hair still managed to shine in the weak grey light seeping through the kitchen window below the half-drawn and yellowy blinds. Frank thought her style and beauty incongruous to the stained tiles, scuffed cabinet doors and fly-specked strip light. It made him feel especially inferior to her, and deeply alienated from his employers. He felt like he'd been put in the apartment as a form of punishment. But what had he been expecting? Special treatment? No, but was the support of his colleagues or a proper briefing too much to ask for? Although even he harboured doubts about the vivid nature of his responses to Lucretia, Kram didn't know that. She wasn't a viewer, so how could she pass judgement on variants in transmission and receipt? She just disliked him and it made Frank seethe.

Kram shook her head again and pushed the three folders away from her. 'There is nothing certain about what you see. No guarantees it's factual. You're not one hundred per cent accurate. No one is, or ever has been with remote viewing. And this investigation is only a trial exercise for us. Testing the water, nothing more. And it looks a little shallow and cloudy to me. We hoped you could give us something beyond lurid sexual fantasy.'

Too outraged to respond, he leaned against the sink unit and closed his eyes. All he managed to do was hold a hand up to stop her. She ignored the hand. 'I think you're getting too close to the target. Your emotions could be interfering with the viewings. Corrupting them. She's a beautiful woman and we know how susceptible you are to the ladies. It's in your profile, Frank. The perversion you see must come from the extra sensitivity you've developed.' Her voice had gone sarcastic. She stubbed the cigarette out in his mug. 'From the details of your first viewing, it looked like you were watching some kind of perverted role play between her and Eldrin. A love-hate thing. That we already had some intelligence about. Only you inferred that she was probably in danger and just obeying his will. When she lets her three charming dinner guests walk her like a dog, you think she's using her infidelity against Eldrin. Punishing him, but getting him off too. But in the new ones –' She prodded the reports again '– when she fucks the high-school kid and the businessman, Eldrin is nowhere to be seen. She's acting on her own volition, is she not? And according to your last account, she takes out an untraceable organised crime outfit, single-handedly, with their own weapons. Quite a feat and not at all compatible with her hapless and submissive nature. And yet, from the tone of your report, she's still the victim to you. Crow has this hold on her and makes her do these disgusting things.' Frank looked at her; shocked at her condemnation of Lucretia's behaviour. He'd thought Kram invulnerable and cold. But this outburst sounded personal. 'I know your history, Frank,' she continued with the attack. 'You obsess. You go too far. You become partial. Because what you want to do is see more. More, more, more. Nothing is ever enough, so maybe you supply it yourself. You see what you want to see. That's why you got kicked off the last project. You allowed your sexual predilections to compromise the integrity of the operation. You're supposed to be a professional observer, not a voyeur. Three bodies in a hotel room? Come on. Things like that get noticed, and by us first.' She sighed and then lowered her voice. 'I'm disappointed. There's little here to work with.'

'Don't,' he said, his voice thin with emotion. Both his hands balled into fists. 'Just don't bullshit me. Debunking what I see. I don't make this up. I never did and I never will. I know what I saw. If you don't believe me then put a tail on her. Bug the apartment. Conceal a camera in the smoke alarm. Do whatever you think best, but don't insult me and don't waste my time. Do you know how many missing aircraft I helped recover, before the other side got to them? At least then I knew what I was looking for. I was briefed. But what am I doing here? What is it you want me to find? Whenever I've managed to view the targets, I have seen exactly what is detailed in those reports.'

Agent Kram looked at her watch and yawned. 'Try and see it from my point of view, Frank. It's all a bit preposterous. Especially the biting part.' She started to snigger as she stood up. Before she turned to go she dropped a card on the table. 'And I'm not the only one who thinks this way. There is disapproval from above. I'm making a recommendation that we drop this approach and use more conventional means of surveillance.' She slipped into her overcoat and shook her umbrella out. 'Don't call me unless you have something concrete. And I want results. Adios.'

When she reached the front door, Frank imagined himself overwhelming her, dragging her back to the kitchen, shoving her head in the sink with the dirty dishes, hiking her skirt up around her waist and grabbing hold of her pussy, before sinking his open mouth into her back. Then he shook the thought from his head, disturbed by the vengeful fantasy. Lucretia's influence?

But had he any right to be angry at her? He couldn't explain the uncanny power of the viewings and dreams either. He felt like a magician who had begun to pull rabbits out of hats he'd only stashed silk scarves inside. Nor could he explain the fact that he only broke through to Lucretia, never Eldrin, who he repeatedly failed to connect with. Kram was right: his claims were preposterous. Maybe he was mad at himself. There were things that Ally Kram didn't know. Not only had he doctored the final report to make it appear she had to wipe out Robe, Socks and T-shirt in self defence, but there were other details he'd completely neglected to enter into his reports. Evidence that confirmed his theory about Eldrin's manipulation of Lucretia. Things that only he could know because Lucretia had told him so, because he'd disobeyed orders. Three weeks into the investigation and Frank had broken protocol. But Kram didn't know that and couldn't find out because she'd close the operation down and pull him off the case and then he . . . he wouldn't see Lucretia again. They would no longer be lovers.

Lovers.

He had no friends at the agency and it looked like the operation was on its last legs. From now on he did things for himself, and for the beautiful, tragic blonde in apartment 40.

Frank broke rules the night he'd viewed her in the motel room getting trigger happy with the gang bangers. She came home in a mess. Couldn't even get out of the cab that pulled up out front, sometime after midnight. The Iranian driver was panicking and banging on the glass doors to the lobby, desperate to have her out of his car. Thought she'd suffered an overdose and Frank didn't blame the guy. That's just what she looked like – someone who'd had her fix and someone else's too. In a way, he supposed she had.

But as he led her into the building, he experienced misgivings about his role as saviour. She leaned into him, her legs giving way and her stiletto heels made loud, scraping noises against the marble floor of the reception. Through her leopardskin coat he sensed the thin material of her dress sliding against her body, over her curves and into the perfumed hollows that had already been flayed and then caressed by unfamiliar hands that very night.

When he slipped one arm around her torso to hold her upright, his hand found a breast. The sensation of this profound softness in the palm of his hand shocked him and he dropped his arm to her waist. But against his hip, her buttock then began to rub as she tried to move. On his shoulder, her head rested with face upturned so he could not prevent himself from gazing down at those beautiful features; lips parted, glossy, inviting and within kissing distance. Too close; the proximity of her mouth broke rules; only one with whom she was intimate should have admired her beauty from such a negligible distance. And drunk: the polluting smell of alcohol wafted from her mouth. After the night's work and the safe return of the attaché case, still clutched in her left hand, Frank guessed she needed to drink. But more significantly, he could smell her perfume. Into his head it went and inside his head it began to work.

Mostly, her eyes remained closed and while her mouth moved to form words, no intelligible sound came out. 'It's OK, Ma'am. OK,' he said, when she tried to speak.

Embarrassed for her, wary of her – she could still be armed – and aroused by the physical contact with her and stupidly afraid that another resident might appear in the lobby, curious about the commotion, and see them together, he rushed Lucretia into the elevator. Excited by this sudden and dramatic contact with the target, he also became aware that she was at his mercy. A reprehensible and inappropriate thought, but one not without a vicarious thrill attached. He fought the notion, but it returned.

Inside the elevator, she seemed to pass out. Lurching forwards, she swung around his neck. All coordination had gone. Holding her around the waist with both arms, Frank eased her to the floor. As she descended, their bodies pressed together. And had it not been for her obvious inebriation, Frank could have sworn she was deliberately tormenting him. One of her hands would not release the back of his neck. He felt her hard, lacquered nails scrape against and then grip the nape of his neck. It fired a mighty shiver through his body. The other brushed against his crotch.

Moaning, she pressed her cheek against Frank's and then giggled into his ear. He tried to pull away, but she kept her face squashed against his cheek. 'Steady, Ma'am,' he said, as her lips played with his ear. 'You're drunk, Ma'am. Here, let me . . .' But it was no use, he lost his balance when her whole weight pulled on his shoulders and neck. Frank fell across her, down on the elevator floor.

Resting on his knees, he struggled to disentangle himself. Leaning one arm out, he then depressed the correct button on the elevator control panel to set them on course for the fourth floor. 'Nnnn,' she murmured, seemingly annoyed at the upward motion of the lift platform, as if she were a groggy but disobedient child, forced into that inexorable march upstairs to bed. There was resistance in her; she did not want to go home.

Her heavy eyelids opened a fraction and Frank suffered a momentary paralysis as he stared into the eternal blue and black of those incredible eyes. 'Not finished,' she said, or he thought she said. And then, with some determination in her voice, she said, 'More.'

Managing to stand upright, he held her arms by the wrists and was about to haul her back to her feet when he became distracted by the view offered between the parted lapels of her coat. Between the drapes of leopardskin, Frank looked at the bra strap crossing a delicate shoulder. His glance became a stare and moved to the lowered neckline, her cleavage and then a stocking top visible below the satin hem of her slip.

Her eyes opened a little wider and she blinked at the treacherous tumescence in his trousers. She wet her lips and smiled. One of her hands pulled against his grip, trying to force its way inwards again, towards his groin, but Frank used all of his strength and self-discipline to hold the insistent hand still until the elevator doors opened at the fourth floor.

Standing behind her, he slipped his hands under her arms, pulled her to her feet and then staggered across the red carpet of the landing to the front door of her apartment. As he moved with her back against his chest, her buttocks bounced against his erection. Panicked and afraid, he even considered ringing the bell and then running down the stairs of the fire escape, back to the safety of his desk on the ground floor, leaving her inert shape propped against the front door of the apartment. Eldrin had to be in there and the very thought filled Frank with dread.

Changing his stance to get her standing upright, Frank caught sight of his red, perspiring face in one of the wide mirrors of the corridor. In the reflection, he also caught a glimpse of Lucretia's face. Angled towards his throat, her eyes were open and dreamy-looking. It made him think of the spent high-school kid on the park bench. He shuddered.

Propping her against the door, sat in an upright position, he then searched the pockets of her jacket, finding a purse, some mints, loose change and her keys. Willing to risk anything but contact or confrontation with Eldrin, Frank decided to make a silent entry. And Lucretia, the sleepy girl, would have to be carried. So over his shoulder he draped her. Bending his knees to take the weight, he placed his shoulder in the middle of her stomach so her torso hung down his back. With one hand he supported the rear of her thighs as her legs pressed against the length of his body. Before he opened the door, he could not resist a gentle squeeze and stroke of those slippery lower limbs. Behind him, Frank fancied he heard her moan.

With the door to the apartment open, he entered the half-light. Several lamps set high on the hall walls had been left on as if to welcome a latecomer. 'Hello,' he said in a half-whisper. 'Hello,' and then waited for a reply or any sound of movement. But none returned. Relieved, he pushed on through the hall and towards the bedroom, where he'd delivered her shopping the last time he was inside.

After a moment of trepidation, fearing he might see the sleeping lump of Eldrin beneath the covers of her bed, Frank opened the bedroom door and into the room of mirrors he carried her. The bed boasted no occupant, so he laid the sleeping princess down. But the moment her long and elegantly dishevelled body bounced silently against the duvet and mattress, she spoke. 'Who? You?'

He lowered his face, terrified again and eager to explain why the doorman of the building was inside her bedroom after midnight. 'Ma'am. It's OK. It's Frank. From downstairs. I had to carry you up.'

She smiled. Were her eyes closed or slit? Could she see him? He couldn't be sure. But he was certain she understood. 'Feet hurt,' she said.

'OK,' he whispered through the gloom and moved down to the base of the bed to take her shoes off. Relieved she hadn't screamed, it seemed his last duty was nigh. Gently he cradled each ankle and took her slingbacks off her feet. Even in the half-light, the patent footwear shone and he could smell the expensive leather mingling with the perfume she must have sprayed down her shins. Placing both shoes on the floor, beside the bed, he was about to depart, but stole one final peek at her body – an elongation of athletic limb, crowned with the dull lustre of blonde hair on a pillow.

'Mmmm,' she murmured, followed by a sweet rendition of his name, 'Frank,' before apparently falling asleep. Debating whether it would be proper to roll her into the recovery position, his eyes strayed to the shadowy divide between her thighs. Her legs were parted and her skirt had ridden up to her hips. Between the sheen of her stocking tops he caught sight of her unclothed sex. Immediately, he was struck by the invitation of its salty warmth.

He lingered to stare at the lightly furred sex of this wealthy and promiscuous tenant. Seductress and killer whose legs now moved further apart, as if his desire to see more had been communicated to her in sleep.

And then he did a terrible thing. After a quick look over his shoulder, and after taking a moment to strain his hearing into the dark corridors and rooms of the penthouse, he moved silently, holding his breath, along the bed until his face hovered above her disordered lap. And then he dipped his curious face so it hovered no more than an inch over her exposed sex.

Closing his eyes, Frank inhaled the secret musk of lingerie and the ripe fragrance of an active vagina. In her sleep, she stirred and moaned as if it had been his tongue slipping through the briny lips of that wanton place. Carefully, he then applied a trembling hand to the front of her thigh. Pausing, he watched her face to see if it moved. Nothing; the contact didn't seem to register. Slowly, he then stroked his hand up and down the front of one leg, and then the other. Again Lucretia moaned, but this time she bent one knee, raising the leg and moving it aside as if to offer complete access.

What was he thinking? His heart had been still, but now it pumped between his ears and he had difficulty swallowing. Then her hands clenched on the covers, unclenched and then clenched again. Rotating the back of her head against the pillow, she continued to moan. And Frank continued to caress her thigh, his touch light, the palm of his hand smoothing the nylon against her skin, his head craned to hear the whisper – the aural evidence that he was actually touching Lucretia's incredible legs.

'Yesss,' she whispered to the dark, to her phantom lover. Or was he a phantom? He had already declared his presence. Perhaps she knew, and wanted this and could keep a secret. Whatever he thought, it was a half-thought; something not thought through and ripe for coercion from some baser part of his brain function. Because soon he was kissing those legs and tasting them, and then the naked inner thigh too. His nose nuzzled under her slip and soon sought the spicy and most tender part of her. Just a touch. Yes! Just the tip of his tongue, probing out, made contact with her labia and then withdrew from the place where so many had already been, this same night. The thought of it both repelled and motivated him to continue. Sick with himself, but unable to stop, he began to lick her, drawing the end of his tongue in lazy swipes and circles around and across the delicate lips of her sex. Up above his busy head, he heard Lucretia gasp. Out the corner of one eye, he watched her bite the index finger of her left hand.

When she began to rotate her buttocks on the bed, he stopped. This was wrong; taking advantage of a drunk and vulnerable resident. He was risking the entire operation for a touch and taste of the half-conscious woman he was supposed to be observing. But fighting against these brief and better instincts were his memories of what he'd seen her doing; sucking strange cocks, riding anonymous groins, submitting to blows from handheld implements of correction, allowing whatever violation and penetration her lovers desired. His appetite won. He wanted to see her mouth accept his cock the way it had done so many others. He wanted to spank her lovely, yielding buttocks like the others had done. Wanted to yank her on and off his sex until he'd expended himself and flushed these tormenting thoughts of her from his mind. Frank wanted to join her and become engulfed by her world.

Sex had pulled him down before. It had made him self-destruct. And sex was about to reclaim him from this opportunity he'd been given to make good, to start over with his gift intact and valued by the highest office. There was no use resisting what he was. Up there in a place he should not have been, he suddenly wanted to fall. Wanted to fall hard with her.

'Fuck me,' she said in her sleep.

His breath caught in his throat. Dizzy and ungainly, he climbed on to the bed and situated himself between her open legs. Closing his eyes and turning his head would have done no good. Into his mind flooded images of her face contorted with passion, her legs kicking out in the ecstasy following deep penetration, her beautiful mouth whispering obscene encouragement, as if he was already inside her and there was no going back. No man could have withstood that temptation, despite the fact that he would lose everything. Of that Frank was sure.

Pushing her slip up to her belly, he cleared a path. Simultaneously reaching up her body to cup her breasts and dipping his face through the darkness, he rediscovered her sex with his mouth. Sucking her lips into his mouth, Frank made the sounds of a man in a desperate feeding frenzy. Great white shark of the clitoral bait, he lapped and then sucked more of her into his mouth. Withdrawing a hand from the breast it had been stroking, he next slipped one and then two fingers inside her. Her back arched on the bed and she bit into the side of her hand. Tickling her inside, he readied Lucretia for a thicker intrusion.

Carried away, encouraged by her response, no longer thinking, Frank unbuckled and unzipped his trousers. Leaning across her, supporting his weight with one arm, fisting his cock with the free hand, he rubbed the head of his phallus against her sex. Again she moved under his body. Seizing the top of his arms, she dug her claws into his triceps and pulled at him, coaxing him further up the bed and further inside her.

There was a glorious moment of resistance around his cock, and then an engulfing sense of freedom that was both deep and warm. Exhaling, nearly shouting with relief, he sank his entire length inside her and felt her body lock and tense beneath. Her mouth was open, her head thrown back, the balls of her feet then pressed down into his calf muscles.

Not long. Not long before he would come. The nature of his transgression, the impact of who he had penetrated, and the risk of discovery mingled with the delightful physical sensations of lying upon her with his cock planted deep. Lucretia! This hotel assassin, barstool temptress, jailbait junkie, whip jockey, street walker, upper-crust slut-highness, began to buck under him. Ramming her hips against him she sucked his cock with her sex. Throwing her head from side to side, she said, 'Fuck me. Fuck me,' demonstrating her reckless self-abandonment at the hands of another stranger. Ripping through her dress, he found her breasts. Smothering them with kisses before sucking her nipples into his mouth, he could no longer restrain his moans and the word 'yes' repeated over and over again like a mantra to banish all conflicting thoughts of resistance and propriety.

And her mouth . . . He wanted to taste her mouth, sensing the hot breath and slippery lips beneath him. Clamping his hands on her jaw, Frank stuffed his tongue between her lips and then sucked her tongue back out and into his own mouth where he could relish her taste. All the while he pumped and heaved and threw himself into her, pummelling her long body up the bed, trapping it against the headboard and then speeding up his thrusts.

Feeling her legs writhe around him, hearing the faint ululations from the back of her throat, he sensed her climax and began to grind his crotch against her sex, pushing his cock right to the back of her in readiness for ejaculation. And it was soon delivered. Holding her wrists, pushing her hands down into the duvet, he summoned the last of his strength and breath to move in and out of her body at a frenzied rate. Feeling her legs rise and then encircle his waist, Frank came. Gasping, his face pressed into the side of her head, he felt a warm tide flow from himself and into her body, taking all of his strength and honour with it.

Moaning, her mouth found his throat. And as she kissed and nuzzled appreciatively, he fell asleep in her arms.

* * *

How long had he been asleep? He couldn't work it out.

When Frank awoke, he was lying on his back beside her. Someone was leaning over the bed, staring down at him. Yes! He was sure he was being watched from close by. Frank sat up. Too quickly. Clutching a numb head, he groaned and then looked about. No one there. Had he imagined the presence, and the eagerness he detected, the appetite?

His body was stiff with fatigue and cold after coming down from the exertion of sex. Around his body, his clothes were screwed up and sticking to him in the places he'd perspired. And he had difficulty staying upright. Experienced disorientation too. It was like waking up in the early hours of the morning, drunk, in front of the television, but without fully regaining consciousness as he stumbled upstairs to bed.

The only light inside the room had filtered through the open door of the bedroom, from the wall lights in the hall. It made the mirrors on the walls of her room look like pools of mercury. He peered through the gloom at her sleeping shape. Still in a state of undress, she had curled her legs up to her chest and tucked both hands under her cheek. He suspected a half-smile. Her unclothed chest gently moved as she slept. He saw the white of her bosom.

Clutching his face in his hands, Frank then tried to stop the spin. But when his eyes were closed he wanted to fall back into the dreamy high he'd been stirred from by the sense of the watcher. What had he done? He began to think. Now the fire of lust had spent itself, he was swamped by the full gravity of his error. A thickening in his throat made him swallow. And then he became aware of an irritation on his neck. It felt numbish – both the skin and the muscle beneath – like his gums after an operation at the dentist. But as the numbness began to fade his flesh began to smart. Distracted, Frank reached out a finger to his neck, but stopped, suddenly. Something moved again in the room, near the bed.

Peering about, he saw nothing beside the dull silver of the distant mirrors. Were the shadows moving? He blinked, but still could not tell.

Sobered by the perceived danger of his situation, which had spooked him into seeing, or at least sensing, a presence, Frank rolled off the bed. Confused but desperate to escape the oppressive, deceptive darkness, he staggered like a drunk to the bedroom door. But as he retreated, he heard a footstep behind. Turning fast and falling back, he saw motion; something dark and thin fading away from him, back towards the bed, where it seemed to hover like a protective presence over its prey. He clawed at his face, shook his head, screwed his eyes up, opened them . . . Nothing there.

Now he was seeing things, but the fright renewed his urge to be gone. In here he had once seen her beaten. With so many mirrors facing each other, the place stretched to infinity. Had the lights been switched on, he would have seen an image of himself forever duplicated; a figure crouched over and terrified.

Stumbling, hands against mirrors, a door jamb and then the walls of the hall outside, he fled towards the reception of the apartment. The door was still open as he had left it. Closing it behind him, Frank fled downstairs to the light.

Behind his desk, under the bright lights of the lobby and the grey glow of the security monitors, reality returned to him. It was as if he'd woken from a strange dream, aroused and frightened. But as he was reminded of what he'd done in that dream, what act he'd committed, he became sick with guilt and self-disgust. And for the rest of the night he sat behind the desk, half-conscious but all the worse for such a debilitated state of mind. Every fear and recrimination was amplified and exaggerated. Awful fates were imagined. Thoughts of the next day were heavy with dread. It didn't make sense; despite his voyeuristic transgressions of the past, his behaviour that night terrified him. It was like he'd not been in control. He had been another person up there, more savage than man. And already, he could imagine the schizophrenic implausibility of these words as they were recited in a court of law.

But the following evening when Frank returned to work, mystified as to why the police had not disturbed his fitful sleep and arrested him at the apartment for immoral conduct, he received the biggest surprise of all.

'Something happened last night.' It was a statement, not a query, and she was looking away from him when she said it.

'Yes,' Frank replied.

They were sitting in her car; she in the driver's seat, him a passenger beside her. Arriving at work that evening full of trepidation and fear and guilt, he barely had time to hang his coat and change into uniform before she called on the house phone and instructed him to meet her in the basement garage. She would be in her car, waiting. Bewildered, but clutching a straw of hope that the meeting might offer him a reprieve from what he'd done the night before, Frank descended the stairs to the garage.

When she spoke, she faced her lap, in a position of intense remorse. 'I am sorry for involving you in this.'

'You're sorry . . .' he began, shocked as much as puzzled. But when she looked at him she silenced him with her beauty. Her eyes were moist.

'I cannot help myself,' she said. 'I am terrible. I know this.'

'I was at fault. I had no right to . . .'

She shook her head and then reached out a gloved hand to touch his cheek. 'Yesterday was one of the craziest days of my life. One I wish to forget. For always. But I feel other days and their craziness will just cover it up. It will always continue.'

'I don't understand.'

'It's the way.'

'The way?'

She nodded. 'The way of the . . . Oh, how can I explain to you what this is?' She stopped herself, clearly frustrated, and then whispered, 'No.'

Mystified, he feared for her sanity and his own if he stayed near her any longer. But leaving her then – so elegant in the dark pinstriped suit and high-heeled shoes, her make-up immaculate, her face shadowed by the finest veil? Never.

'My lover started it. Put this darkness inside me. What happened last night between us, has happened before. It's hard to explain. I have certain needs, Frank. An appetite, if you like. And it was given to me, by my lover, for his own pleasure. So he could watch me. And for his own pain when he sees that I can be just like him. What he has made me.' Frank wanted to tell her that he knew all about her appetite and her needs but let her continue. He was exhausted with relief because she was not angry and had not reported him to the police.

'Many years ago when first we were together, he was different. Dangerous, yes, but not so harsh and he saved me from a terrible fate. So you see, I became

106

attached to him. Devoted. In debt to him and his . . . tastes. And now we have gone so far together, we have lost sight of where we started. And I do these things for him, Frank. You know of the way I can love and be loved?' She was looking right into him and he blanched, panicked by what she had said. Was she referring to his viewings? She smiled. 'My three dinner guests. The three men who visited me. At the end of the night, you put them in cabs. Helped me. Cleared up for me. Then I knew you understood. You must have known what happened up there that night. What they did to me.'

Frank exhaled with relief and then said something trite about consenting adults behind closed doors. It drew another smile from her; this one pitying like he had displayed some great innocence.

'Yes,' she said, and stroked his face. 'But it goes deeper. It is like a sport. A dangerous sport now. I can't stop myself any more. At first it was for him. Just for him, but now . . . I don't know. It's what we are.' And then she withdrew the hand and covered her eyes. When Frank heard her sob he gathered her to his chest.

Convinced he was to be her saviour, he whispered promises of protection and muttered plans for her escape from that sadist who kept her and forced her into a growing and reckless darkness. He longed to tell her about the investigation and the surveillance; that she was in even greater danger from the agency. But Frank held back, realising her confession and trust and apparent forgiveness for his violation fanned the embers of the dying investigation back to life. Maybe from her he could now extract details to make sense of intelligence gathered from the remote viewings; enough to save her and sink Crow. 'Who is he?' he asked as he comforted Lucretia, stroking her hair and enjoying the gentle weight of her head against his chest.

'One who is not to be trusted. Nor underestimated.'

'Leave him.'

She shook her head and sniffed. 'And go where? Alone? I'm not strong enough. I have no money of my own. We've been together for so long and this is all I have. It's what I'm used to. I'm not even supposed to be in this country. The best I can hope for is imprisonment, or ... or worse. Like before. What he saved me from. I would rather die than go back to the men he bought me from. And anyway, he would kill me if I ever tried to leave him. There is nothing that can be done for me.' And then she gathered herself and drew away from Frank. 'Sorry. I have no right to put this on you. It is my problem.'

'No. After last night I am a part of it. I took advantage of you. I've ... I've always coveted you. Watched you. Desired you. I am no better than he is. Than any man who has used you. I was just waiting for an opportunity ... I owe you something. I want to help.' It was true and he would have done anything to guarantee seeing her again.

'No. No. No. It is for the best that you forget about last night. He would hurt you if he thought you were interfering. He is ill, an invalid, but still devious. He manipulates me. He has plans for me yet.'

'Plans. What plans? You have rights. You don't have to –'

'Don't, Frank. Just forget what I have said. It is impossible. I should never have seduced you last night. It is just ... I need someone I can talk to. And that first day, when you carried my bags, I saw in you a kindness. A sympathy I wanted to exploit.'

'Seduced me? You were drunk. It was me who took –'

'Advantage? No. I was not so drunk.' She bowed her head. 'I liked you.' She touched his chest and sniffed again. 'Just for a while, I needed to be loved by someone good.' The touch became a caress. 'And right under his nose.'

Frank swallowed. 'He saw? He came into the room? I knew it.'

She shook her head. 'No. If he had, you would be dead. Like the other one I once had feelings for. He owns me now.'

All he'd suspected of Eldrin she had confirmed: he was dangerous, deceitful, sadistic. But they were together. Crow had a hold on her. Absurdly, he felt an envy so great it manifested as a chest pain.

Lucretia moved closer. 'Frank? Can I tell you something?'

He nodded as she wrapped her arms around his neck and stared so intently into him he barely withstood her gaze. 'I am frightened. He has changed since we fled here. We are in hiding and he has grown worse. He's so paranoid now. Convinced that we are being watched. Even with all the blinds drawn in that horrid apartment, he is convinced someone can see him.'

Frank stiffened. He nearly made a specific inquiry about organised crime, but held back. 'What is he mixed up in?'

'It's best you don't know, Frank. It involves bad business. A lot of money is at stake. He tried to be too clever and now certain people are angry. They feel betrayed. He takes his anger out on me. Makes me do things. I'm guilty too, now. I'm trapped, Frank, between him and what I have done. But what I need is a friend. He doesn't have to know about you. Will you be that, Frank? I shouldn't ask. But I need someone.' And as she spoke she looked at him in a way to affect him with such feelings of passion and desire and love that he knew at once he must have her as his own, and would go to any length to help her and protect her. Perhaps subconsciously, as she looked at him, he even felt some sympathy for Eldrin.

What she had said was vague, but somehow convincing at the same time. No real detail was ever included in her stories: names, dates, actual events, nothing. And as implausible as it all seemed to him later, back then he would have believed anything.

After she had finished speaking, and as he was about to flood the air with questions, they came to be kissing. She was squashed against Frank and their mouths were sealed in a desperate union like those of two people denied each other for a lifetime, who have suddenly come together and found a missing part of themselves in each other.

As if it were required of her, and as if she wanted to serve him to secure his interest, her face then fell into his lap. Content to just kiss and worship her beauty, without pressing for any greater intimacy, he felt awkward and a little guilty as she unzipped him with determined fingers, still gloved in soft leather. A part of him wanted to tell her that it was not necessary; that she didn't have to offer her body to guarantee companionship and trust, but when the softness of her lips enveloped his sex, Frank was, once again, without his will.

Deep into her mouth she drew him. Wide were her jaws, because even the base of his cock felt the slippery embrace of her mouth. And she caressed with tongue and cheek with such intensity and rapture, he felt it was him being worshipped; that it was him who was irresistible. And such feelings naturally and inevitably made him believe they were meant to be together.

'Take me, Frank. Please. Like you did last night. I need to feel you again. Inside me.'

Stretching her long body across him, her suit and underwear rustling maddeningly in his ears, Frank lowered his seat to the horizontal position and watched her long legs straddle him. The muscles taught beneath the dark and smoky film of nylon, her legs shepherded his own limbs together and into a position that would provide her with room and mobility. Unbuttoning her blouse with nervous fingers, his was confronted by the sight of her pale and shapely breasts, suspended in the dark, see-through mesh of her brassière. And when his eager hands pressed against her breasts, she clenched her eyes shut and he felt her skin shiver. Pushing his face forwards, the hard pellets of her pinky nipples were brushed by his lips, lapped by his tongue and then scooped inside his mouth. As he ate at the luxury of her breasts, her leathered hand gripped the base of his cock and positioned it upright. With a sigh, her hips descended into his unzipped lap, and the garters on her thighs became taut. She bit the side of her free hand Her cries became muffled, as were his, still engorged on her breasts.

Slowly, agonisingly, she raised and lowered her delightful frame and weight upon him. Sinking through her, until the lips of her sex were tickled by his floss, she would then pause with all of his length pillared inside her, and her eyes would glaze over from a sensation she seemed to find so intense he suspected she would cry. And it was a struggle to hold back; to clench every muscle in his sex to postpone the inevitable eruption. 'Want to come,' he whispered before her lips engulfed his breath.

'Not yet,' she said, and slowed her pace to preserve him. 'Is there much of it?' she then asked, and by asking the question was nearly answered not with words but with physical evidence.

'Yes,' Frank said, imploring her for release with his eyes.

'Mmm. I want all of it. Inside me.'

Seizing the back of her head, he laminated the beauty of her face against his weary and shadowy features. With his other hand, Frank held her by one buttock and began to thrust upwards, deep, seeking some imaginary rear wall that would prevent him from going any further.

And then the elevator doors directly opposite the windshield of the car opened. He could see them over Lucretia's shoulder and stopped thumping his groin against her.

'Don't stop. Not now. It's cruel,' she cried, and her voice was surprisingly deep, but not in a way as to be unwelcome.

'Someone is coming,' he said in a hissy whisper. 'Don't move.'

It was Mrs Barnes-Dubois, her face a portrait of sullen arrogance as usual. Behind her stood her elderly and dutiful driver. Lucretia looked over her shoulder at the intruders, and then shook her blonde hair loose, knocking her little hat from off her head. Laughing wildly, she then began to pump herself on and off Frank's lap, digging her claret nails into his shoulders to facilitate the violent pounding of body against body, of sex through sex. 'Forget her. I don't care about her. Or anyone.'

'But she'll see!'

'Fuck her!' she said, with a demonic fury that further fuelled his anxiety and increased the action of her hips.

And sure enough, Barnes-Dubois had seen the car. Looking right at Frank, she strode across to the vehicle and stood beside the driver's door. Frantic with panic, Frank tried to push Lucretia from his lap, but she was strong. In her haste to reach completion, she seized his arms at the elbow and seemed to immobilise them with her grip, making them limp and strengthless. It was the same abandon he'd observed in his viewings as she rode the laps of strangers, friends and enemies alike.

Barnes-Dubois rapped her knuckles against the glass and appeared to have difficulty seeing inside the car. Up and down, left and right, her confused eyes moved, peering at the glass rather than through it. It was then Frank remembered the windows were made of one-way glass. Even if they were only tinted, the garage was dark and she would have seen little more than vague shapes, moving through an inner opacity. But by the motion of the car, rocking on its suspension, she must have been wise as to the activity within. Horrified and outraged, she turned on the shiny heels of her court shoes and scuttled away to her Bentley.

'She knew. She knew we were fucking. Oh, Frank.' And Lucretia's long body then began to shake against him while the beautiful blue of her eyes rolled to white.

Holding handfuls of her long thighs and sheer stockings, he thrust in anger at the foolish risk she had taken, and with a desire so overwhelming he became dizzy. As Barnes-Dubois's car slowly drove past the bonnet of Lucretia's squeaking Mercedes, Frank came. And in the sleepy paralysis, the half-conscious swoon that follows the expenditure of all energy and vitality inside a truly wonderful lover, her face fell into the crook of his neck. Then, like the night before, he experienced a vague discomfort against the skin of his neck where her mouth touched.

It was followed by a dreamy somnolence and a sense of immense inner well-being; all lulled through him to the rhythm of a tongue lapping and wet lips kissing.

Silent and entwined, they lay together for some time. Like the night before in her bedchamber, he had no idea for how long they stayed in the position. But nothing could have tempted him to even fidget. In his mind he pondered a cinema reel of memory; a complete reminiscence of Lucretia. In a strange wholeness of recollection he reviewed her and felt nothing but delight, and acknowledged the hopelessness of his love for her. He welcomed all future pain, as if it were a gift as long as she was the cause. Any contact, even if it were indirect and agonising, would be wonderful, as long as it came from her.

She spoke and broke Frank's reverie. It was some kind of explanation. 'I wanted you. You gave me a taste last night, Frank. I lost control again.'

He smiled with approval and then they kissed, as if signing and counter-signing a contract guaranteeing an insane future together. After their lips parted, she gracefully eased across to the driver's seat and lit a cigarette. And as he looked at her, still stricken with disbelief by what had just happened, and sleepy with the visions and with the sense of her being inside him somehow, of having taken possession of him, he watched her dab the shorn pelt of her sex with her brief black panties to stem the flow of his cream on to Eldrin's leather seat covers. Sheepishly, she looked at him. They laughed, and Frank felt the last vestiges of resistance, reason and caution dissolve into nothing.

Eight

And for a while, Lucretia started to come to Frank. Most of the time she was soft and wanted him to be hard. 'Are you going to be mean to me?' she once whispered, her eyes half-lidded as he cornered her on a stairwell, desperate for contact with her.

That morning she had been able to steal a couple of hours away from Eldrin's perpetual tormenting and surveillance in order to go shopping; an indulgence he allowed her less and less during the weeks following the beginning of the affair with Frank. Only this time, when Frank appeared in the garage, he was shown a cold and coquettish aspect to her character. Virtually ignored, he was then humiliated in an exchange between Lucretia and a smirking Mrs Barnes-Dubois, who passed them on her way to the Bentley.

Teasing him with incredible views of her legs through the slits in her skirt, and taunting him with a glimpse of pale cleavage through the lacy border of a mostly transparent blouse, Lucretia led Frank up to the ground floor, his arms burdened with her purchases. He was confused and unable to think what he may have said to offend. His frustration became anger.

Trapped, stifled and bored for days on end, upstairs in the dark of Eldrin's chambers, where she incubated as a dangerous sexual plaything – his torment, his delight, his assassin – it seemed there were no guarantees as to her mood or affections whenever she either flitted down to Frank, or returned from an excursion outside the building.

'Mean?' he said, holding her elbow and steering her through an emergency door that opened into the stairwell. And then there was a brief struggle as Frank fell into the role she assigned him that day, fighting for Lucretia's wrists. She raised her chin to show Frank a haughty face – challenging him and demanding he express the precise effect she worked. 'Mean? Like this?' he said, and tore her blouse down and across her chest, before seizing her breasts, wanting all of them in his mouth and hands at the same time; the very sight of them painful to behold. 'Yeah?' he said, no longer recognising himself. 'Think you can fuck with me like that? Make me carry your crap up from the car, while you condescend to me in front of the other residents? When you know how I feel about you? Is this some fucking game, Lucretia? Do you think I'm a sick fuck, like your lover? Am I to be toyed with?'

And her lips parted and her eyes narrowed when she saw his passion. 'Why should you put up with me? Don't know why you do,' she whispered, her voice hoarse, her breath laced with the scent of gin and tobacco. And when she said that, comfortably reassured by his full attention and obvious pain, he bent her body over so her fingers spread on the carpet of the stairs. She looked back, through her hair, over her shoulder. Her mouth opened, but not with outrage. He had merely surprised her, but evidently pleased her in doing so. Determined to prove himself worthy of her passion, and urged by a new-found confidence and reckless energy that had begun to course through him since making her acquaintance, Frank helped himself to her beauty.

Even though it was black and tight, he managed to yank her skirt up her thighs until it circled her waist. Buttocks smooth and pale under silk confronted him. Eight suspender straps passed under the antique-looking panties and pulled black seamed stockings right up to her sex. Glossy and sleek, these legs automatically parted so she could maintain her balance. And down there, in a stairwell bathed in yellow electric light, in a place where he carried the residents' garbage down to the basement skip, he spanked those pretty cheeks pink, and finally red.

Whimpering, her eyes wet with tears, she begged Frank not to stop. Asked him to make it sting. And he did, despite realising the risk of exposure, of someone happening across the perverse coupling on a stairwell. Because on the other side of the wall, as he dealt the heavy slaps against her buttocks, he heard doors open and shut, and heard decorators whistling inside a ground-floor apartment.

'Why do you behave like this?' he asked, pausing to question his insane behaviour.

'Maybe so you notice me.'

'You know I do. I told you how I feel. That I want to help.'

'I need to be shown.'

Thinking then of what she could run away and find elsewhere – what depraved cravings she had been indulging long before his arrival – he became monstrous. Holding a handful of her hair, so silky in his clenched fist, he pulled her head back and pushed her body downwards, so she had to support her weight with her knees. 'Can I be enough for you?' he said, filled with a desire that felt like rage too.

'Maybe,' she whispered. An evil smile spread across her mouth. 'Maybe,' she repeated.

After tearing her panties down the back of her legs, Frank quickly unbelted his trousers. Her breath speeded up. Soon she began to pant. 'Yes. Yes, Frank. Show me.'

Moist after being spanked by the help, and at the additional prospect of being taken on the stairs, her sex allowed Frank to slide inside her effortlessly when he pushed forwards. Holding her hips and digging his fingertips into the soft flesh, he began to move through her, slowly. Riding her back, he then dug himself deep.

'Harder, Frank. I want it hard.' Part of him still found it difficult to equate this beautiful face and this elegantly dressed body with such an appetite and with such dark urges, even after all he had seen.

'No,' he replied.

'Bastard,' she said in a hissy voice.

'Not yet,' he said, and thrust quickly and suddenly to take her breath away. 'Not until you tell me why.'

'Why I need to be fucked like this?' With one eye peering through her blonde hair, she saw the shock on his face. She grinned. 'Why I have to have this all the time and why one man is never enough? Mmm? You want to torture yourself with that, Frank?'

'Stop it,' he said, unable now to control the increasing vigour of his thrusts inside her.

'You're just like him,' she said, laughing to herself. 'Want to keep me to yourself. Afraid of what I can do. What every woman you've ever known can do if she pleases. Always wanting to know about why and how and where. As if you could handle it.'

'No.'

'Yes! To have me all to yourself, you have to take me. Just take me and show me why I should be yours.

Go on, Frank. Take me. I know you can. I've always known it was you. Knew it the first day I saw you.'

'You're lying,' he said, his voice hoarse.

She shook her head. 'No, I'm not.'

And the few remaining restraints and fears and doubts and inhibitions were gone. Looking down at that long and supple body – the legs splayed, stockings creased, one high heel dislodged, breasts swinging free, smudged mouth open, blonde hair fanned across the stairs – he thrust at her harder than he ever thought appropriate or possible.

'Don't stop,' she cried out, while he gritted his teeth and yanked her body on and off his erection, pulling her back hard and then grinding his groin into her buttocks.

'That hard enough?' he said, breathless, angry, excited, and beneath it all, in love. 'Is this what the performance was for? So I could take you like a slut in a stairwell?'

And she came after he said that; her mouth opened above a chin smeared pink with lipstick and saliva. Above cheekbones peppered with eyeliner, her wet eyes looked back at him through strands of tousled hair – eyes full of adoration and longing.

'But I want to come here,' he said, and gently circled the rim of her anus with his wet index finger. Somehow unhinged now, he wanted to break every rule of decency and every taboo to become squalid and swallowed by lust. 'So you can feel me all day and all night, and know how much I fucking ache for you, Lucretia.' This made her groan with approval. And Frank forced his sex, still wet with her own fluids, inside that tight ring.

'Say my name. Say my name and call me beautiful while you fuck me, Frank. While you fuck me like a dog, Frank.'

119

'Lucretia. Lucretia. Lucretia, my . . .' Thinking his heart would burst and that he'd never get his breath back, Frank's mind passed into a red place. His cock squeezed every drop of its vigour into her tight insides. He thought he would faint. And through the madness of their desperate loving, he watched the pale skin of her body, where it was exposed through her disordered clothes, and he longed to taste her there. Really taste her, by filling himself with her. Biting her. Eating her. No, devouring her and drinking her sweetness until he found euphoric oblivion by having her warm and mineral vitality inside himself. It now seemed the most natural thing in the world to crave.

After she allowed him to suckle from a buttock, they lay against each other, panting. In a daze they both stared at the tears in her stockings and the claw marks on his skin where the perspiration had begun to sting. And she laughed her wild laugh before she gave him one of her special nips on the back of his shoulder. Sharp at first, the pain then became exquisite.

When she finished he tried to stand, but fell against a wall, barely able to support his body. Struggling with the intoxication she always left in him, Frank watched Lucretia walk away to the masquerade upstairs, straightening her clothes as she went.

'I'm sorry. I'm so sorry,' Frank said, pacing back and forth in the staffroom on the day following his performance in the stairwell. It was during a stretch of his day shifts and Lucretia had slunk downstairs to find him morose during his lunchbreak. 'Ripping your clothes! What was I thinking? I – I forced you, Lucretia. Because I was jealous and horny and . . .'

Smiling, she continued to pull on her cigarette.

Frank ran his fingers through his hair. 'As if you don't have enough of this. With what that sadist puts you through and makes you do. I don't know what came over me. It's this energy. Something inside me. I'm so restless. Dissatisfied. It's like life isn't enough. Am I making sense? No. Nothing makes sense. You know, I ran ten miles last night. Not managed that since high school. But it only took the edge off this anxiety. Just let a little pressure out. Today, I ran six miles before work. All hill work. What's happening to me? It's all I can do to take my mind off you. I'm convinced I had a hard-on through the entire night. All I did was dream about you.' Frank wasn't exaggerating. There was a new power inside him; a dark energy that could not be burned away. He felt like he could run for ever, and not at the usual wheezy canter, but swiftly and with a purpose he chased but could not identify. Even though his appetite was enormous, something was missing from every meal. Sleep was either as deep as a coma or disturbed by a relentless arousal that made him feverish. And his viewings were clearer than he thought possible. Every building he walked past in his neighbourhood, and every apartment block around Lucretia's building, bombarded him with momentary flashes of insight into the lives within. Could love do this? It had never been like this before.

'We could stop.' She was looking down at her boots. Pointy-toed boots, made from patent leather with a spike heel. Stretching up her calf muscles to the hem of her skirt, her actual legs were concealed but at once made more appealing.

'No!' he blurted out, feeling nauseous at the mere suggestion of an end; of not being near those boots or ever finding another woman who could wear these things in such a way.

121

'But you worry so. It makes you ill and unhappy.'

'No, no, no. Never felt better. I'm more alive than ever. Everything works better and faster and for longer. It's physical but mental too. Like I've caught something. A virus that's doing me good.' Only he didn't know why he felt this way, and was reluctant to question its progress in case it stopped. Defining himself, or even remembering who he'd been before he met Lucretia proved increasingly difficult.

'But when you are rough with me, it pains you.'

'Because it's not right. I go too far and can't stop.' Like her. Yes, like the way she would go too far.

'These are just roles, Frank. And I like it,' she added in a shy voice.

'Really?'

She nodded. 'It's fun with you.'

Immediately his panic was doused. 'But can't we just –'

'Be like other people?' She shook her head. 'I can't. But you still can.'

A curious thing for her to confess, and sincerely too, he could tell. This was a choice. 'Why do you say that? All I'm asking is why things have to be so aggressive. To always go so far?'

'Be so intense? Yes. For me it must be that way now.'

'Because of Eldrin? Of what he introduced you to?' He still had to be careful and not let her know how much he'd seen.

'Maybe it was I who made the introduction.' She laughed at the look of horror on his face. 'This world has changed so much. Women have changed too.'

'Yeah, but they still want kids and homes and things.'

'And the perfect man?'

He nodded. She laughed. 'Men are only perfect for a while and this life is long.'

She was younger but again this apparent wisdom or cynicism or experience seemed incongruous against her beauty and youth. But what she said only reinforced his designs to save her. When she sat back on the small table beside the refrigerator, she crossed her legs and smiled through the veneer of smoke drifting across her face; a signal for him to stop asking questions and to grasp the reason she had come looking for him. Although time was always in short supply, whenever he pried about Eldrin's business, or asked who they were hiding from, and inquired how they came to be in the building, she somehow changed the subject with an act of love he was unable to resist. For the investigation he learned nothing, but his curiosity about sex was always satisfied.

On his knees, he cradled her right leg in his hands. Tracing over the supple leather and hard heel of her boot, his fingers then slipped up to the top of the leather and found a slippery knee. Angling her head to one side, pleased with the adoration in his eyes, she smiled and stretched her left leg out too, offering it. The tip of the boot heel touched his lips. Under her skirt her legs rustled and a wave of hot blood seemed to hit the tidal barrier of bone structure in Frank's face. He cleared his throat. 'How much time do you have?'

'Not long. He will wake soon. Once the medication wears off.' Immediately, Frank tried to speak, but she gently pushed a spike heel inside his mouth and held it in place. 'But I have time to play. Take off your clothes.'

Reluctantly, he took her heel from his tongue. 'I can't. Not like this. Not here. Not now.'

She leaned forwards and replaced the heel with a finger. The nail polish was so fresh he could taste pear drops. 'You are delicate, Frank. Inside. And I like that. Perhaps you think you have seen it all, but inside you are still fragile.' She removed the finger from his mouth and sucked it. 'There will never be enough time while I live here with Eldrin. We have to take chances when they arise.'

Stripping off his jacket and then his shirt and trousers at work would ordinarily have made him feel foolish, but the look of misty-eyed desire she gave him, at the sight of his unrobing, encouraged Frank to obey.

'Lie on the floor,' she said.

Grinning and hoping her face would soften, he stretched out, propping himself up on one elbow, expecting her to slowly strip before joining him. But her face never softened and she never removed a single item of clothing. Instead, she walked across to him and towered over his naked body. Her mood had changed. She stared down with an intensity he found disarming. 'Lie down. Right down.'

'What?'

'Shut up.'

He lay flat on his back. Close to the outline of his body, but careful not to touch him with her feet, she walked around him. Taking tiny steps, she assessed and perhaps even admired him. 'Good. You must learn to trust me. I trust you. I submit. You must do the same.'

'But I –'

'Quiet. Don't say another word until I am gone. Promise? You must promise or I am gone.'

'Promise.' Role-playing games; she had mentioned them. They were important to her. During his viewings she had played various roles and used her lovers accordingly. Through roles she sifted for what she wanted to express in herself and satisfy; he could

124

feel it. She used her inner instincts in much the same way as he did when viewing. And if he could love and secure her through these mad rituals then so be it.

'Close your eyes,' she said. Frank put himself in the dark.

Fear spread through him when he heard her raise a leg next to his naked body. Inhaling sharply, he felt the first sole indent the skin of his stomach. It felt smooth. Tensing the muscles in his stomach, he readied himself for her weight. First there was an epicentre of pressure that he pushed up and against to withstand, and then her other leg swung up from the floor and placed the left foot beside the right. Both silver tips of her spiked heels grazed his yielding skin. Her weight was concentrated through the flat oval of each leather sole. She had done this before; he had seen her and feared her spikes, but wanted them too. It was as if she knew.

She took a step. Fearing a puncture, he strained every muscle in his torso. 'Relax,' she said from above, her voice manifesting in the warm darkness of his head. 'Take my weight. Support it. Nurture it. Cradle me. Know that I'm strong and dangerous and can go right through you like a sword.' She laughed a little girlish laugh. 'Look up.'

He did. Her soles covered his nipples and her long perfumed body seemed to totter, ever so slightly, like the peak of a giant tree in a wind you could not feel on the ground. But his eyes were immediately drawn into the dark tunnel created between her knees. Pale thighs in sheer stockings rose up to a panel of white panty gauze. The flesh behind this fine screen looked pink. He sensed it was moist. Between his legs his erection rose, flopped to the side of his belly and then stood tall.

'You like? Men used to pay for this. Men like you. Men who got their own way far too much.'

Taking shallow breaths, Frank tried to smile.

Pressing both heels down into his skin, she ended his attempts at a smile. Her features, so far away, darkened. In that moment he saw his hopelessness and his end. Debased on a linoleum floor, he looked up and watched her draw the skirt up her slippery legs to her stocking tops. Then, slowly, she crouched over his body so her face was closer. Balancing on one foot, she stretched the other out and planted the tight leathered foot beside his cheek. It threw a shadow across his face. Transferring her weight on to that foot, she gently removed her other boot from his chest. As he exhaled he felt a domino-pattern of painful indentations begin to go hot across his torso. 'You think we go too far and yet by the look on your face, I can see you have not gone far enough. You like to watch, Frank. That is not enough. You need to go further. How far will you go to please a woman? To get what you want? What you need from her? Perhaps a weakness must be exploited. Is that not how love begins?'

It was dark with her squatting over his face and he could smell her sex. Frank eyed her panties squashed between her legs. Interfering with his desire for her was a sense of unease. Was she accusing him of spying? Laughing at his silence and sudden stiffening, she rocked forward on to her knees. Spreading her legs she pressed her sex against his mouth. 'But you trusted me, so you get a sweet.' She gasped at the contact his mouth made on her salted softness. Sliding her fingers through his hair, she dropped her head back between her shoulders. 'Fuck me. Fuck me with your mouth, Frank.'

Playing with her sex, he trawled his tongue back and forth across her lips, sometimes pressing his tongue against them too, without sucking. Was it his saliva, or her moisture that made her panties so damp? Reaching out behind her, she gripped his cock with one hand. Tortuously, she began to pull it up and down, squeezing just enough to massage every muscle and feel every contour. 'Sometimes I'll want to be hard with you, Frank. But mostly, I'll be whatever you want me to be.'

Removing her sex from off his face, she moved down Frank's body and rotated her hips above his groin. The very tip of his phallus brushed her silk-plastered sex. 'You say you want to help me, Frank. To help me escape. I want to believe you. I do. But promises have been broken before. I've tried to forget you, but our bond just strengthens. So maybe there is a chance for us to be together. Maybe.'

Pulling her wet panties to the side, she lowered her body down to his sex. As it pushed through her, she opened her mouth but screwed up her eyes and nose. Beside a faint croak, she was silent until she found a rhythm and accustomed herself anew to his dimensions as they were pushed through her with the added weight of gravity that worked on her body. Moving on him rapidly, she began to groan in time with each descent. 'I want to be with you, Frank. I do. Maybe neither of us have a choice any more.'

'That's right,' he told her, watching the elegantly dressed body rise and fall in his lap, all the time feeling like a naked patient suddenly surprised by his specialist.

'Tell me when you're going to come. I want to feel you all day and I want to taste you all day.'

Moments away from climax, her request hastened his end. 'Now. Right now. Drink it.'

In one swift and balanced movement she seemed to detach herself from his penetration and lower her face to his sex. After a final jerk in the warm palm of her hand, Frank came. Catching the first spurt in mid-flight, she then covered only the head of his cock with her mouth and worked the rest of him on to her tongue. Staring deep into his eyes, she swallowed without fuss. 'You taste good. It's important to me how a man tastes. I throw the bitter ones back.' She smiled. And then she took from him again. Down on the floor, her delicious mouth left a mark on the inside of his thigh. Frank tried to tell Lucretia he loved her, but she had gone before he could finish.

Nine

Lucretia was not a woman to be shared, but coveted. Why Eldrin allowed her to stray was the biggest mystery to Frank. Considering Eldrin's illness – whatever it was – surely a house bound invalid would become possessive or excessively dependent on such a female prize? But Eldrin Crow knew of Lucretia's infidelities; some were even carried out in the next room. While he seemed to punish her, he also appeared to delight in her excesses. But why had she not run from him earlier? In his enfeebled condition, he would be easy to evade.

Doubt, hope, trust; the cycle of emotion exhausted Frank more than his sleeplessness or the energy it took to facilitate and sustain his viewings. Maybe his feelings for Lucretia were interfering with his attempts to locate and view Eldrin. Perhaps it was his loathing of the man who seemed to own his lover. But whatever the reason, right from the beginning of the investigation, Frank had failed to view Eldrin sufficiently to truly know him. Unless Lucretia was directly involved with him – making love or a party to one of his strange rituals – Crow remained an enigma. And was it a coincidence that shortly following Lucretia's first assurances that she would be with Frank, the young beauty became a prisoner?

Food was delivered and the curtains never opened in the apartment. Lucretia's shopping excursions stopped. Her hastily taken phone calls to his desk suddenly ceased. As had her visits to her car and the safer communal areas of the building in which they met to conduct the affair. There was no explanation, no final word, not even a note. Frank burned for her touch and longed for her teeth and the wonderful delirium they would bring. Enraged, jealous, sometimes despairing, never free of his thoughts of her, Frank threw all of himself into a fresh campaign of almost continual viewing. Only now he was looking for himself; the agency's stipulations were all but forgotten. But it was never easy. Just as he attained new powers of psychic vision, he suddenly encountered a considerable block to his clairvoyance. It was as if they didn't want to be seen.

Holding a pair of panties Lucretia left him with after their final liaison – a quick entanglement in an elevator – Frank spent the next week deep inside his own head, trying to relocate a path back inside Lucretia's apartment. But interruptions plagued him the whole time he worked the front of the building. Courier packages arrived for other tenants; decorators moved in and out of the building; real-estate brokers assessed empty flats; guests came and went. In addition, when he tried to find her in the safety and quiet of his own apartment, the agony of separation from Lucretia and the building she lived within prevented Frank on concentrating for the required length of time.

Lucretia only came to him in fragments. He became a collector of glimpses, the way it used to be when he was starting out in psionics. Piecing together these moments of intangible and perverse rite to find cohesion, continuity and meaning was the hardest task of all. Never catching the whole picture or scenario, seeing the end of scenes, the aftermath or just the beginning of some new strategy of Crow's, he could only speculate as to what his intentions were.

Was Crow aware her affections had found a new home? Were these his last desperate attempts to control her; the last scenes in this drama Frank had been instructed to watch? Was his hold upon her still considerable? Or was Lucretia only going along with Crow's demands out of habit, or in order to fool him into a false sense of security as she waited to choose her moment to escape? Or was this all wishful thinking – the only way Frank could cope with watching her get used like that?

But if she did flee – and Frank felt his very sanity depended upon her escape from Crow – he'd already decided the agency would only hear of it once she was long and safely gone. He would protect her with his life.

Body parts were a good source of introduction to Frank. Starting small, the image could grow. Sometimes, when he dreamed or concentrated his recall on certain of her provocative features, she would gradually appear to him and his viewing would commence. For a while at least.

Idle but arousing thoughts of her legs once placed his vision inside the apartment with her. Toes squeezed together, a pale foot dipped, the toenails Corvette-red, he saw her slide a pair of nylons up her legs. Sheer and black, they appeared to be of an impossible length until the hose completed a perfect fit on her legs and the opaque tops were secured to the garter fastenings of an antique girdle. It was made from purple and black satin.

From a nearby chair, looking withered and pale in a black suit, Eldrin watched her dress. Legs crossed, his grey eyes were fixed, unblinking, above the rim of a glass he drank from. And then the scene was gone.

Again shiny in fine hose, he once saw these incredible legs zipped into the clinging leather of long boots. Across the square black and white tiles of a marble floor, he then saw her walk towards a low couch where Eldrin lay. Inhaling oxygen or gas through a mouthpiece, the pallid Crow stroked his long erection as she neared. His gown was open and part of it trailed on the floor. In his free hand, he fondled a silver chain that gradually sagged to the tiles as her swaying buttocks approached. Sinking to her knees, she opened her glossy mouth above his phallus and waited for the gift he stroked muscle to produce. Her eyes were closed. Frank lost them before Crow came in her mouth.

Snatches of her slender feet raised at a 70 degree angle – mounted on the pedestals of spike-heeled shoes – came to Frank the night he idly thought of the golden chain she sometimes wore on her left ankle. Like a fetish diva, she would teeter across the chess board of their apartment's floor space, committed to some fresh task her master had bidden her to perform. Sometimes she wore slingback heels, but always a pair of high-heeled sandals, with straps as thin as whiskers, to complement the long backless dresses that Crow would not be long in removing. And Crow's scrutiny was always present, as if competing with Frank's gaze, then taunting the remote viewer with a moment of indulgence, before finally triumphing and ending his episode of second sight.

Rolling sleeplessly at home in his bed, his vivid recollection of Lucretia's face once inspired a vision that kept him awake for the remainder of the night. Sucking the white flesh of Eldrin's cock, so rigid with hot blood, Lucretia's features were alive with adoration as she looked up her jailer's lean body. Fingers spread, the red nail paint bright against her keeper's belly, she clawed at the bands of muscle while she slid her mouth on and off his erection. Then the phallus was released from inside her wide mouth. Appearing in the oval of her parted lips, she then rubbed it against her chin and cheeks as if worshipping a blasphemous relic, hoping to extract a miracle from its length.

When Frank remembered the touch of her hands and shivered as if the pressure of her long fingers was real, he saw these same hands clenched on wood. He almost heard the scraping sound of her silver rings as she fisted the support, clinging on as if for life, while the ghostly shape of Eldrin rode her back; a back lined pink from a cane's kiss. Gouging through her anus, sinking his width deep, he stretched Frank's lover until the only sounds she could issue from her wet mouth were croaks, as if seams and timbers were being rent asunder inside her.

It hurt Frank to see such things. It registered like a physical pain. A scalding beneath his breastbone – hot embers under smooth stones – and a burning in his belly – the dry, chemical fire of jealous rage. And it was her enthusiasm that rankled most: the sparks of sun in her ocean eyes; the animate face, so eager, so greedy; the lash of tongue and the thinning nose; the grasp of fingers and the claw of nail. A pretence? Or an unscrupulous delight in the extreme sensations made in equal parts by pain and pleasure? Damn her! Frank would swear aloud. Is she so invulnerable to the stipulations of deeper attachments – like loyalty and commitment? Was she the destruction of every man by becoming the epitome of sensual freedom they dared to dream of?

Entrapment within one's own excesses, seeking pleasure of an increasing intensity, predatory instincts; destructive obsession: was Frank becoming Eldrin? The thought troubled him, but he was unable to stop looking and longing.

A pale face, suspended in the dark of its own misery and confinement, watches her. Propped up in the vastness of his bed, cold among the pillows, the staring eyes are a colour of freezing sleet at dusk. They chill her slender form. Resplendent in shining rubber, she stands before the mirrors. Feet together, head down, hands crossed at the belly, a thin chain falls from her collar . . . She is gone.

And then again, in his chair, out of bed but weakened in the plush cushions of red velvet, Crow's sharp face directs questions at Lucretia. She kneels on the floor before him, head bowed. And she is naked, according to his wishes. Beside the occasional sly smile, Lucretia remains indifferent. Crow's actual words are a mystery to Frank. But of the tone and emotion involved in the exchange, he is not left ignorant. Crow seems to be without something; has gone without it for some time. Not a drug, but whatever he craves Lucretia is in possession of it. This he finds infuriating as if she were to blame for its absence in him. His inquiries and accusations are weathered by her invulnerable beauty and this impassive side of her nature. This power in her frightens Frank. In Eldrin he can again identify his future self, but also denies the notion again; refuses to let it take hold because, by this time, the very thought of her not belonging to him is intolerable.

Eventually broken by her silence, Eldrin will resort to other means. Her lover of many years can still reach her in other ways.

Eldrin leads her into the second bedroom she had once been led to by three young guests. And in there

– the equipment room – she is recreated. Before Crow, who sits on a chair beside the wooden frame, and before the silent witness of Frank's remote presence, Lucretia dresses.

For such a beautiful woman, masking her with anything but a transparent veil seems foolish. And yet even with a tight rubber hood, coating her from collarbone to cranium, Lucretia still manages to exude the most astonishing beauty. It shines from her eyes and exhibits itself in the red of her lips; the only parts of her face left uncovered by the holes tailored into the garment. And her breasts only seem larger and her narrow waist more compact when the rubber top is zipped up her back to join the hood. From her waist to her toes only her buttocks are left free of clinging rubber. Spike-heeled boots stretch up her thighs to the V of her groin where the panties cover her sex. Unhurried, careful, her eyes inscrutable, Lucretia rubberises herself into Edwin Crow's living doll.

Dressed in this manner, she observes silence. She kneels before him again while he strokes her head and talks to the rubbered face. He tells her he must punish her.

Strung up by thin chains that are attached to wrist and ankle cuffs, Lucretia hangs in the centre of the wooden frame. Crow stands beside the apparatus and inspects his tools while talking to her in a soft and patient voice. Again, she is asked to reveal her secrets, her distractions, they who have come between them, he who has come between them. She remains mute.

A paddle is weighed in his hand; a crop whistles through the air close to her ear. But he decides on the thin cane, long banned from classrooms, in order to complete the re-education of his mistress. He holds it before her face and speaks to her again. For some time now, she has been ignoring his wishes and wilfully goading his fury with her disappearances from the apartment. She had given herself to others without his consent and driven him mad with her refusal to share what she managed to snare, out there in this city in which he is hunted. And why does she keep so much from him? Does she favour someone over him? Who has she found when he needs her most?

Only a partial confession is extracted when he uses the cane against her buttocks. Partial, because Frank becomes convinced that although Lucretia never names him, she must be telling Eldrin there is another. He sees the revelation register on Crow's face, and in the speed of his arm after she had muttered something over her shoulder. Despite her cries, as Crow applies the quick strokes to her unclothed buttocks, and the tears that seep from the eye sockets of the hood, and her pulling and straining against the cuffs that hold her fast, she refuses to speak again. Another cane is used, and then another.

Lined red, Frank catches glimpses of her punished buttocks. He actually sees the quick bite of the rod, indenting her cheeks, turning the pale flesh to stripes. It is as if he is being made to watch so both Lucretia and her new lover are corrected. And as Lucretia is punished for being so desirable as well as unfaithful, Frank is then to be tormented by the sight of Crow thrusting through her at a furious pace. Still trapped within the wooden gibbet, Eldrin unseals her anus and sex by opening the slit in her rubber panties. Holding her squeaky waist, he then enters her sex from behind. Knowing her weakness for enforced use, Frank watches her lips begin to mouth encouragement as her captor works himself through her. Eldrin's groin slams against her buttocks. The entire frame judders against the metal bolts that fix the device to the wooden floorboards. He continues the penetration for an hour. And when Frank believes he can stand to see no more, Eldrin merely moves his thick erection from her sex and plants it in her anus.

After Crow has left the room, Frank notices the dreamy languor of joy that appears in Lucretia's eyes. An exaltation and a sign of pleasure like it is she who has enjoyed success in the inquisition.

Crow returns to the room, not penitent but softer in his approach. When he kisses her full lips, caresses the side of her rubber head and moves his hands over her hardened breasts, she bites her lips to fight pleasure while failing to deter it. It makes Frank seethe when she appears to reciprocate. Crow's treatment is cruel and Frank cannot understand why she has not put an end to him and his tyranny in the same way she ended the gang at the hotel.

Removing her from the shackles, Crow guides her to the bathroom. When the door to the equipment room is closed, Frank's vision ends. He cannot understand why.

But Crow could not always be vigilant; he had to rest more than she did. During one of these periods when he fell into an uneasy sleep, Lucretia finally fled.

'I've left him.' Lucretia came through the door of his apartment. It was two in the morning and she had disturbed Frank from his own poor rest. He was running a fever. Swathed in black, there was an air of solemnity about her. It was the first time Frank had seen her impeded by any kind of responsibility.

He made them coffee, his nerves alight with the excitement and relief of their reunion. But it was not all he felt; he sensed a greater period of trouble and patience, as if another trial was about to begin. He joined her in the living room. Dressed in his robe, he sat in a chair before her and shivered. He half-expected her arrival to be part of a dream. During the previous week he had rehearsed so much to say to her. Now she was here, it all seemed preposterous. 'Talk to me,' was all he could manage.

Lucretia lit a cigarette. Wearing a long black dress beneath her furs, it was her intention to conceal her body. Even her feet were booted and her hands were gloved in leather. Beneath the garments, her pale body whispered. This was the first time she had come to his home or strayed so far from the apartment building. She smoked in silence.

Frank found words. 'Tell me what happened. I've been going crazy. You never called. What was I to think? He punished you. I know it. He found out about us and imprisoned you. Made you suffer.' He swallowed and tried to fight the emotion he felt. His voice was breaking and his face was wild.

But how could he have known what had befallen her? A guess? She should have seemed surprised at his disclosure, or at least asked him how he arrived at such a conclusion. She never did. Lucretia looked up and stared into him; her gaze unnerving, too penetrative. But she seemed pleased with what he had said. 'He knows. Knows everything. Always finds a way to know, Frank. And yes, I have been punished.'

'How can you just accept this? I don't get it.'

'There is a darkness inside me. It is what I have become. Some of me, the person I used to be, is left. But not much.' She paused to collect herself. A profound sadness seemed to have momentarily risen inside her. 'The dark is with you now, Frank. I put it there. The answers to all of your questions are inside with it. You will learn to hear them soon.'

'It's always been there, Lucretia. You and I are alike. It's why we belong together.' He sighed, exasperated, and pushed his fingers through his hair. The skin of his brow became smooth. 'We've never had time to talk. To really talk. There is so much I want to explain. Meeting you was no accident.' He stopped there. Could he tell her? He must think straight, choose his words. Was this the right time? 'We need time. Time to talk. I have to get you away from him.'

Lucretia smiled. 'I know who you are, Frank.'

He looked at her, held his breath.

She exhaled a thin plume of smoke. 'Were you not like me, you would not have survived me this long. There is no other way.'

What did she mean? Thinking her upset after Crow's torments, manipulation and excesses, Frank never pushed her; he had too much to say. 'We have to get away from the city. As far as possible. I have some money. Maybe Mexico. You could fly down. I could join you. You're free, baby.'

Lucretia smiled. 'And not for the first time. His demands can suffocate. His illness worsens and so do his obsessions. All of my energies have been occupied with reassuring him and placating him this past week. It's why I have been unable to come to you. I am sorry. But I went through this to protect you.'

A sudden anger flashed through Frank. He knew exactly what the reassurance of Crow had involved. He felt it had been carried out at his expense. Lucretia saw his rage and looked at her boots. She touched the corner of one eye. It was all Frank needed to banish his anger. His mood changed in a heartbeat. 'You knew I'd wait. That I'll always wait. And you've been through so much. I understand more than you know. Trust me.'

She smiled. Her eyes were wet. 'You want me for ever, Frank? You must be certain.'

'Always. I want you for keeps. You know that.'

'I will be the only one.'

'No one can compare with you. When I first saw you I felt my destiny change. You know it.'

'Many men have fallen because of me. It is not an idle boast. But only a few have survived me. Only the gifted ones. Eldrin is gifted. It drew me to him as it draws me to you. It is the way I am.' She lit another cigarette. 'But there is risk if you truly accept me. Nothing is easy. Nor will anything be the same again. Not for you.'

'Yes, yes, yes. I know. I just want you.'

'It can be wonderful too, despite the pain. I have the same pain.'

'I need you. I can't go back to what it was like before. I've had enough of that life.'

'Then come to me.'

Frank crossed the room and sat beside her. Never had she looked into his eyes with such intensity and feeling. Never had her teeth gone so deep. Never had she taken so much from him. Between his legs, his erection quivered in response to the pain. Dreaminess followed. When he began to faint away, her beautiful mouth fell into his lap. And when Frank climaxed inside her mouth, their bond was complete. And she had not lied when she said she would be with him for ever.

As he clung to her, his face wretched with pleading, he knew she was about to leave him again. 'I have to go,' she said, pushing one finger against his lips to silence his cries. 'I can't stay here. It is not safe. But I will return to you again. Soon, I promise. So don't look for me. But do whatever you must to survive the wait. Obey your instincts, Frank.' He lacked the strength to rise and follow her when she left.

When Frank awoke, she had gone.

Ten

Windows and doors and walls are no obstacle to Frank. Into her apartment he goes. Over the antique furniture his vision travels. Along the shelves and cabinets that hold the porcelains and silver, he searches for her. Around the rooms his inner eye sweeps. Dismissing the rare oils that hang on marbled walls, he is not there to admire the trappings of her wealth. Across the Turkish rugs and down the hall he speeds, seeking her in the most private place.

Ensconced in the master bedroom he finds her, preparing for an evening out. The jewels had been affixed around her throat. Diamond earrings cluster in her petite earlobes. That haughty but handsome face has been exactingly prepared with the best cosmetics. Her blonde hair shines, demanding and then absorbing the chandelier's light. But no dress, even if it cost a thousand dollars, is a shield to his foraging senses. He even fancies he can smell her.

No, Mrs Barnes-Dubois cannot sense the predator; he makes no sound, nor does he manifest before her. But inside her he will go to make preparations; to lay the bait for this priceless catch. This night, Frank has gone to court her.

On the other side of town, oblivious to the screech of siren, the bellows of the drunks and the smashing of glass in the street below, Frank sits naked in an armchair. Deathly still, consumed by a trance, he sends his other self out to forage for food; a particular sustenance he has grown to need, gradually and then desperately.

A contradiction to claim to love Lucretia like he has never loved any woman before – with a need that bores his insides – while he hunts another in her absence? But who started the connection between them? Who tutored him in the way of achieving a complete indulgence for even the darkest and most grotesque of his cravings? And who left him the moment he was enslaved? Lucretia. And would she blame him, or rage and spit? No. He knows she would merely feel some sense of pride, tinged with jealousy, that they were, as she had always suspected, the same. Follow your instincts, she told him. And even if she had asked Frank to be true to her while she was away, such a noble gesture would have been impossible. He has changed and is now destined, or doomed, to pursue whoever catches his eye.

Upstairs, as he watches her reapply lipstick, Mrs Barnes-Dubois keeps her driver waiting; something she often does without a thought. Downstairs in the garage, he polishes the windscreen and double-checks the interior to make sure everything is perfect, knowing how she is. And although she never keeps important people waiting, he is merely the 'help' like Frank, and does not count. Tonight, if Frank's experiment works, her delay will be the longest yet.

Padding across to her wardrobe, she considers her collection of shoes. Manifesting his invisible self around her body, he fills himself with her essence: the movements, contours and attitudes he has experienced when she walks past his desk, or pauses to make one of her many complaints about the state of the communal areas. In the bedroom, he then absorbs her; the thickish but shapely legs elongated from the designer heels she wears; the large bosom, freckled by the St Tropez and Caribbean sun; the plump mouth and insolent green eyes; teased blonde hair, sprayed hard and annually maintained for the same price as a family car; gold-heavy fingers; heart-shaped rump. And with so much of her inside him to nurture the joining, his desire begins to rage. A need to scoop mouthfuls of this soft flesh and seize handfuls of this mature glamour spreads. It is a compulsion to handle and rip and spread.

Into her mind he slips to begin the process of suggestion. Distracting her with the shiver left behind by the trace of a man's fingers on her neck, he then lulls her with the impression of strong arms circling and broad hands sliding. Sowing a thought about a handsome mouth kissing down from her mouth to her nipples, where at last it would sup, brings the goosebumps out on her arms. And eventually, he infiltrates her subconscience with an image, if not the outline, of the most powerful sensation yet. Unsteady on her feet, she then embraces the sensation of a young cock pushing at the mouth of her sex, promising to stretch and fill her with its thickness and vigour.

Alone in her room, she closes her eyes and her cheeks flush. Glossy lips part and a sigh is uttered. Blinking, she tries to collect herself, but no, he will fight resistance. Ghostly hands grip her shoulders and sneaking fingers slip her dress upwards so she can feel the cool air on the back of her thighs and on her parts only half-veiled by thin fabrics. Almost looks over her shoulder, but as she has not felt so aroused in such a long time, she lets the sensations play.

An eager hand ruffles under the hem of her dress and then strokes the panty-tissue of French silk across the wet flesh beneath. Tilting her head back, the weight of her skull rests on her shoulders as if she is trying to expose the tender skin on her neck to a rough chin and hot breath. So Frank puts it there, and just grazes the back and side of that neck with enamel also, so she knows animal instincts are at hand; eager to mount and penetrate and mate while the mouth bites.

Shoeless, she moves back to her bed and lies down to face the ceiling. Her eyes close. Pushing back across the satin sheets with her stubborn heels, she slips the hem of that sparkly black dress up to the top of her thighs to expose her thickish but tempting legs. She wears sheer black tights that shimmer up to her hips. And inside the panty and nylon shield, her red fingernails slide.

And as if he were actually there in the flesh, Frank makes it feel like he is on top of her, naked and hard and wild of eye. Raising her legs and parting them, he arranges her beneath him, and slips the head of his cock through the mouth of her sex. It is followed by the longest and heaviest girth she has ever seen.

The imaginary cock moves slowly inside, before withdrawing, and then easing forwards, once again, and a little harder due to less resistance from her widened sex. She makes the sounds of a woman juggling a hot potato with her tongue. By subtle increments he eases projections of himself into these sudden and fresh and overwhelming thoughts she experiences. Frank, the uniformed concierge, the big, shy brute who wants her like no man has ever wanted her, is a man who will be as discreet as he will be passionate. And he is up there, inside her, right now.

'Yes,' she says. 'Yes.' And inside her panties and tights, her fingers move like they are polishing a coin.

Frank, he thinks. It is Frank, he thinks.

'Yes. More. Yes, harder,' she says, and pushes three fingers inside herself to give herself the brief pain of the imagined entry. Then she tickles the pinky walls of her sex with those precious nails. Frank, he whispers again with his inner voice. And inside her head she can see his taut buttocks contracting and the definition of the muscles on his back.

'Oh. Oh. Oh. Fuck me,' she says, talking trash to the spirit-man in her head, who is now making the brass headboard slam against the marble wall as the very force of his thrusts shuffles her entire body up the bed. And then her imagination is married with his imagination, and in the sharing of their sixth senses they meet; astral travellers join as lovers.

Now she can see her dress torn down over her breasts, and the shoulder strap of her bra dislodges and hangs by an elbow, so the white meat inside those lacy cups can be feasted upon. Between her legs, the sheer Italian tights are ripped so his shaft can bury itself deep, oiled by her need.

Frank, Frank, Frank, Frank, he thinks.

She gulps at the air, and then her lips move as if that plump, spoiled and pretty mouth is trying to form words. 'Fran . . . Fra . . .'

Frank! Frank! Frank! Fuck me, Frank! It takes all of his energy to suggest this to her and to accompany the words with the spectre of his cock and balls slamming against her buttocks, while his unshaven mouth works her breasts.

'Frank. Fuck me, Frank. Go on, fuck me. You bastard. You bastard. Fuck me, you bastard!'

Yes. Deep and hard, so she will feel light and helpless. Succumbing for a short time, she will absolve herself of everything other than the proof of her own desirability as this brute pleasures himself. On all fours? he then suggests. How good she will look; how total his mastery of her body will be, and how complete her submission.

Her body is swivelled on its front and then firm hands grasp her hips to guide her up and on to her knees. She can imagine this; the ideas just come to her and she responds. Yes, she enjoys the aggressive needs of this spectral lover; he who delights in watching her shapely buttocks judder while he moves through her at the speed she knows will precipitate a climax.

Seeing herself on all fours with the hired man, she makes an 'O' shape with her mouth and ascends to her own peak. Her wrists ache from the exertion of producing so much friction on her little bud. 'Make me come, Frank. I'm coming on your cock, Frank.'

This far, why not further: you have been taken by force. I came to you and took what I wanted because you made my state of arousal insufferable. Risking everything, I would never have found peace had I not taken you so abruptly. Remember how this happened. See me now, handling you, steering you to the bed, my mouth fixed on yours, my hands sliding over the parts of you I have worshipped from afar.

She turns her face to the side and lets the hard sounds fall out of her mouth. Passing in and out of a dreamy place, shudders wrack her body and Frank inserts a final idea: his climax occurring at the same time as hers. His body stiffens over her, just as her legs lock and her head cranes back. And then his body will pause rigid above her, before collapsing when the whitest seed is spilled inside her.

But ultimately it is Frank who is surprised by the psychic exchange. Because as her orgasm swamps her, she thinks of his cock spilling its seed over her face, and over her breasts too. These images are transferred back to Frank. There is so much of his cream, like it is a testament to her beauty and a younger man's adoration. And her imagination then creates a final image of his cock re-entering her sex to pulse inside her, right at the back of her womb, while she whispers, 'All of it, Frank. Give me all of it.'

Holding her to his vaporous chest with his invisible arms, he reinforces the sense that they have been together. Then, finally, he retreats to watch her from above as she lies alone on that bed. Her hand is finally still inside her underwear.

Had he imagined the entire incident? The next day, when Frank awoke from a deep sleep, he had significant doubts that such a psychic connection could even be made with Mrs Barnes-Dubois. In Nevada, when he was still in the services, their NSA-funded operations to transmit messages over vast distances had inconclusive results. All attempts to communicate with captured pilots in Iraq failed.

But when Frank returned to the building, the day following the extraordinary viewing, to begin a week of night shifts, the old Colombian concierge who he relieved said a curious thing. It was a warning. He asked Frank to prepare himself for some 'ball breaking', as he put it. Twice that day, Mrs Barnes-Dubois had asked after him. 'She wanna know when you on duty, man. You musta pissed her off, man.'

Twenty minutes after the Colombian had left the building, the house phone rang. It was Mrs Barnes-Dubois. 'Frank, yes. What point is there in having a new satellite system installed if one cannot watch the channels one desires?'

After an inner yawn, he said, 'None.'

'Precisely, so when you have a moment this evening, I would like you to attend to this matter. Am I understood?'

'Perfectly.'

She hung up. And for a while his old self returned: the anxious, dithering Frank who liked to watch but feared failure in any greater participation; the self that amused Lucretia until she removed this part of him for her own designs. Frank became bewildered. Was this coincidence? Barnes-Dubois had never pursued him before in this manner, or ever asked him up to her apartment. But then, her tone of voice was hardly likely to ignite any desire for her. She was just her usual unpleasant and demanding self. He would go up there, fiddle with the television, declare it faulty if there was nothing he could do to improve her reception, and then return to his desk to complete an incident report. There was no ulterior motive. Of this, he convinced himself and felt relief. But the feeling was short-lived.

He had been in her apartment before. Instantly he recognised the features in the hallway from the dream. He felt light-headed. And to see Mrs Barnes-Dubois prepared in manner similar to the image in the viewing was overwhelming. The connection had been made.

Speechless, Frank followed her down the hall towards the living room, where he presumed the television would be. Unable to remove his eyes from her body in the backless black gown, his reticence and anxiety began to erode. The desperate and baffling desire that he associated with his new hunger replaced the doubt. Watching her from behind, it was as if he was already experiencing the warm sensations of her naked flesh against his own. His focus on her curves sharpened in a direct correlation to the thickening in his groin. She would see his excitement. Let her, the new and firmer inner voice suggested.

And their destination was not the living room. She turned off the main concourse and led Frank to the master bedroom. Immediately, his presence of mind returned with a clarity and an alacrity he never associated with sexual feelings of such power. Thick and red and seemingly inexhaustible, his arousal waited like lava behind the insubstantial peak of a volcano. And it would not wait for long.

The television was in her bedroom. 'I'm damned if I'll waste another moment fiddling with it. I wish they'd never started messing around with it in the first place. I'm missing my shows.'

'I thought you were going out,' he said. In response, she looked mean, as if he had said something rude. 'You look so elegant,' Frank added. 'But I guess a real lady is always a lady. Even if she's just watching television,' he added and put a pinch of small-town guilelessness into his voice so she knew she was still his better.

'Thank you,' she said. She stopped frowning and her eyes softened. All day she had recalled the previous night and the vision he had sent her. Inside of her, he now detected a great vulnerability she had not allowed herself to feel in years. Despite the power of her voice and the fortress of her arrogant face, there were no defences inside. Frank took deep and soundless breaths to remain calm.

Unsurprisingly, there was nothing wrong with the television either. She had merely made the wrong selection on the handset and sent the impressive equipment into the standby mode. Convenient? 'Just watch out for this button, here,' he said. Standing next to him, the hairs on her arms reached out to touch the sleeve of his cotton shirt. He could hear her breathing and could smell her warm, strong breath on his cheek. Usually it smelled silvery, like when she was chiding him. But now it was different; she had been drinking brandy. Nerves. Frank smiled to himself.

With his body still facing her television set, he turned his face to the side and looked into her eyes. Such pretty green eyes, where the girl still lived, and not at all unbecoming with those lines at the side that plastic surgery failed to erase. 'You smell so good,' he whispered, and she saw his face darken with desire. Her primal intuition detected the signs of male desire, even after ten million years of evolution. Frank's nostrils widened, his jaw set and he seemed to inflate and bristle all over. He heard her swallow. She seemed unable to escape his gaze.

He turned the television set off and threw the remote control on to the bed. The silence in the room became a gravity of pressure. He had to act before it squashed her back to her senses. 'You are a lovely woman, Ma'am.'

'Carol. Call me Carol.'

'Spoiled and despotic too.'

She barely had the air to say, 'How dare you.'

'But so desirable. Your attitude only makes you foxy.'

She looked nervous. One of her eyelids twitched as his mouth moved closer to her lips. 'Beautiful,' he said, and then filled his mouth with her.

Never felt a woman tremble so much. Holding the top of her arms firmly, he prevented her from toppling over as he kissed down and into her mouth. 'The nastier you are to me, the more I want you,' he said, briefly breaking from the kiss so she could breathe. 'And you should be careful when you display your body in those dresses, Ma'am. More than once, I've been tempted to reach for you.'

She closed her eyes and placed her hands against his chest, as if to push him away, but there was no strength in her arms. His teeth found her neck. She fell against him and said, 'No.'

'Mmm,' he answered, and grazed the skin of her throat with his teeth. It smelled of soap.

'We mustn't.'

Pulling back, he looked down at her, deep into her eyes. 'I am going to have you.' Frank spoke slowly. 'Right here. I no longer care.'

Again she shuddered, and this time kept her lips and teeth shut as he probed at her mouth with his own. Sliding his hands down her naked back, he placed the tips of his fingers inside the waist of her dress and stroked her garter belt. To allow a moan to escape, her lips parted. Quickly, he drew her tongue from out of her mouth and sucked at it, hard. Against her stomach and his groin, they both felt something hard as bone. Into her ear, he whispered, 'I want to be inside you.'

This time her moan was louder, and her head had fallen right back on her shoulders. 'We can't. I'm expecting a friend. A gentleman.'

'Then he can watch me fuck you,' Frank whispered, to which she made a crying sound.

On his belt, the pager began to beep: there was a guest at the front door. 'Fuck it,' Frank said, and threw the pager to the ground. Barnes-Dubois's eyes were frantic. Moving forwards and supporting her weight so she wouldn't stumble, he moved her to the bed. Threading his fingers through the shoulder straps of her dress, he then lifted the bootlace straps from her shoulders. The dress fell to her waist. Now it was his turn to swoon; her large breasts were hammocked in a material both black and sheer. Large nipples demanded he suck them like pacifiers, just to delay the aggressive penetrative plans he had for the lady.

When the mattress struck the back of her knees, she fell on to her behind. Kissing her neck again, Frank pulled her dress from under her buttocks and then down her legs with uncompromising hands. Straightening his back, his lips parted to suggest disbelief – she had slipped into a directoire garter belt and black stockings. 'They will only make it harder for you,' he said. 'It'll make me rough, I'm afraid. And I'll last longer.' She swallowed. The pager beeped like an insect trapped on the wrong side of a window. Oblivious to its incessant pestering, he said, 'Take your panties off. And then give them to me.'

She continued to stare at Frank in disbelief. 'Now,' he said, in an even but direct tone of voice.

Slowly, with tentative fingers, she began to slide the black briefs down from her hips while he admired her body. 'I can't,' she said.

'Well, I can.' Leaning over her, his lips a moment from her own glossy mouth, he gently knocked her hands to one side and then slid her panties down to her knees.

'Bastard,' she said, in a voice he'd never heard before, before pushing her mouth into his. At the back of Frank's head, her nails clawed his scalp.

Clenching his hand in her thick hair, he moved her biting, sucking mouth from his own and eased her further up the bed. Kneeling over her, he then stripped his tie, shirt and T-shirt from his torso. Stroking his hand up her legs, and watching it slide over every contour from her ankles to her hips, he experienced a dire need to feel her, any part of her, against his sex. His cock became impatient within its wrappings. Once free of his trousers, shorts, socks and shoes, which he tore from his body with some-thing approaching rage, he selected her mouth to satisfy the craving.

Immediately, her crimson nails were shining against his stomach. Below her half-lidded eyes, her mouth opened to engulf his sex. Sitting astride her chest so his balls tickled her bosom, he held her head steady and then commenced with a series of short pumps inside her mouth. Breathing quickly through her nose, Mrs Barnes-Dubois relished what she had been fed. She closed her eyes and hummed through her nose. 'That's it. Take it all. No teeth. Good girl.' Encouraged by his words, she held his shaft with both hands and rubbed it while she sucked. 'Mmm. Get me good and hard, so I'm ready for your tight pussy. Oh, yes. Like that. That's so good.'

Clenching tight, he slipped himself from her mouth and let the desire to come expire. 'Not yet,' he whispered, and moved further down her body to insert his sex between her breasts. And the sensation of her brassière, of the gauzy fabric against his skin, with the full weight of her heavy breasts behind the silken cocoon, brought him back to the point of climax. 'I'm going to come on your beautiful breasts, Ma'am. And then you are to eat it. You understand?'

She nodded her head.

'I can't give you much choice in this.' He was no longer thinking; he spoke from impulse. 'When I'm in here with you, when I'm inside you, your mouth, your beautiful pussy, and your arse too ... Don't look so horrified, I am going in there too. When I take you, I am in control. It's important you understand that.' Squashing her heavy breasts together, he thrust through them before pulling back and letting go.

'Bastard,' she whispered, but leaned her head forwards to watch his ejaculation. When it was over, she seized his cock and cleaned it inside her mouth. It remained between her cheeks until it was soft and she had acquired all of its remaining spice.

Using his mouth to play with her sex benefited his swift recovery. And as he tasted her and then tickled her deep inside with one, two and finally three of his fingers, he looked up her body and watched her eat his cream off her bosom. She seemed to consider the spillage on her cleavage as a savoury dip that the crackers of her red fingernails were drawn to.

Indulged by her wet sex, and feeling its hard briny tang at the back of his throat, Frank then attended to the uncompromising nature of his need. Pulling her legs up and against his chest, by holding her stocky ankles, he began to nudge and tickle the mouth of her sex with the end of his erection.

'Put it in me. Do it,' she said. Then pleaded, 'Please, Frank.'

To which he slapped her left buttock hard.

'Bastard!' she cried out.

Swivelled on to her tummy by his hands, she clutched out with her fingers to purchase a grip on the bedclothes. Before her nails sunk into the slippery sheets, the flat of his hand had engaged her rump several times. But as he spanked her, she groaned and her eyes developed a dreaminess. He sensed her desire for something hard.

Holding her body down against the bed, Frank whipped his hand in and out to strike the flesh of her buttocks over and over again. Slapping her broad cheeks, he began to sweat and she began to whimper. Breathing harder than ever, she looked over her shoulder when he pushed his thickness inside her. Writhing her head against a pillow with two fingers clutched between her teeth, the wealthiest resident in the building grunted every time his sex packed through her womb.

Not resting or pausing to breathe, his inner will drove him to continue a deep and aggressive rifling of her body. Clawing at the bedclothes, she whispered obscenities and encouragement for even harder treatment. Holding her wrists against the bed excited her more than anything. After biting his forearms, she gritted her teeth and then screamed from behind her locked molars.

Still wearing a stained brassière, creased stockings and garter belt, he thought her more beautiful than ever. Flushed of cheek and mad of eye, she bucked against him and began to smash her hips back towards his own, demanding a deeper penetration and greater friction. 'Come on my cock,' he whispered, when he recalled something she had said during the remote viewing. 'Come the way you come in my dreams, Ma'am. Come hard and feel me come inside you.'

She shouted something incomprehensible, and as she fought the cage of his fingers that still held her down, her legs locked and she cried through her climax. 'Now, Ma'am. Feel me. What I've wanted to put inside you since the first time I saw you.'

'Yes. Come in me. Come . . . Bastard.' And Frank stayed buried deep until every spasm had faded and until every drop had been delivered in the royal purple of her womb.

But as her torments to the humble concierge had been prolonged and intended to wound, his use of her that evening was long and destined to change things between them for ever. At the time Frank knew he was playing a dangerous game, but he exalted in his own recklessness and thought only of a desire for fulfilment. He no longer feared her – had seen her too naked and exposed to be wary of the superficial rank and the threat she represented. He accepted the challenge to tame her into his plaything. Knowing she was trouble and that they should never have come together in this way, there was also something about her Frank could not be without.

After securing her ankles with her brassière, he tied her wrists together with an expensive stocking. Strapped into position, she beamed at Frank over her shoulder. 'Are you really going to? I've always wondered what it would feel like. Wanted it, often. But a woman in my position, well . . . it just wouldn't do to carry on like that. Unless it was with someone . . . like you. I once asked a friend if he would, you know, take me in that place. But he declined. I frightened him off. I can't believe it's going to happen. Will it hurt?'

'Oh, yes,' he said. She shivered as he lubricated his sex and then loosened the bud of her anus with a finger.

'Be careful with me,' she whispered in a girlish voice.

Frank smiled. 'Just a little bit at a time. Just a taste. To get you ready for tomorrow. And the day after that. And so on. When I will come up here and take you in the ass.'

Her whole body shuddered and she closed her eyes. 'Promise?' she whispered.

'No,' he said, and slipped the first quarter of his phallus inside her rectum. Pausing, he listened to her cries. 'And when I come and see you, make sure you are prepared like you are tonight. And I want you to smell good. And when I undress you, surprise me.'

'You're inside me,' she whimpered. 'Inside . . . Feel how wet I am, Frank.'

And he did, before slipping his entire sex inside too.

Exhausted by the long, slow and often tortuous loss of her anal virginity, Mrs Barnes-Dubois eventually fell silent. Her whole body, still dishevelled in her best lingerie, relaxed into the bed. Frank left her tied to the brass bedframe when he bit the top of her leg. It was instinct. He never gave it much thought, because it was the most natural thing in the world for him to do. It was a part of love. Brandy-thick, caviar-salted, liqueur-rich: she tasted good and stopped writhing once she'd learned to enjoy the soft pulling sensation inside her flesh.

Maybe he took too much, because his head was then hot and full of mist. When he stood up and reached for his scattered clothes, he lost his balance and began to stagger. Untying the bra and nylons from her limbs was the greatest challenge of all. Mrs Barnes-Dubois had fallen asleep by this time. So Frank left her alone on the bed and made his way back downstairs. But in her dreams he remained.

Eleven

Despite his longing for Lucretia growing stronger with each day since her departure from the building, the attentions of Mrs Barnes-Dubois had at least taken the edge off Frank's craving. As if suddenly unleashed into an awareness of how impoverished her predominately sexless life had been, before his infiltration into her dreams and then bedchamber, she now seemed eager to make up for lost time. Too eager. Although Frank enjoyed her, he secretly hoped the mutual curiosity and her infatuation would burn itself out. In truth, Frank had no idea what he had started. He was now a creature of impluse, not reason. Nightly, throughout that first week of their union, she demanded his attentions and the biting that concluded each encounter. Did his teeth give her the same ecstasy that Lucretia's drinking mouth had supplied him? The dreamy visions of morphine?

'I don't appreciate being kept waiting. You were summoned over one hour ago,' she said to Frank, through a crack in her door on the fourth night of that shift pattern.

Inside his stomach, he felt a now familiar and ominous tug of annoyance. 'I have other duties. Security responsibilities,' he lied.

The skin around Barnes-Dubois's mouth tightened. She opened the door and beckoned him in. As soon as Frank stood in the hall, she slammed the door shut. 'And I can't stay for –' he began to say, but the sight of her outfit ended his excuses, again.

She raised her eyebrow, but seemed pleased with what she read on his face. She was dressed in a chiffon gown, black and transparent, and Frank could see through the gauze to her shapely body beneath. Beneath the gown her voluptuous curves had then been further enhanced by the constrictions of a leather corset. Her breasts were pushed up to spill over the top of the garment like a sweet dough made from the purest flour. Dark stockings were attached by six suspenders to the corset. Between her hips, her sex was unclothed. 'Never make me wait again.'

'Yes, Ma'am.'

'I may have overlooked your invasions into my room this week, but don't imagine for a moment that you can take liberties with me, young man. My contributions to the maintenance pay your wages. I am one of your employers and I will enjoy access to you whenever I wish.' She strode down the hall towards the lounge, expecting him to follow. 'Now we have dispensed with that unpleasant but necessary business, I suggest we continue where we left off last night.'

Smiling, Frank followed her into the split-level room. Despite the grand piano, bar and dining table to seat twelve, there was still enough space to house a small orchestra. 'Perhaps, a drink first,' she said.

'Not while I'm on duty.'

There was a perceptible straightening of her back. 'Then make me one.'

He sighed. 'As you wish.'

'This is a duty to you?' He didn't need to look at Mrs Barnes-Dubois to see her expression.

'I like seeing you. It's exciting.'

'Then why the reticence?'

'I don't want to get fired. I like my job.'

'Do you know who I am? Would it be beyond me to pull a few strings and save that wretched position you're usually so willing to neglect?'

He handed her a gin and tonic. 'I don't want it to be that way.'

She laughed derisively. 'Then we are to be equals in this?'

Eyeing her lingerie and flesh through the dark smoke of the robe, his desire mingled with wounded pride – the powerful force that had led him into her arms in the first place. His appetite returned in full. But was he willing to overlook this insistence of her mastery? Times had changed and he had already made his position clear. 'No. We are not to be equals.' A smile started to form on her face until he said, 'I will come to you when I choose, and will pleasure myself as I wish.'

She lashed her drink across his face. 'Bastard!' That she had been reduced to craving satisfaction from a lowly doorman rankled; with fang and claw it fought against the hunger he had nourished inside her. 'I could have you –' Seizing her around the waist, Frank kissed her mouth hard before she could finish. Withdrawing her hands to beat against his chest and face, she made the mistake of looking Frank in the eye. Everything on her face softened. Her hands fell uselessly against his shoulders.

'Don't ever resist me,' he warned. Holding her by the elbow, he led her across the room to the leather sofa and bent her over the back. Reaching out with her hands, she spread her fingers on the cushions. She peeked over her shoulder. With a growing look of horror, she watched Frank unthread the heavy

160

leather belt from around his waist. He doubled the strap over and then held her in place by pressing one hand between her shoulders. 'This is going to sting. It is unpleasant, but clearly necessary.'

'You bastard!' she shrieked at his mimicry.

'Mouth like a tramp. I like that about you. But should I tolerate such an outburst?' The leather of the belt licked around her wide rump. She closed her eyes and gritted her teeth. Lowering his aim, he lashed the billowing chiffon against her thighs twice more. She shuddered, but made no sound. Still angry at her bullying, Frank continued to belabour her backside with the belt, enjoying the way her body jolted from the shock of contact with the leather. Between his legs, his sex hung heavy. Was this a game? Or had playtime become so deeply fused and confused with real life for both of them, they know longer recognised one from the other?

Her voice softened when she spoke during a pause in the punishment. 'Are you my master?' She kept her eyes closed. 'Frank?'

'It's why I came to you. For your spirit and your beauty. But it needed taming. You were out of control.'

'Yes.' She nodded her head. 'Will you correct me often?'

'Increasingly. But you can make things easier by dressing like this.'

'You like it?'

'Makes me wicked.'

A shiver ran across her skin and her face contorted like he had just entered her. 'You shouldn't have to put up with me.'

'That's true.'

'So what will you do when I'm a bad girl?'

Frank answered with the belt until she danced as if hot coals had singed her feet.

161

Without further delay, he unzipped his trousers and raised her gown. 'What are you going to do?' she asked.

'Be quiet.'

'But ... Oh Frank. Oh God, Frank.' Slipping through her moist sex made his legs tremble. And right from the first moment of penetration, he had to remove his eyes from the criss-crossing laces of her corseted back. The very sight urged Frank to come. He let the need subside and then made her legs bang against the rear of her own furniture as he thrust inside her. 'Did you dress for me?' he asked.

'Yes.'

'Why?'

'So you would like me.'

'So I would do this?' Gripping her pale shoulders, slippery beneath the gown, he pushed her body down until her face was buried in the sofa cushions. Squashing his legs into the back of her thighs, he hammered himself into her, relentless, denying her speech, or the ability to concentrate on anything but the force and sensation of a ruthless penetration.

'Yes. Yes. Oh, yes. Like this. I need it like this. It must be like this.'

'No. It must be harder.' And she choked and then shrieked as they came together.

Haunted by all the images of the investigation – Lucretia's mouth sucking stiff flesh, her long and willing body held down under a flail, shiny heels indenting flesh, youth stolen in the back seat of a limo, Barnes-Dubois bent over leather upholstery – Frank was soon able to think of little else but sex. Lust twisted his insides. Never sated and always dreamy, he became unable to concentrate on even the simplest tasks. And there would be no respite from himself until Lucretia and he were reunited. But her message never arrived. A week passed and there was no word.

For the remaining two night shifts of that week, compulsion led Frank back upstairs to stare longingly at Lucretia's door before moving on to Barnes-Dubois's penthouse.

'What are you doing? Tell me, Frank.'

He ignored her cries. Barnes-Dubois lay on the bed where he had dropped her. Hurriedly stripped down to her underwear, by his own hands, she had curled up in the centre of the wide bed to watch him. Grim-faced, eyes set on the task, he opened two flat packets of her expensive hosiery.

'What? Are these not right?' She stroked her thigh to draw his attention to the nude stockings attached to her girdle.

'They're fine. These are for your wrists, ankles and mouth.'

'No!'

Wrestling her arms down to the bed, he loomed over her. She stared up and deep into his eyes. Her anxiety over his intentions became anticipation. Her fear of the unknown transformed into a fear of herself.

Copying the knots he'd seen the female naval officer use on her girlfriend, Frank secured Barnes-Dubois's wrists together in the small of her back. Holding the stocking like a leash, he pulled her torso up until she rested on her knees, easing the nylon through his fingers. Her head and chest were then lowered back down to the duvet. Against the bedlinen her face turned to the side. She continued to question him, so he used another of the stockings to gag her mouth. Having enjoyed the music his leather belt had made the previous night, he again unthreaded it from his trousers. She made muffled sounds Frank ignored.

Thinking of Lucretia, of how she had been loved, of what she craved from ruthless lovers, he combined thoughts of her with his awareness of the delightful malleability and willingness of this powerful widow. As he removed his watch and rolled the sleeves of his shirt up to the elbow, Frank spoke to her: 'Turn your face away. Go on. Do it!' His leather strap connected with her buttocks and made a wet sound. 'Good. Now watch in the mirror. You'll be able to see the look on my face as I punish you. You'll witness a lack of compromise. And a determination to love you with strokes. You will be helpless as you are punished. You will see a plaything dominated by one she has wronged.' She moaned, but the sound was soft; one of relief and anticipation and not one of misery. Leaning down to whisper to her, he removed a strand of blonde hair from her ear. 'Watch your own struggle. See your own tears. And understand my desperate need for you. To me you are so desirable that I cannot remain alone downstairs. Just knowing you are up here hurts. Share my pain.' Then he kissed her cheek, before getting busy with the belt.

For the first half a dozen lashes, he heard her sharp intakes of breath. For the next six, her yelps were dispersed by the sheer stocking between her teeth. His final four strokes were accepted in silence. Not once did she take her eyes from the vision in the mirror. Kneeling helplessly in directoire corsetry, stockings and her long-line brassière, like a kidnapped heiress starring in a Tijuana skin-flick of the 1950s, Mrs Barnes-Dubois smiled through her tears. Down both cheeks, her mascara had run in black lines.

Dropping his belt, Frank continued to act as if controlled by an inner directive. Securing her ankles together with a third stocking, he then readjusted the nylon between her lips by tying it tighter. Squeezing one hand between her thighs, now that her legs were squashed together, Frank stroked her sex. Sopping pubic hair had stuck to the lips of her sex. 'You're so wet, Ma'am.' She made a muffled sound. 'Perhaps too loose for what I need,' he added. 'No, I shall clearly need to pursue another means of entering a glamorous slut.' Her eyes widened and there were renewed cries from behind the gag, and then frantic tuggings against the wrist and ankle bindings. Frank's knots held fast. 'Yes,' he said, looking her in the eye, via the reflection in her dressing mirror. 'To fully master you, Ma'am, you must accustom yourself to these new limits. I was easy with you last time'

Leaving her alone for a while, to think of her impending fate, Frank walked to the lounge. He helped himself to the 25-year-old scotch from behind her bar while he listened to her Beethoven CD. In the kitchen, where he devoured an excellent Swiss cheese sandwich, three fresh cream cakes and a tray of after-dinner mints, he picked up a bottle of extra-virgin olive oil. He took the oil back to the master bedroom with him.

Having left her with little hope of mobility, she remained in the centre of the bed. Only now she was lying on her side, facing the door. She remained silent on his approach to the bed. Casually, he undressed before her. She watched his erection as if hypnotised. Sitting beside her, Frank then lubricated two fingers with the olive oil. Then he poured it upon his sex and rubbed it into the skin to produce a slick shaft. With the two slippery fingers, he began to play with her anus. She gasped. Closing her eyes, she began to fidget. And to his surprise, she was soon pushing her buttocks back at his hand, seeking more from the fingers that tickled and probed. 'It will be slow at first, but not for long,' he informed her.

Resting comfortably on his knees behind the great heart of her buttocks, Frank held her hips and gently nudged the head of his phallus between her cheeks. Her entire body stiffened and she whipped her head from side to side, before returning her gaze on the reflection in the wardrobe mirrors. 'Now,' Frank said, and her breathing quickened. Every one of her fingers and toes straightened. Her head craned back and rested between her shoulders. Her eyelids were clenched shut. 'There. Feel it? Just an inch. Now more. Just a little more.' She hissed. Frank withdrew and then re-entered, withdrew and re-entered, pressing further each time, but only by modest increments so she could accustom herself to the violation. That was, until it was time to say, 'All of me. All of me is inside you, Ma'am. You have an employee's cock deep inside your ass.' To that she shrieked against the wet underside of her gag.

He then attached her wrists to her ankles behind her back. When he finished, she lay on her front, with the soles of her feet facing the ceiling. Between ankle and wrist, the nylon cord was taut. Frank removed the gag. Saliva and friction from the moving nylon had melted her lispstick and it covered her chin, giving the skin a pinky veneer. She breathed quickly. 'Are you uncomfortable?' he asked. Between his legs, the erection glistened after being withdrawn from her backside.

'Can't move my legs and arms at all,' she answered.

'Good. Did you like me in your ass?'

She looked Frank in the eye and nodded her head. 'I'll do anything. You know that. Don't you, baby? You own me now.'

With an expression of one who had been told what he already knew, Frank nodded with approval. 'Now open your lovely mouth. I haven't come yet.' And soon, she was unable to speak again. And while her mouth worked on his cock, so recently withdrawn from her little bud, he stretched his head towards her feet and found his own sustenance from the top of her right thigh. In fact, he took so much this time, she fainted.

After untying her wrists and ankles, Frank left her to sleep through the remainder of the night, with his seed drying on her chin.

Twelve

It was uncanny to ascend what he thought was his peak. Besides the week when Lucretia was incarcerated at Crow's leisure, Frank had become more skilled as a remote viewer than ever before. And even though Ally Kram left him with fewer clues than Mrs Barnes-Dubois, these crumbs were sufficient.

For her own protection, Agent Ally Kram offered Frank little trace of her real self. Deliberately left behind to thwart Frank, after her visits to his apartment, was the refrain of her attitude (still a lingering discomfort in his rooms), the undeniable sense she did not care for him, or trust him, and a threat to kill him if he ever tried to view her. And he believed she would resort to extreme tactics if he took a peek into her head or life. A rush in itself. Pretty girls with bad tempers and guns; something he learned to adore in the services. And not for a moment did Frank believe she had nothing to hide. Those that operate the best defences are the most interesting targets.

Merely thinking about her was not going to be sufficient to track her through the psychic ether. But nerves made her careless. And the concentration of all her energies to feed him the 'tough girl' act gave him the only clue he required. Three Marlboro 100 cigarette butts, stained indigo by her lipstick, became his passport to her inner life.

Sitting comfortably behind his desk at work, shortly after midnight, and not long after he had left Mrs Barnes-Dubois in an exhausted sleep for the second night running, Frank listened to the slow pulse of his own blood and drifted inward. Holding one of the cigarette butts in the palm of his right hand, he began to concentrate his thoughts on Agent Ally Kram. He had taken the butts to work with him sealed in a plastic sandwich bag, after retrieving them from the coffee cup she used as an ashtray during her last visit. Alone, they were not without an erotic appeal because they came from her lips, of which there remained a dark and incriminating stain.

With ease he slipped deep into his subconscious world and thought of her mouth as she sucked the smoke into her lungs. A sophisticated smoker – and the tobacco helped to keep her trim. They aided her concentration. Yes, she began to smoke to look older and now inhaling was directly linked to the very machinery of her thoughts. A complicated girl with a self-examined life who had become an addict. Frank warmed to her, reached further, pictured her face . . .

Then he caught something: the image of a whisky bottle on a coffee table. Next to the bottle was a tumbler. Inside the glass he could see ice cubes and bourbon. Beside the tumbler there was an ashtray. The ashtray had not been emptied for some time and she had been smoking the cigarettes down to the filter, which were stained with a lipstick the colour of a fire engine. The shade suited her. Under the table he saw a pair of slingback shoes. They had high heels and were made from suede the colour of charcoal. New shoes. She liked to buy new shoes; like the cigarettes, they helped. He looked beyond the table. He saw more.

On an agency expense code, and probably under a false name, she had been installed in a spacious, one-roomed suite with cream walls and a white ceiling. Although it was night she had left the curtains open. An aluminium tray of take-out curry festered under the lamp at her bedside. Make-up debris was littered on the dresser with the mirror, and there were items of underwear strewn across the floor. In the bathroom, the towels on the floor were still damp from the shower she took that morning. Messy girl, he liked her.

On the bed, her long body stretched out, Agent Ally Kram lay awake. Facing the ceiling, she smoked another Marlboro 100. Too preoccupied to pay much attention to her immediate environment, or to get undressed after work, she wore half of her suit; a skirt with a pinstripe, and one of the white, sleeveless T-shirts she wore under the jacket which was now crumpled over the armrest of the only chair in the room. In the half-light of the reading lamp, her tights shimmered against her legs. Both her fingernails and toenails were painted the colour of her lips. Moving her head on the pillows had mussed up her red hair.

Although her eyes were open, they focused on nothing in the room. It was as if she stared through the ceiling. Frank sensed confusion; she was disturbed by events in her life she had no control over. Once she was alone and the tough façade gone, he discovered a tenderness and vulnerability in her both surprising and appealing. He recognised himself in the opening stages of the investigation: bemused, anxious, afraid. On the floor beside the bed lay a brown paper file. Well thumbed, but now cast aside, he knew it had been a source of frustration for her. Perhaps she looked for a meaning or pattern in the information that would not reveal itself. Frank knew the feeling.

Returning to his conscious self, he felt troubled by what he had seen and intuited. Dare he use his psychic ability yet again for unethical use? Since the infiltration of Mrs Barnes-Dubois's subconscious mind, and then her physical life, he had begun to feel like a doctor taking great liberties with his oath. Remote viewing a woman in private no longer felt like a game.

But warring against this reserve, which has never been difficult to talk around, was his perpetual state of arousal. Battling his sympathy and begrudging respect for Kram was an overwhelming fascination with her beauty and style and guarded sensuality. He just had to see inside her; the very compulsion made him light-headed like he was lost at high altitude. Carried by the utterly seductive delights of voyeurism, Frank slipped back into his trance. Lucretia won again.

Growing weary of her exhausting thoughts – the wretched fatigue of too much introspection – Agent Kram extinguished her cigarette. Easing herself off the bed, she reached for the drink. Holding the glass and taking repeated sips, she stood by the window and looked out at the nightscape. And Frank came in.

She was lonely. Stuck in a purgatory of indecision. Deceived by one she trusted. She had no one to confide in. Frank went to her with feelings of sympathy and encouragement. You don't have to do this alone, there is another, he thought for both of them. He then inserted a flattering idea of himself. As with Mrs Barnes-Dubois, Frank recreated himself inside her idle thoughts as someone more attractive than he actually was. Hard of body, wide of smile, bountiful in humour and affection, he helped Ally Kram reconsider his character. She smiled. When he visualised himself naked for her, her smile faded but her tongue absently played with her front teeth. So well hung? She had not expected that. And such stamina from all that running. Abundantly sexual from his curiosity about strong women too. Perhaps she had underestimated him? With an act of intimacy there was even a chance he could take her mind away from this endless doubt she suffered about her job. It would be an intimacy charged with the harsh feelings they harboured for each other. It would be hard and uncompromising in bed; a fight for control. She could use his cock; put it right where she needed it and then would allow him to overcome her when she wanted to be held down and just . . . No, she shook her head and sniggered.

Too late for second thoughts – those were just her natural defences. The seed had been planted. Her cheeks developed colour. A light returned to her eyes. How long had it been since she touched herself down there? It had been over two weeks. So busy with trying to fathom the investigation, she had neglected nature's gift of stress relief. She was frustrated, thwarted, preoccupied, but the whisky must have loosened her. Yes, that is why she was entertaining these crazy thoughts about her subordinate.

Padding across to her dresser, she opened the top drawer on the right side. In there, Frank saw a froth of lingerie: rolled bundles of pantyhose, tangled brassières, a camisole, some birth control, tampons, panties thin as slingshots, and at the bottom, towards the rear of the drawer, he spied a penis.

Shocked, he nearly spun out of the viewing. But some keen and deeply rooted desire to stay submerged kept the vision firm, despite an interfering ripple. It was not a real male organ, but a lifelike reproduction made from latex. Who actually buys

172

these things? He had often wondered. Now he had a better idea.

Quickly, Ally stripped off her T-shirt and the white sports brassière she wore beneath. While Frank choked at the sight of her immaculate breasts, she unzipped her skirt and then rolled her pantyhose down both legs. Once she had stepped free of her panties and hosiery, she flopped back on the bed and made herself comfortable. Freshly naked, her body shone in the dim light as if adding its own illumination to the room. Like drops of blood, her toenails glinted.

Sharing his thoughts with her, Frank imagined his hands caressing her breasts. He could see it clearly. She could too. Using fingertips, he stroked the curve of her breasts. Then his thumbs flicked her nipples. Gently cupping her breasts, he squeezed so her nipples protruded towards his lips. Circling her hardening pips with his tongue, he occasionally paused to speak to her in a whispery voice. He spoke of her astonishing beauty.

Responding to this image her imagination flaunted at her, Ally reached between her legs. Trimmed short, her floss lay flat against her belly in a neat V-shape. It made the lips of her sex look pinkish. With her long fingers, she played with her sex, as if teasing it before rubbing the tickle out of existence. Then she applied the heavy-looking phallus, with its obscene purple of engorgement, to her clit.

Yes, that is Frank's cock down there. And those are his fingers touching you in just the right way. And while he plays with your sex, he cradles the back of your sweet head with his other hand. Now your hair slides between his fingers like red silk. It tickles the webbed skin between his digits. Your head is moved into a specific position to accept his cock. You like to suck, to feel a man's body tense, and to hear the whimpers of his impending surrender to the power of your mouth. The greatest skill is the mere welcome your mouth offers. But you only suck him for a while, because your need for penetration is overwhelming. Plus, you don't want this thing to go off on your tongue, even though the idea of a hot ejaculation inside your mouth arouses you. Deep inside you is a greater need to be stretched and filled at depth.

The urge became an ache.

And then she took over. Suddenly, Frank found himself afloat in a psychic dream in which he was used by another's will. Releasing his cock from her lips, shiny with saliva and polished lipstick, she stroked his shaft through her hand. The fingers were long and their embrace easy. They never stopped those long squeezy-rubs until she sat astride him and placed the tip of his phallus back in her dew. With a long groan, she sat down like she was descending on a hydraulic chair. Frank passed inside her. Inside Agent Ally Kram!

On her bed, in his actual real-time vision, she pressed the latex toy through her sex and shuddered from her tautness around its girth. It was like Frank now saw two motion pictures; one superimposed over the other, each effortlessly interchanging and gaining prominence. While Ally Kram actually fucked herself in bed with a false cock, he received the projections from her imagination of what she dreamed of doing to him. Dual psychic transference: in theory it was supposed to be light years away. Riding his belly, she arched her back so it appeared more slender than ever. Clawing his chest, she used the muscles in her thighs to move her up and down and to push and pull his manhood through her. But in real time she locked her legs straight and withdrew the toy from her sex with a measured efficiency, before plunging the shaft back inside her sex. It went in hard. At the end of each stroke from her bedside friend, which she now ardently wished was Frank's living flesh, she threw her head back and widened her jaws. The scream was silent.

But in her dream, safely previewed behind the claret velvet of closed eyelids, she was still bucking over his naked and handsome body. She had even given him a Calvin Klein torso, exploiting corporate homo-erotica for her own pleasure. Clawing the skin over his stomach muscles, she fish-gulped conditioned hotel air and dug the pink heels of her feet into his thighs. Securing him fast, in a position that facilitated her release in the lap of a minion, which magnified her charge, she bounced on his cock and ground herself into Frank's pelvic bones to ascend the foothills of her climax.

To Frank's astonishment, her imagination then delivered a magnificent showreel of one girl's hidden depravity. This one would go far. As she climaxed in a quick succession of peaks, perverse snapshots cascaded through her imagination, travelled the psychic highway and were delivered behind Frank's moist brow. These were scenarios she favoured whenever the lights were out and her fingers were busy beneath the sheets.

Skirt up, legs apart, pantyhose ruffled around her knees, painted fingernails spread on a toilet seat, the special agent thought of a stranger aggressively thrusting into her sex from behind.

Bound head to toe in a PVC catsuit, so only her beautiful eyes and red lips were visible, she imagined herself belted tight to a wooden frame. In a star-shape she offered her body to a room full of muscular young men who watched her with love-struck eyes.

In an office upholstered in leather and wood, an eminently handsome man with a stern expression told her to bend over his desk. She complied. She wore a red jumper with an embroidered J over her left breast. White bobby socks were folded around each ankle bone and her skirt was both short and pleated. Her hair was tied into bunches and she wore glasses with square black frames. The man was older than her and addressed her backside with the flat and hard palm of his hand.

Limbs bound together, body straight, she hung from the ceiling of a plain room – the kind found in cheap boarding houses. She was reduced to a shapely silhouette. A dark and sinister presence paced around her. He flexed a cane. Her skin pin-pricked beneath the antique corsetry; her arms perspired within the tight single glove that pulled her wrists together behind her back. Inside the leather hood that clung to her face like a silken sea creature, her lips parted. She drank in the air, his psychotic eagerness, and the scent of her own excitement . . .

Frank yearned to see more, stretched out to her with all his remaining energy, but the final image proved too much for Ally Kram. Finally, her climaxes tailed into a fatigue that clouded her head and filled her body with morphine. At peace at last, Ally Kram smiled a sleepy-girl smile and pulled a pillow over her face to muffle a giggle.

Released from the chains of her worries for one night alone in a hotel room, which had become a prison cell for her, she had inadvertently shown Frank her sexuality at the most profound level. And for a few priceless seconds, she gave no thought to the volume of her cries. They passed through the walls and ceiling of her room, and carried beyond to two lucky salesmen, also alone in bed and stuck for inspiration.

Damp in his shirt, Frank sat behind the front desk of the apartment building, shaken by the intensity of yet another woman's submerged desire. Baffled and aroused, he then began to pace the lobby. Running his fingers through his hair, he tried to fathom Ally Kram. What was the motivation for what he had seen: plain fantasy or real experience during the episode of self-pleasure he had instigated? The final image she left him, of herself strung up and bound in a boarding house had been too vivid. It was different to the other revelations. Details had lingered more than they would if the fantasy had been a collage of observations and imagined props.

Hard to say, also, who had gotten the better of who. Ally Kram had climaxed while Frank was left in heat and alone at night. It annoyed him. He felt cheated. Too many images from her fantasies endured in his mind. He'd never find peace until he once again relished the spice of a woman in his mouth. Dreams only lit the fuse or started the timing device. They were no longer sufficient and served to awaken an appetite in him he thought insane. Opening the safe behind his desk, he seized the spare keys to Mrs Barnes-Dubois's penthouse apartment. Thinking of Agent Ally Kram, Frank entered the elevator and began his ascent.

Thirteen

There was a knock against the front door of his apartment. Frank paused on his way from the bathroom to the bedroom. Dressed in only his shorts with a towel around his neck, he walked to the front door. Sensing the presence of a woman out in the hall, his stomach became alive with nerves. Within her he intuited feelings of caution and a need for secrecy and reticence. Could it be Lucretia?

Hurriedly, he unlatched the chain and turned the dead bolt. Pulling the door wide open, he held his breath in expectation. Exhaling, he said, 'You.'

Agent Ally Kram nodded. Uncomfortable with looking him in the eye, she peered down at the bottle she held in her gloved hands. 'Me.'

Standing to one side, he let her enter the apartment, and a cloud of perfume with a sharp scent was unleashed. It suited her. 'You weren't expecting me.'

'No.'

'You don't have to look so disappointed.' She tried to smile, but bashfulness killed the smile before it could widen her mouth. She was wearing more lipstick than usual. 'Here.' She held out the bottle. It was champagne. 'A peace offering.' Surprised, and still in the grips of the dejection he felt at the absence of Lucretia, Frank never reached for the wine.

Kram stepped back. 'I understand. It was stupid of me to come and expect you to be nice. After all I said before. You probably hate me.' She put the bottle down on the floor, turned and walked swiftly down the hallway towards the stairwell.

'Wait.' Frank followed her and put his hand on her elbow before she could take the first step. 'Hold on. I'm surprised, not angry. You usually don't bother with knocking.'

Fishing in the pocket of her woollen overcoat, she then pulled her hand out and opened her fingers. In the palm of her hand was a silver key. It had been attached to a Magnum shell. 'Take it. I should never have used it against you. Only . . .' She never finished.

Frank folded her gloved fingers back over the key. 'You should keep it. Just in case.' The moment became awkward. Frank released her fingers. 'Come on. My lasagne's gonna burn. We can wash the black bits down with your champagne.'

Kram looked up at him and smiled. 'Really?'

'Sure. I made too much anyway. Get so hungry after a run.'

She asked about his run and he told her, before going into the bedroom to change. After completing six night shifts, he'd awoken in the early hours of the afternoon and immediately embarked on a five-mile run along the dockside. Taking in the park on the way home, he'd then run over ten miles instead before returning to shower.

By the time he returned to the living room, wearing jeans and a T-shirt, his feeling of disappointment over Lucretia had eased. Kram had removed her coat and hung it over the back of a kitchen chair. The sight of her made him realise just how hungry he was.

Co-ordinated with a long black skirt and rollneck jumper, she wore tight leather boots with a square toe. Her make-up was discreet but enhanced her strong features. Her eyes seemed bigger than ever. She was smoking. 'I took the liberty,' she said and held up the cigarette between her long, white fingers. Some of the strength had returned to her voice, but she was still anxious.

Frank smiled. Although he never smoked tobacco, he wasn't opposed to the smoke, and hidden under his mattress was an ounce of Mexican reefer he'd bought off the kids who played basketball behind his building. It helped with the visions. He poured drinks to help her relax. Kram gulped her champagne like Lucretia.

'Like your outfit,' he said, from behind the kitchen counter as he eased the lasagne dish from the oven. The golden top bubbled but wasn't burned.

'Thanks,' she said. 'Saturday night, you know.' She laughed nervously and started a second glass of champagne.

Why was she here? And was it now becoming a date? After he placed the food on the kitchen table, he found oddments of cutlery to set a second place. He kept busy so his puzzlement would not show, but sensed she had come to him to make a confession. The thought excited him.

'You work out too?' she said from the door of the kitchen, looking his body over.

'No. Just run.'

She sat down at the table. 'Yeah.' She sounded mystified. 'I thought you were bigger somehow.'

Frank remembered the details of the vision he had instigated in her; especially the body he had awarded himself, which she then further embellished. He smiled as he handed her a fork. She looked up at him

180

with a guilty face. 'Sorry. I'm such a bitch. I didn't mean anything by it. You look all right. Good. You look good, I meant to say.'

Frank nodded. 'I prefer lean and rangy.' She blushed; they were flirting now. She liked him; he could sense her attitude towards him had changed. But she still fought the notion too. Knowing what she did about his sleazy past, why did she now find herself attracted to the man she set out to hate? It confused her, like the incredible clarity of that crazy dream had confused her. She thought she'd dealt with that. Frank brought garlic bread to the table from the oven.

Towards the end of the predominately silent meal, she offered her explanation. 'So why am I here, you wonder?'

'Sho' ain't to see my muscles,' he said, cleaning his plate with a crust.

When he looked up, she was staring at him. 'No, seriously. I thought it was time I was straight with you about the investigation.' She cleaned her teeth with her tongue; he watched it move under her thick lips. Under the table, his cock remained hard, as it had done since she took her coat off. 'I've had enough of being on my own with all of this. I need to talk to you. I need you. Your input.' Gazing back across the table, right into her eyes, the way he did with Barnes-Dubois, he saw Ally Kram's cheeks flush pink again. Immediately, she looked down at her hands. Unable to stay averted for long, she looked back at him. Her pupils had grown.

'Go on,' Frank prompted. 'It's a bit late in the day to brief me, but I'm all ears. I've always been curious about what you know.'

Kram took a long swig of champagne from her glass; she'd drunk the best part of the bottle alone.

181

She lit a cigarette – a Marlboro 100. Red lipstick on the filter caught Frank's eye. 'Same as you,' she said. 'I know the same as you.'

For a moment they stared at each other in silence. Frank was the first to speak. 'You mean you know sweet FA?'

She nodded, exhaling a plume of smoke between pursed lips. He wanted to kiss that mouth, but managed to keep most of his mind on what she was confessing.

'So what do they usually tell you before an assignment?' he asked.

She shrugged. 'No idea.'

Stunned, Frank asked, 'This is your first job too?'

She nodded, embarrassed.

Sliding his hands behind his head, Frank looked at the ceiling and whistled. 'If it's any consolation, you had me fooled.'

Kram drew on her cigarette. 'But I'm the fool. I went into this with my eyes closed. All I know about the agency are the rumours I heard in the Bureau.'

'You were Bureau?'

She nodded.

'It's a sweet gig. Why did you leave?'

'Given no choice.'

Frank leaned across the table. 'Discharge?'

'Dishonourable,' she answered softly, her eyes moistening. 'I guess one of the reasons I tried to dislike you was the fact that we're so alike. Couldn't keep it in our pants.'

Frank started to chuckle.

'Stop laughing at me,' she said, her face suddenly hard. 'I got involved with a con. Someone I was chasing for a long time. It got messy and he escaped. I was fired. But we have to leave it there.'

I saw something of what you did, Frank thought, remembering the final vision she had transmitted

182

back to him fuelling her climax: the dark and vague apparition of herself, suspended in the room of a boarding house. But the information only made her more interesting to him. He wished he could tell her. 'And I thought you were so die-hard. A real cop.' He shook his head in disbelief. She was still suffering; he wanted her to suffer a little, but not in this way. He had other ideas, for later. 'Thanks for telling me. You know my story. You know my shame. But you can find your way again. We both can with the agency. There is a reason for all this secrecy. I haven't given it much thought, but I've a hunch they have a strategy. To see how well we do without direct command. This ain't the military or the Bureau. Perhaps we're supposed to operate on our own initiative.' But saying that filled him with a sudden remorse for what he had done to the investigation. Of the few instructions he was given for the assignment, was there one he had not disobeyed?

Ally Kram smiled through her tears. She nodded. 'Maybe you're right.' She sniffed and wiped her eyes with a tissue. 'Look at me. A big girl with a big mouth. That's all I am.'

'Come on,' he said, smiling. 'It's freezing in here, but it's four hundred degrees by the sofa. This place sucks.' He offered his hand to his supervisor. She sniffed and then accepted the hand. Her fingers were cold against his palm, but the merest touch of them thrilled him to the core of his soul.

'You cleaned up,' she said, looking about the room and putting herself back together inside.

'I get restless. When I'm not at work, I don't know what to do with myself. Feel lost. So I run and I clean. Keeps my head straight.'

Sitting beside him on the sofa, she nodded. 'You're lucky. That's what I need. A distraction.'

'We could go bowling.'

Ally Kram laughed. 'You know, this is the first night I've had out since we were posted here. I just wait and wait for instructions. But all they say is, "Sit tight." Just sit tight. Nothing else. So I had to see you.' She looked at him with an expression of both shame and gratitude. 'Thanks. It's helped.' She stretched her legs out and Frank heard her boots creak. Under her skirt something whispered. He swallowed. She caught him looking at her legs and read admiration and curiosity on his face; a brief power transference. Smoothing a hand down her thigh, she said, 'I wore a long one, because the first time we met, you tried to look up my skirt.'

He shrugged; his turn to be embarrassed. 'What do you want from me? You have great legs. You wore a short skirt, and, well . . .'

They both laughed, then sat in silence for a while, watching the candles Frank had lit on the mantel-piece. 'Have you looked at me?' she asked. 'You know, remote viewed me?'

Frank cringed. He shook his head. 'Didn't want to get shot.'

She giggled. It made her sound younger. Then she looked at her lap. 'Will you hold me? I'd like that, Frank.'

Accepting her head against his chest, he filled his lungs with her smell. Perfume, shampoo, soap, new clothes, her fresh sex – he could smell and define all of these things. Slipping two fingers under her chin, he raised her face and looked into her eyes. They were glazed with drink and desire. There was no resistance to his kiss.

'Thought you were a pantyhose girl, chief.'

'I'm full of surprises.' It was the truth. Naked and kneeling between her thighs, Frank ran his open

184

hands up the back of her legs. Long and toned by exercise and striding about in high heels, every contour and dip and curve now whispered under his palms. She had dressed for him. Thong panties with a sheer front over a shaven sex; thigh-high stockings that were black and sheer to the toes of her long feet so he could see the red of toenail beneath; a brassière with transparent cups. His mouth filled with saliva at the prospect of a good meal. She had class but wanted him to appreciate her wildness with this touch under her designer clothes. He had willed this from her; recreated her to his taste as he had done with Barnes-Dubois. This was a wonderful gift he had cultivated and one he would never relinquish. He knew this instantly and had thought it before, but was again unable to let his reason interfere with what he was about to start. Only a submerged murmur of alarm hummed inside him about this new life of his and how it had become destined for pure sensual excess, like Lucretia's.

'I had an idea tonight would be special,' she said, when most of her face was covered in shadow on the pillow.

'You did?' he prompted, wanting to hear more of her fall towards him; needing to know how his power had grown and how Lucretia had begun to flourish inside him.

'Yes,' she answered, her voice now faint, choked like she needed to clear her throat. 'Been having these dreams, Frank. It's like you came to me one night. It was so clear. Like I could even feel you . . .'

'Inside. You could feel me inside. Like this.'

She gasped as he entered her. Slowly, after just the tip of his phallus had been ruffling through her wet lips, he sank his thickness through her, until he was completely inside her sex. 'I dreamed this too,' he said in all honesty. 'Since the first time I saw you, I wanted you.'

'Really?' she whispered, moving her body against the mattress and writhing her head against the pillows. 'You wanted me?'

'All of you. Wanted to be inside you. You're so sexy. And elegant too. You –' He wanted to say she reminded him of Lucretia, but knew it would have ended this time between them in a heartbeat. 'Thrilled me. Right to the centre of myself.'

Slipping her feet on to his shoulders, he kissed her ankle bone and then leaned over her body. Cupping her breasts, he made her gasp again. Tweaking her nipples and then smoothing his hands around the bulb of her breasts, he incited a whimpering sound from her wide lips. The world of women seemed to be his own; something to partake of whenever his passion demanded it. Whenever his thoughts focused with the intensity of a laser sight, he could identify his target and separate her from the herd and its respectability, manners and games. He could make any one of them his own for a time; take them and taste them; fill himself with their softness and scents and sounds and sweet, sweet life. Even his supervisor. The thought drove him mad.

Thrusting with all his might, his thighs were soon slapping against her buttocks. The bed slammed against the discoloured yellow plaster of the bedroom wall. Within the cacophony of bed spring and wood banging on brick, he could hear her moans, interspersed with pauses when she gulped at the air.

'Take me. Have me. Fuck me, you bastard. You dirty bastard, fuck me.' She hated him but wanted him. Needed to surrender unconditionally, if only for a short time. But was that not all he wanted, a short time with each of them? All of them; every damn one of them who passed him in cars or on foot, or made

186

the mistake of sitting beside him, or who dared to glance in his direction?

Filled with his own sense of power and desirability – something he had never imagined would be his – Frank ground his pelvis against Kram's sex. Gripping her hips, he began to yank her body on and off his cock. Poking himself deep and from beneath and above and side to side, he made her body ride and crawl all over the bed until she slapped his chest to slow him down and speed him up at the same time. Snatching her wrists from the air, he pressed them into the sheets beside her head, as he had done in the dream. Her teeth set into a snarl and her eyes flashed a challenge at him. In them he witnessed an intensity that frightened him; this was no girl he could toy with. This woman had already been to the dark places he had only begun to visit. Flaunting rules and discipline and professional conduct, she was a bigger sinner than he. And again, he was starting something he could not see the end of.

'You like this? Huh? When I hold you down and just fuck you, Ma'am?'

She tried to bite his face, but he moved out of her reach. Unleashing the cry of an animal, she began to buck her hips upwards. Rubbing her parts so fiercely against his wooden muscle, she found the heat and speed to finish herself. Jaw open wide, head back, she became silent. Legs tight against his body, every muscle tensing in her arms and across her stomach, she found deliverance. Then she collapsed and all the strength disappeared from her body at once.

Seizing the hair at the back of her head, Frank withdrew his cock from her sex. With one hand clenched on a steel bar on the headboard, he moved his body further across her chest until his knees were planted beside her ears. For a moment she looked up at him, her eyes filled with alarm, but relaxed once his

187

phallus rested against her top lip. Raising her head by the hair he fisted, he stroked his cock with his other hand and watched the thick spurts of his seed lash against her chin and cheeks. She closed her eyes but opened her mouth. Moving her head against his hand, she tried to catch the last of him from the air, as if desperate for a taste of this man who had handled her so roughly in a dingy room. Obliging and wishing to complete his dominance, Frank massaged the last spurt of cream deep inside her mouth. Under the skin of her throat, he watched the delicate cartilage rings work in a swallowing motion.

But when she came to him that night, she'd merely activated an already deep and profound hunger. An appetite that had already compelled him to run ten miles that day just so he could think straight. Dawn was a long way off, and Frank was hungry.

Imagining but not expecting that she would find her wrists bound to her ankles when she left the hotel that evening, so her body would bend into an elegant curve, it was her curiosity and her desire to relive another dangerous tryst that allowed him to bind her. And then gag her with her own sweet panties.

'You were rude to me.' She never saw him when he spoke in such a deep and sincere voice. Frank sat behind her; somewhere in the dark, just watching her. But she felt his voice inside her; it made her want to hurt in a way she found pleasing. 'You must have known I couldn't let you get away with it.' She wanted to ask him what he would do, but could do nothing but make muffled sounds over the silk of her own panties, taut between her teeth. She just had to lie there and anticipate his desires; imagine the force of them, stoked to an intensity by her nakedness and compliance in his rooms.

'You can't blame me, Ma'am. And, after all, you did come here to make amends. Just see it as make-up sex without the relationship.'

She flexed her arms and legs. There was a pleasing itch around her wrists and ankles where her own knotted stockings prohibited her limbs from parting. The bed sunk under her buttocks; he was moving out there in the dark. A rough hand stroked her bottom and legs. Three fingers slipped between her thighs and made her shiver. Playing with her clit, they lulled her into a vague feeling of reassurance that he would be gentle with her, despite the tight bindings that prevented her from any resistance. She felt relief and disappointment at the same time.

He kissed the hair away from her ears and his stubble rubbed against her cheek. The tip of his tongue licked the last of her foundation away. 'This will hurt,' he whispered.

She gasped.

'Sometimes you need to be loved like this. I can feel it. It's like you and I communicate on another level that doesn't require words. We have an empathy. I don't think I'm guessing. I know you like to be tied down, Ma'am.' What he said was intrusive, maddening. She struggled, but his hands held her still and his bare cock rubbed between her buttocks. They clenched. 'I'm going to be hard with you from time to time. No one need know and you will always be my superior at work. I'll never question your authority. You know that. But there will be times when you have no authority. In here especially. You will find me unwilling to put up with your attitude. In fact, I can honestly say, the more stubborn and wilful you are, the harder I will be. You cannot be so beautiful and so unobtainable. It makes me suffer. So when you give yourself to me, and you will with an increasing regularity, I am going to be hard.'

And there was no change in the rhythm of his strokes against her buttocks. The strap fell evenly; she could count one thousand and one, one thousand and two, between each hot, stinging lash around her fleshy cheeks. From just below her tailbone to the top of her thighs where she let the downy hairs grow, she knew he had turned her skin pink. And soon the sensations changed: pain became an incredible warmth, and in the heat of her skin the blows stopped registering as blows. Under the warmth her flesh was numb. Against the top of her inner thighs, her own fluids spread and became sticky as the air dried them.

Eventually, when she stopped hissing, he stopped the beating. After dabbing the tears off her cheeks, he kissed the end of her little nose. And she was left with an incredible sense of belonging and dependence; it had been a long time since she'd felt so wanted and needed. Fighting this was a sense of disbelief that again she had relinquished power and responsibility to a man of extreme desires and too great a sensitivity to all things. Where these feelings met in a man, she found what she required to escape the world.

Moving her on to her hands and knees – her wrists and ankles still strapped together by her stockings – he then readied her anus with a mentholated jelly. Smoothing the outside of her anus with his fingers, he made her bottom cold and slippery. And then she heard him lubricate his cock in the darkness behind her. Clenching her eyes shut, she waited for the new sensation he would give her. It would overwhelm her; she would be lost inside a suffocating and blinding storm of physical sensations and primal emotions; airless like a vacuum; a place where she would utterly submit, bound to a pole like a sacrifice and skewered deep.

And when he mounted her white back and sank through her, the exquisite moment of discomfort was abetted by another sense of penetration, at the back of her neck, where the skin was especially soft. It felt like his teeth had gone inside her too.

Fourteen

'I'm a bitch.'

'Yes.'

'Mean and demanding and spoiled.'

'That's true.'

'Is that why you punish me?'

'It is. And because I want to find the girl in you.'

'The sweet girl?'

'Yes, the soft girl. One who can give. In all the tears and the struggling, I want to find the girl who can give herself freely.'

'Yes. Yes. Yes. And you have to be a bad man to do that?'

He kissed her cheek. 'Afraid so, my sweet.'

'And am I beautiful too? Is that why you hit me with the stick?'

'Yes. To make you mine. All mine. To take the nastiness away for a while, so I can enjoy the beauty of the sweet girl.'

Ally Kram started to wriggle in her bindings. Her eyes were closed and she wanted to squeeze her thighs together and touch herself, but was unable because she was tied in a star-shape. Across the bed, her arms and legs were stretched out to the bedposts where they were strapped with leather thongs. She had brought them with her inside her Versace handbag.

191

Her face sweated inside the rubber hood. It kept the white sheet on the mattress clean. The hood had been in the bag too. Around her mouth, the scarlet lipstick had begun to smudge. He could see it through the hole she breathed through.

She had been in his room for a long time; they started early that day. He was inexhaustible; craved the taste of her. And this was the fifth time they had met since she came to his apartment with a bottle of champagne. At work, Mrs Barnes-Dubois took the edge from his yearning for Lucretia; after work, his time belonged to his supervising agent.

And he knew she had done this before; given herself completely to a cruel man. One she had hunted and tracked down and then fallen for. There were never any photos of the relationship; the only mementos were these accessories she had brought with her to play with, and her memories. Standing above her, near her, Frank paced around his room trying to fathom her out. Searching for her source, he removed all other distractions; the only world that mattered was in that room and nowhere else. The windows and curtains were closed, the heating was on and the only lighting came from a 100 watt bulb, unshaded and hanging above the bed to light her supple body.

Inflamed passions, a total absorption into this game of bondage and blows and whispers and taunts and reprimands, her body ascended to its peak through the stimulation of mind more than body. Through the extremes of her thoughts and emotions Frank was able to see her inner life. And after what he saw, he knew that if it had not been for his love of Lucretia, he would have fallen hard for this woman. But had he not met Lucretia, would he ever have done anything more than just peek inside another extraordinary mind?

Using the short cane Ally Kram kept inside the elegant case with the green velvet lining, Frank stroked the back of her legs. Tightly wrapped in shiny rubber stockings to her buttocks and pussy, her calves and thighs looked wet where they caught the electric light. And it was only when he touched the exposed skin of her buttocks that she shivered and stopped talking.

He felt frightened to see a woman so reduced but made more powerful than he could have imagined. The sight of her was overwhelming. He took a breath, steadied himself and isolated the target in his mind. Frank drew a bead. When the thin wood whipped the air and then stopped dead on her pale flesh with a 'plakk' sound, he had a vision. From inside that rubber hood, a beautiful head was having decadent dreams.

Court shoes, shiny stockings the colour of fine sand, a pinstriped suit, a white T-shirt, leather gloves and a shoulder holster were worn by her the day she handcuffed a tall man to her wrist, whom she led to a dark Sedan with tinted windows. She had found and captured her man in an upstairs room of a boarding house, as he carefully sealed items of women's underwear inside specimen bags. While he worked, he listened to Mozart. The door had been unlocked; he had been waiting for her. Such was his interest in the pretty girl who once shot bullets at him, he'd long decided that the smell of her hair up close, the action of her putting the cuffs on him, and the feel of her leathered fingers searching between his splayed legs was worth incarceration. She'd only gotten so close to him because she understood him; was inspired by his work. Frank never saw much of his face. Indoors it was always covered by a rubber hood. Outside between the porch and the Sedan, it was shadowed by the brim of a Trilby hat.

Frank raised and flicked the cane down again, and again, and again. Kram never made a sound, but he could see the shaven pink lips of her sex were wet. The vision continued; he took a deep breath.

As she walked the prisoner to her car, the tall man complimented Ally on her appearance; he was flattered she had dressed so well for him. She insulted him; he smiled. He suggested things to her; terrible things in the most simple way, using only harmless words. She told him to shut up and then called him dreadful names; he smiled and brushed the inside of her wrist with one finger. Her body stiffened all over, and underneath her expensive sunglasses, she closed her eyes for a moment. Then he told her a secret; one of her own secrets. She allowed him to lead her back to his room in the boarding house.

Frank put the cane to her thighs, using more force to make a louder but duller sound – seasoned wood on tight rubber. Then he rounded ten fast strokes against her buttocks because he wanted to see more; to see what happened in that room for the entire week before she was found by her superiors, alone and stripped of her underwear.

Antique techniques of binding were used on her body in that boarding-house room. She had only ever seen such contraptions and their knots in confiscated magazines from the 1950s that were kept in the Bureau archives. As if frozen at the moment of her potential poise and balance, she found herself suspended in exquisite immobility from the ceiling, with only the toes of her boots touching the bare boards of the floor. Legs strapped closed; arms recreated into useless ornamentation behind her back in a single glove, made from hide with a mirror finish; her head positioned at a slightly downward angle, as if she were asking for permission from a figure of authority;

eyes blindfolded with a black, silk scarf; lips painted a wet red. Beneath the leather straps and cuffs, and the chains that were attached to the surgical harness under her arms, she wore a hand-stitched corset of black silk, virgin stockings with dark seams that he kept in a special drawer in a special attaché case and tight ankle boots joined together by a short chain. And she maintained that position and only spoke when the ball gag was slipped from between her lips – another item the tall man had made especially for her, in anticipation of their union.

On the single bed near the open window, her own clothes were neatly folded; except for her underwear which now slept safely inside polythene, peaceful until the eventual awakening.

After eight hours in the harness in which she was subjected to long silences and long suggestions, her weakened body was relieved and laid out upon the bed, face down. All of her parts were then massaged into tingling life by skilled fingers, and the denser flesh around her sexual parts was caressed and tuned by a cane into a level of sensitivity equal to the finest nerves of her sex. And the cycle of bondage and punishment continued for one week. Willingly she lived in a dark world of pure sensation. A nirvana of emotion without thought or care. And only once each day was she permitted to take him inside her mouth. And in the evening before she gave herself to the harnesses and the straps again, he would enter her and move inside her for prolonged periods of time. But he never came inside her; she would have to be his bride for that honour, and that was impossible.

After Frank had repeated what he had seen in the visions – the caning and the long, intense periods of penetration – he gave Kram the conclusion she had grown to love from the man who ruined her and now

195

haunted her. From the silver cup she brought with her in the designer handbag, she drank his seed while it was still warm.

Fifteen

'Frank. This is ridiculous. I can barely walk. We must go back to the car and take it out.'

'No.'

'But Frank, it's making me feel dizzy. I will have to sit down.'

'No!'

Mrs Barnes-Dubois fell silent. At his side, she continued with the short steps in her hobble skirt that reached her ankles. Matching the skirt, her short jacket was buttoned up to her sternum and pushed her large breasts up and forwards. Beneath the gossamer blouse, a long and deep shadow formed inside her cleavage. Beneath the clothing she wore transparent French knickers, a wide garter belt, stockings and a curious device he'd picked up in a specialist store with blacked-out windows. The longest part of the device stretched a good eight inches inside her sex; its smooth and thinner counterpart, not much bigger than the average thumb, moved inside her rectum with every tiny step she made through the park. Occasionally, a passer-by would look at the tightly wrapped woman in the hat and veil, who crept forward with one hand on the elbow of her younger companion who wore a black suit. They made a strange couple; like something from the

197

past, from high society, or from a private party in which only a few indistinct polaroids ever emerged.

During his four days off work, his activities with Supervising Agent Ally Kram should have exhausted him. In between the long sessions they had spent alone in his rooms, he had either run like an Olympian or slept like the dead. On his return to work and the tyranny of Barnes-Dubois's demands, he found himself unwilling or unable (he was never sure) to let go of his desire for seduction and the new varieties of stimulation his lovers provided. Barnes-Dubois and Kram had become his disciples; each of them had steadily relinquished all responsibility to him. He had both women performing and dressing in ways neither could have imagined possible a few weeks before. For Kram, it was an extension and a return to a disastrous but invigorating episode in her life; for Barnes-Dubois it was a transfer of all her energy and motivation from her eminence in society to a state of absolute servitude. She was always wary but thrilled by what Frank would ask her to do, now that he was no longer willing to just pop upstairs during a shift and appease her need for attention. But her caution was all part of her pleasure.

'But what if someone should see me? My friends frequent this park.' She spoke softly, appealing to his sympathy.

Frank withdrew the short crop from inside his jacket.

'No. I object. Are you mad?' Mrs Barnes-Dubois tried to hobble away from Frank, across the concrete path that led to a popular picnic area. While she moved as fast as she could, moaning with every step that her spike heels rang out against the slabs, Frank idly cleaned the length of the black crop with a white handkerchief. A girl passed on her rollerblades and

198

then looked back over her shoulder at the struggling Barnes-Dubois, and at the young man who polished the stick. She shrugged and disappeared around a corner. When Mrs Barnes-Dubois reached a wooden bench, Frank caught up with her. 'Now, now, Ma'am. It's foolish to run away. You can't get far in those shoes. They're too high and tight on your feet. And that skirt doesn't allow you more than a few inches of movement, so you cannot possibly get away. Silly thing.'

She was breathing hard and her heavily painted eyes were frantic behind the veil. 'Frank. No. Enough.' She tried to smile. 'Let me remind you we are in public. I have a position. This is ridiculous.'

'I do believe it is now my prerogative to decide on where and when our relations continue. Did we not have a deal? You made me a promise.' He raised his voice. 'This morning when you asked me to put my cock in your ass, you said to me –'

'Frank! No!' She reached her hands to his face, hoping to stopper his mouth with her leather fingers. He caught her wrists. Holding them together against her tight belly, he turned her completely around and bent her over the bench. 'No!' she shrieked. But he answered her cries with a flurry of blows against her compact rump. It made the sound of ice cubes breaking on patio tiles. Down the back of her thighs, where the suspender straps indented the cloth of her skirt, he then trailed a harder series of lashes. The last one struck behind her knees.

When Frank released her wrists there was no further struggle in her. Although her face was wet with tears – he could see them shining beneath the veil – she now made the low panting sounds familiar to her when desire took hold.

Strolling past them, as Frank stood away from the bench and straightened his sleeves, an elderly gent paused on his walk and tipped his hat. Nodding in approval, he then admired Mrs Barnes-Dubois's ankles before continuing with his walk.

Taking his arm, and leaning into his body, Mrs Barnes-Dubois then allowed Frank to lead her back to the car. Now and again she made a sniffing sound, but never uttered another word until he peeled her shapely legs out of the skirt on the back seat of the car. 'We must be getting back now,' he said, removing her damp knickers and then the wet device from her sex and anus.

'Drive slowly,' she called out to her chauffeur, who sat patiently on the other side of the one-way glass, fixed between the front and rear seats of the Bentley. And with a sigh, she then eased her body back into the leather upholstery and allowed Frank to position her ankles on his shoulders.

Sixteen

For over two weeks there had been no word from Lucretia, and Frank needed a sign to indicate when they would be together again. At most, he agreed to give her another week and then he would begin a search for her.

But would she blame him for easing the agony of the delay with Ally Kram and Barnes-Dubois? He still could not be sure, but was aware that he could not curb his appetite for these strange adornments and practices of the flesh. Ideas just appeared in his head and he was compelled to fulfil them immediately and exactingly. It made him recall Eldrin's tastes and the rituals he committed Lucretia to. Of the dark and silent one, Frank could find no trace in apartment 40 either. Even with his heightened clairvoyance, the man eluded every one of Frank's further attempts to catch a glimpse into the invalid's life. There were no visitors to the apartment after Lucretia's escape either, no deliveries, no messages, and the other porters in the building swore Eldrin had not left the building on their shifts. Crow was just waiting up there in the dark. Did Lucretia create this effect in every man?

On his runs or long walks home from work, Frank was now unable to turn his remote viewing off. No longer dependent on the relaxation and concentration to facilitate a viewing, Frank found himself slipping into a psychic search as easily as a schoolboy slips into a daydream while staring through the dusty window of a classroom, gazing away from the stiff airs and droning voices of afternoon mathematics lessons. Reality held little interest for him: affairs of the world, the routines of other lives around him, nature's relentless cycles of change and repetition. All he saw were the glimpses of illicit evidence left inside the heads of pretty but careless dreamers. Through street-facing windows where women cooked and read, in the stores and restaurants where their determined faces revolved around him, on the sidewalks where the business girls scurried to and fro, he picked up their messages, as if the closing of a bedroom door allowed him a glimpse of naked bodies still twisting in the sheets.

He would never have suspected the raven-haired woman, with the thin nose and pleasing freckles, who sat opposite him on a subway train as he made his way home one evening, was about to transform herself that night into an uncompromising proposition in spike-heeled boots. In her mind she played with ideas for her outfit and recollected nights spent in basement clubs where the music was deliberately deafening and the smoke impenetrable in the corners. Frank took these thoughts into his own mind. As if it were his own experience, he saw her pointy boots walking the backs of anonymous men with grey hair who wore leather chokers for her leash. He saw her gloved hand whipping the fresh cock of an adventurous young man, who'd never recovered from the spanking a drunken neighbour had delivered to him as a teenager, after he was caught stealing the flimsier items from her washing line. And, finally, before she stood up and left the train, smiling to herself, he saw the freckled girl's soft hands beating the back and shoulders of her own boss, who crawled around his mahogany desk in a $1000 suit, trying to kiss her feet whenever they were mounted in elegant slingback shoes. A man who doubled her salary after she agreed to trample on his face.

And once Frank emerged from the subway and made his way to the supermarket, he saw a young woman in a denim shirt and jeans, hanging around the front of a liquor store. And she gave him a vision so profound, his whole body shivered cold despite the warmth of the afternoon sun. She could have been a teacher or doctor with such an intelligent face, so how could she even consider giving herself to the biker gang who drank in the bar across the street? When she imagined all four of them attending to her body with rough hands and mouths, on the floor of a tenement room, Frank imagined it too. So by the time he had reached the supermarket, despite the day's thorough business in the park, car, and then Barnes-Dubois's own apartment, he was hungry again.

And this appetite grew when he spotted the young woman with short blonde hair and blue eyeshadow, checking bananas for bruises in the fresh produce section of a grocery store. When he concentrated his restless thoughts into a single stream at her beautiful profile – inhaling her smell of perfume and bubblegum and imagining the softness of her neck in his mouth – she suddenly said, 'Oh,' and held the fruit away from her. Blinking rapidly, she could have sworn that for just a moment, she was not holding a yellow banana, but the tanned shaft of a fully erect penis; moist at the tip as if ready for her succulent mouth.

Unaware of his presence in the next aisle, when she went indoors and cradled a box of eggs she again found her thoughts wandering and visualising golden-furred balls close to her chin. Blushing, and more conscious of the way she was breathing than she had been when she entered the store, she then enjoyed the idea of being taken backwards over a freezer cabinet. With her hands deep in cartons of vanilla ice cream, and her short buckskin skirt around her waist, she saw herself thrust into from behind. Taking strokes from a stranger's cock, which felt incredibly thick, while unable to move her feet much because of the stranglehold her sheer pantyhose and thong had formed above her knee-boots, she allowed the notion to take hold and for several minutes she remained standing in the same position, bent forwards while her sex dampened. It was then Frank spoke to her. Her name was Alice.

Alice lived nearby and had not long finished her afternoon lectures. Later, when she confided to her best friend about the incident, she likened the whole episode with Frank to a prolonged dream. It was as if she were only half-awake throughout the entire experience.

Besides the intensity of his eyes, she couldn't remember much about the man she had met in the store. He wore a dark suit, she thought, but couldn't be sure; it had all happened so suddenly. They had spoken briefly and she found herself inviting him back to her apartment. While she had some nerves she did think him attractive; and asking him back seemed a natural thing to do. Although, of course, it wasn't.

Once outside the store, before they set off for her place, the sun had begun to set and the air cooled. Maybe it was the temperature that made her start to shiver, or maybe it was the way he kissed her neck; he just leaned into her and touched her neck with his lips, then tongue, then teeth. After that, she remembered they only made it to the stairwell of her apartment block before the kissing started; hungry, desperate kissing. They were disturbed by a neighbour's kids, so she took him by the hand and led him into her kitchen. And it was there, on the table, that he took her; first with his mouth, and then with his cock.

There wasn't time to undress because they were expecting her room-mate back at any time, so he just pulled her hose and panties down to the top of her leather boots, and then sank his face into her sex. She was already wet, and the way he moved his mouth all over her lips, before pushing inside her with his tongue and then with three fingers, made her come quickly.

Begging him to hurry and to put himself inside her, she clawed at his chest. He refused for a while. Instead, he bent her over the table and spanked her hard. So hard, she remembered a not displeasing soreness on her buttocks that lasted all evening as she sat on the sofa and tried to watch television. And only after the spanking had taken all the strength out of her legs, did he slide his sex inside her; all of it in one long motion.

While he fucked Alice, her shoulder bag, all of the morning papers and a dish with three withered apples inside, fell to the kitchen floor. When her room-mate returned later that evening, moments after the stranger had vanished from the apartment, she asked why the table had been moved across the kitchen. Alice pleaded ignorance, but secretly knew the table had moved because the stranger had been so hard with her; thorough, continuous and deep with his penetration, just the way she liked it best. He took her like he had taken her over the freezer cabinet in the supermarket daydream.

And she would never forget how her body became weightless; shaken like a doll all over the table. He had been ravenous for her; wanted her more than she could ever remember anyone wanting her. Sure, other boyfriends had been passionate, but never with such consistency for such a duration. It was like he had been starved of something. So when he held her by the hair with one hand and squeezed her breasts with the other – instinctively knowing they needed a firm touch – while all the time pounding between her hips, she'd been transported out of her body. It was an episode she would never forget.

No one had ever been in her ass either. Down there she was a virgin, but the stranger moistened himself with olive oil from a jug he'd snatched from a kitchen surface, and then entered her slowly. It was like choking – too much feeling and sensation all at once – but good. A completion, she had thought at the time, so she would continue to feel him in every entrance to her body for a long time after.

The cock in her ass made her thrash about, so he took her to the bathroom and used her room-mate's underwear to secure her wrists and to gag her mouth for that final joining. And that was where she awoke after he had left; in the tub. He'd come inside her the moment her busy fingers, circling and rubbing her own sex, delivered her through a third climax. And then he'd done something to her shoulder; bitten her softly and made her skin go cold and then numb. And as he kissed or sucked at her, she felt her consciousness go out through her skin and into his mouth until she fainted, still speared by his erection.

When her room-mate returned and called out from the kitchen, Alice awoke. Lying in the bathtub, dressed and dreamy and confused, the bindings gone from her wrists and mouth, she had looked about for the stranger. But he had gone. After washing her face, she'd changed her underwear and wandered through the apartment looking for a part of her that seemed to be missing.

After leaving Alice's apartment, Frank had gone back to the store in a daze and bought food; lots of sweet things and carbohydrates. With his groceries under one arm, he walked to his apartment. He was light-headed and smiling. The cold air felt good against his skin. It was one of those moments when he felt fully alive. He'd not taken too much from the girl – that would have made him high, drunken and sleepy and he'd have missed the vividness of the world afterwards. Just a taste was all he'd needed, to take the edge off his craving, like Lucretia did.

Ally Kram was waiting outside the door to his apartment. She was smoking and had been there for some time. Three extinguished butts lay about the heels of her shiny boots. Shadows filled the stairwell and the air in the hall was thick and stale. Her face looked pallid and she wore sunglasses. Frank was not pleased to see her. The sense of severity in her expression and clothes made him feel uneasy. 'Hi,' he said, feeling guilty.

'I can smell cunt on you.' Her voice was tense.

He let go of the grocery bag when her fist connected with his jaw.

Seventeen

The long hair was black now and sunglasses concealed the colour and expression of her eyes, but the woman who was marched through the reception to the elevator doors, flanked on either side by a man holding her elbow, was Lucretia. There was no mistaking her. Frank felt her presence in the ends of the fine hair on the nape of his neck before he even saw her.

Wearing black suits and sunglasses, the two men forced her to walk at a quick march. Each square head looked straight ahead, the faces determined. These were men who did not want to be seen for long. As one of the men reached forward to depress the steel button, in order to summon the elevator to the ground floor, his jacket swung open and Frank glimpsed a leather shoulder holster.

They were armed, Lucretia was their captive and she was going home to Crow against her will. Frank felt cold and could not move.

A clunk, followed by a swishing sound, signalled the arrival of the elevator. The hollow noise of three pairs of feet entering the elevator reached Frank's desk. The doors to the lift closed and Lucretia was gone again. It had been eighteen days since Frank had seen her, but, oddly, he never felt further from her since the dawn of the investigation.

Anger replaced his shock and filled his flesh. He heard the blood pumping through his skull. Such pressure antagonised his swollen jaw. It still hurt from the night before. Choking back tears after delivering the blow, Ally Kram had then left him standing in the doorway to his apartment.

The house phone rang and Frank jumped. Acting automatically, his thoughts in disarray, Frank raised the receiver. It was Mrs Barnes-Dubois: 'I'd like to see you now, please.' There was nothing inviting in her tone; a great effort was being employed to conceal her rage. She had twice visited his desk in reception that morning. Anxious over the breakdown in his relationship with Agent Kram, Frank had been curt with the glamorous widow. Even though she had gone to considerable lengths to please Frank, he remained indifferent to her new spike-heeled boots and leather suit. Following a brief tantrum, she had then gone back upstairs, expecting him to follow and deal with her – a ploy she favoured. But Frank had other conflicts on his mind then, and twice the load now. 'No,' he said. 'I'm busy. I'll call,' he added, unconvincingly, then hung up.

When the phone rang again he could see by the light on the switchboard that it was Barnes-Dubois again. Swinging into his blazer, Frank emerged from behind his desk and headed for the stairwell in Lucretia's wing of the building. He'd walk the four flights to her floor. It would give him time to think of a plan.

Standing guard in the corridor outside Lucretia's apartment, both men kept their glasses on indoors. Feet apart, with hands crossed over their belt buckles, they turned to face Frank as he emerged through the door connected to the stairwell. His smile was weak and quickly died. He cleared his throat and said, 'Excuse me, but if you're guests I have to ask your names. For the register.'

The men surveyed Frank at leisure from behind the opaque lenses of their glasses. Neither square jaw nor smooth brow showed any reaction. With the same build and identical clothing, the only notable physical difference between the men was age. The man with grey hair on his temples spoke first. 'Just put us down as guests.'

Frank glanced down at the clipboard he held before his body. 'Sorry. I need names.'

The younger blond guard smirked. 'Beat it.'

Frank looked up. 'What?'

'He said beat it, and he means it,' the older man said.

Frank thought of what Eldrin was probably doing to Lucretia at that very moment. He imagined a cane whipping through the air and took a step forwards. The open palm of a hard hand met his sternum and held him still. 'You fuckin' deaf, chump?' the younger guard warned. 'Beat it.'

Frank knocked the hand aside and reached for the front doorbell. 'The lady can answer for you.'

Both guards sprung into action at the mention of Lucretia. 'Listen, you faggot bellhop fuck.' The younger guard spoke through clenched teeth. Bony fingers seized his upper arms and he was walked backwards to the elevator. Frank neither had time nor the presence of mind to react. 'Get your ass back downstairs where it belongs.' Both men put their weight behind a violent shove that sent Frank crashing to the back of the elevator carriage.

Dropping the clipboard, Frank lurched at the two men, both his hands balled into fists. But he stopped short when the man with grey hair opened the lapels of his jacket with the tips of his fingers and showed Frank a holster. He was holding a Glock. He smiled at Frank. The younger guard punched a button on the control panel of the elevator and waved goodbye as the doors closed.

Struggling to breathe from rage and the vengeful fantasies already forming in his mind, Frank descended to the ground floor and then walked back to his desk, opening and closing his fingers as he moved. His mood was further antagonised by the sight of Mrs Barnes-Dubois. She was standing beside his chair, her face paler than usual. Refusing to look her in the eye, Frank went straight for the house phone and began to call Lucretia's apartment. No one would answer him.

'I should have you fired,' Barnes-Dubois whispered. Her voice trembled.

Frank continued to call Lucretia's apartment.

'Who the hell do you think you are?' Barnes-Dubois raised her voice; it was becoming shrill. 'Look at me, damn you! I said look at me!'

Frank slammed the house phone into the cradle. 'Get out of my sight.'

Speechless for a moment, Mrs Barnes-Dubois then swung her hand at Frank's face. The underside of a ring connected with his jawbone; on the same spot where Ally Kram had slugged him. There was madness in her eyes. 'I'll finish you.' Her face quivered. 'Have you any idea who I am?'

'A mistake,' Frank said. He caught the next blow with one hand and then marched her backwards, as he had been force-marched by Eldrin's men, to the elevator in her wing. When they reached the doors, he released her and ran back to his desk.

'Frank. Frank. Frank, I'm sorry.' Mrs Barnes-Dubois pursued him. 'Please, Frank. Listen to me.'

There would be no respite from her. You have taken too much, an inner voice said. Frank sprinted through the reception and banged through the front doors of the building. 'Frank!' Behind him, he heard Mrs Barnes-Dubois's muffled cries on the other side of the glass. He never looked around but knew the tear-stained face at the window was one he never wanted to see again.

The moment his feet hit the sidewalk, Frank broke into a run. His chest hurt and there was a rushing sound in his head. He choked on emotion; it tasted bitter. Behind him in the street, Barnes-Dubois shrieked his name. But her voice grew dim after he rounded a corner and pounded down an alley. Hiding behind a dumpster, at the rear of a hotel restaurant, Frank stripped his jacket off. Air cooled against his damp shirt. Feeling constricted and unable to breathe, he tore his tie from around his neck. With a handkerchief he mopped the sweat from his face.

Crouching in the alley, Frank could smell the wet ash and rotting mulch of food and coffee grounds that had collected at the bottom of the dumpster. Closing his eyes, he slowed his heart and breathing down. Looking on the underside of his eyelids at an imaginary spot three feet in front of his knees, Frank thought of his Lucretia: he recalled her voice and made the husky tone and European accent come alive inside his head; he remembered her expensive smell and how it made him dreamy; the touch of her lips was soft but somehow consuming; there was always a hiss when she walked in a tight skirt or crossed her long legs; around his erection, he imagined the engulfing warmth of her sex. And then Frank really saw something.

The remote viewing begins with a glimpse inside the equipment room. Even when distressed, Lucretia is beautiful. It makes Frank's heart ache. Glasses now removed, her ocean eyes are moist. Lipstick is smudged off her lower lip. She has been kissed.

Frank wants to wake and scream, but he must remain calm. He must see if she is safe. Slender, pale, limp: her hands rest inside the tight leather cuffs. Her arms have been pulled out at 45-degree angles and secured by a thin chain to the innermost corners of the frame – a device that looks old and cruel, as if it has been preserved from another age. Crow has used this before; when he wanted answers from her and punished her for the lies, and the truth that is worse than lies, that spilled from her lovely mouth.

Behind her head, the punisher whispers. Sibilant, fierce, determined: his words create anticipation in the captive. Her eyelids become heavy and her lips move.

No, Frank wants to cry and be heard. Resist him!

Crow will be hard. Long white fingers brush her newly black hair from her shoulders. Her neck is kissed, her ears are kissed. A sheer black blouse is untucked from her leather skirt and the white hands slip beneath to cradle and comfort and stroke her breasts. Lucretia begins to moan.

She has no choice, Frank says to himself.

The leather skirt is unzipped and slithers down her legs. It is snatched from around her high-heel shoes, which are then removed in turn. Next, her panties are rolled down her legs until they hang from her knees. Slowly, the white hands slide back up her legs and then stroke her inner thighs. The blouse is opened and she shivers when the cool air settles on her breasts. Seamed stockings and a garter belt are the only other items she is permitted to wear. With most of her spiky and tight second skin removed, she feels more vulnerable. The slim fingers of her tormentor slide inside her sex. She goes stiff within her bonds, her limbs lock fast, she exhales. Thin fingers tickle her inside, move slowly, taunt Frank who shakes in the alleyway, bent on violence. The fingers are withdrawn, Lucretia is effortlessly hoisted up to waist level and, with her flimsy panties still caught around her knees, she is entered from behind. Held aloft, her body moves and her hair sways as each thrust passes in and out, in and out for Frank to see.

Why does she not resist? Why? Why so helpless? Is her spirit broken? What has been done to her? Frank shouts these questions into the ether but they go unheard.

There is something final about this ritual; Frank can feel it. Crow's patience is at an end and she is tired. Rage and jealousy and a peculiar ecstasy motivate Crow and bring the cords of muscles out in his tight body. He no longer looks like an invalid. Eighteen days of misery and rejection must be expressed with cane and flail and cock. Escape and capture, conflict and reparation, obsession and resistance: it has gone on for so long. Lucretia no longer cares about her fate and gives herself to the pale demon on her back. Her only departure is found in an abandonment of responsibility and a slide into unthinking sensation, as she has done so many times before. It is up to Frank now.

Eighteen

'Didn't think you'd have the gall to show your face for a long time. Come to apologise? Well, I don't want to –'

'No. No I haven't. It's not about us.' Frank spoke and gulped air at the same time. From the alleyway where he'd suffered the vision, he'd run to Agent Ally Kram's hotel room. As he ran on the tarmac, avoiding the sidewalks jammed with pedestrians, and weaved among honking cabs and braking motorists on the road, he'd carried with him the sense of a finality in Crow's intentions regarding Lucretia. 'We have to move. We have to go in. She's in danger.'

Kram stopped glaring at him and stepped back from the door. 'What are you talking about?'

Frank staggered into her room and bent double. 'Now. We have to go in now. Into the apartment. Crow's lost it. Lucretia's in danger.'

Kram closed the door to her room. She moved across to her bedside table and snatched up her cell phone. 'Tell me. Tell me what you saw.'

Sitting on the end of the bed, Frank wiped the sleeve over his shirt across his face. 'Two armed men brought her back. Big guys. They look like outfit. They're carrying. When I challenged them, the older guy showed me his piece. These fucks are watching the door while Crow goes at her inside. I got this feeling too. When I was viewing her, strung up on this rack he has . . .' Frank paused when he saw Kram's reaction; he'd reminded her of something. She turned away from him, her body stiff.

When she spoke her voice was unnaturally calm. 'I'm confused, Frank. Help me out. These men – you say they brought her back. From where?'

Frank swallowed. He'd not mentioned Lucretia's escape to Kram. 'She just . . . You know, disappeared or something a while back. At first I thought it was my viewings. An inability to connect with the target. I never saw her go. I got suspicious but didn't want to bother you until I was sure she'd gone. But she must have cleared out because Crow has taken her back by force. This is a kidnapping. And he means her harm, I can sense it.'

Kram looked up and out of the window, but kept her back to him. 'Liar.'

Frank stood up. 'What?'

'Are you fucking her too, Frank?' Kram turned around and Frank did not like the look on her face. 'Mmm? Another one of your conquests? You manage to deduce Lucretia's in danger. That she's been abducted and is about to be cancelled, but you had no idea she had run away in the first place. How convenient. You must think I'm stupid. Crow's found out, hasn't he? About you and her? Was it her cunt I smelled on your breath last night?'

Shaking his head with disbelief and a growing horror, Frank raised his hands in the air as if to plead with her sanity. 'Enough of this. Enough. Just call my report in, Agent Kram. One of our targets is in danger. You have to.'

Kram just stared at him with undisguised malevolence. He'd seen the same look in Barnes-Dubois's

216

face. 'How long, Frank? How long have you been fucking her?'

'Call it in, damn you!' Frank roared at her.

She turned away from him and calmly walked into the en suite bathroom. Through the door Frank heard her make a call. 'Kram. The viewer says the female target is in danger. A code two.'

Frank exhaled with relief. But in the bathroom, there followed a long silence until Kram said, 'You're sure? Under no circumstances? She is? Yes sir, I understand.'

The bathroom door opened. On Kram's face Frank read an undisguised look of triumph. 'We stay put,' she said, moving with more purpose now.

'You fuckin' nuts? Give me the phone. I want to speak to whoever is in charge of this fuck-up.'

Kram stepped back, her body poised for action. 'Keep back, Frank.' Frank stepped away from her. 'We stand down,' she added. 'That's an order.'

'What? But –'

'I called in a code two. That covers a situation like this, when one candidate might grease the other. We've been expecting something like this to happen. It's happened before with Crow. He starts this shit with his girlfriends and can't deal with it. And she's expendable.'

Frank leaned towards her. 'Are you out of your mind? You'll let her die because you're jealous?'

Kram swung a fist at his face, but this time Frank was ready and caught her thin wrist in mid-air. He swung her around and pushed her towards the bed. The momentum carried her across the room and she collapsed on the mattress. Swallowing the emotion that threatened to choke him, Frank could feel the muscles in his face quiver. Even Kram looked alarmed. 'You're pretty good, Kram. A real piece of work. And you're right about one thing: I am fucking her. She's been my lover for weeks now. But you and this agency are wrong about the most important thing of all: she is not expendable.'

Determined not to waste another precious second, Frank turned and fled from the room. Behind him, Kram began to scream orders. 'Stop! That's an order, agent! Get back here! Interfere with the targets and I will take you down. Do you hear me? I have orders to put you down!'

But Frank was no longer listening. Standing in the elevator, on his way to street level, he removed his tie and began to wish he'd taken his service automatic to work with him. Like his instincts had advised him to, in preparation for when this day arrived. He was finished with the agency. All that mattered to him now was Lucretia's safety. He'd take a cab back to his tenement rooms to collect the gun and all the spare clips he kept in the shoebox at the top of his wardrobe. The cab driver could leave the meter running.

In the room of mirrors she was in bed with Crow now. Her legs kicked at the air and her red fingernails clawed his back. Between her legs the devil's white body thrust and ground into her softness. Holding the hair at the back of her head, Crow buried his face into Lucretia's neck and sucked. Her eyes looked glassy; she was lost to the world.

In every mirror from every angle, Frank saw it happen. Sitting on his bed with one hand clenched on the grip of his automatic, he was not only transfixed by what he saw in the remote viewing, but with a loathing and a rage he had never felt before. It would take him to a new place. With his gun, he would go and collect Lucretia and they would flee together. Fugitives, but together.

218

And this viewing, the last he swore he would ever make once Lucretia was his own, had just come to him and overwhelmed him, like it had been transmitted from a hostile source with the intention of wounding him. Now Frank felt like the target. But showing him this would do Crow no good, because Frank was nothing like Eldrin Crow. Crow could stand to watch her with other men and Frank could not. Those days had gone.

After loading the gun and concealing it in the waistband of his trousers, Frank threw some cash and a change of clothes into a small airline bag. Peering from out of the kitchen window, he then checked the street outside to see if Kram had followed him or alerted other agency personnel. Two kids threw a baseball from one side of the street to the other. Besides them it looked clear. The cab was parked in the next street. Frank locked the front door and left his apartment for the last time.

Nineteen

Across the street from Lucretia's apartment building, Frank crouched behind a row of parked cars. Shadow from the four-storey building swallowed the sun's warmth. Even that was against him; it felt like a bad omen. The street-facing windows of Lucretia's apartment were shaded. Nothing unusual about that, but the sight of them filled Frank with dread. It was as if the evil behind the glass and blinds cast its aura into anyone who looked up at them; he felt alone and vulnerable and removed from anything he could draw comfort from. And what was Crow doing to Lucretia at that precise moment?

The cab had dropped him off one block down and he'd made careful progress back to the address. Away from the main thoroughfare of traffic and pedestrians, he'd dodged between the stationary vehicles, checking store fronts and driver seats for Agent Ally Kram or anything resembling agency activity. But Frank found nothing to concern him, which in itself was alarming. Kram knew he was serious about saving Lucretia. Desperate and reckless and angry, he'd also antagonised her jealousy into a rage with his petulant confession. So where was she? A woman like Kram, wounded by his betrayal, would need to exact revenge. But of more significance, what would the agency instruct her to do?

Against his lower spine the steel of the automatic was cold. The weight and shape of the gun made his whole body feel uncomfortable. Would he even be able to use it? Frank thought of the two guards and of facing Eldrin Crow for the first time. All the strength seemed to desert his limbs.

Drawing a deep breath, he crossed the street at a trot, all the time expecting to hear the retort of a pistol. No one fired. He peered through the plate glass of the front entrance. Reception was clear. No Barnes-Dubois: a small mercy. In a matter of weeks how had a voyeur and recluse managed to make three beautiful women fall in love with him? Maybe it was the uniform, he thought, and then grinned until he felt stupid and so nervous he could barely inhale.

Get in there. Flash the piece and look like you mean it. You won't even have to pull the trigger. Grab Lucretia and then split. Once he got her outside, she could hail a cab from the street while he covered their retreat. Lucretia must know of somewhere they could go. And at the first opportunity they would blow the city limits. He had enough cash for a couple of months. Maybe she had a stash too. It didn't matter right now. They could figure the rest on the run. Frank recited his meagre strategy to try and make the word become the deed.

Because he had difficulty executing specific tasks, he only managed to punch in the right security code at the third attempt to open the front doors. Inside the building, he immediately headed for his desk. His only access to Lucretia's apartment would be through the front door and there was a spare set of keys for every apartment in the safe behind the concierge's chair. As he ran across the marble floor, he heard the house phone trilling. Sneaking behind his desk, he glanced at the switchboard panel. Barnes-Dubois was checking in. Frank became angry again. Anger was

221

good – it helped courage. He grabbed the set of keys for apartment 40 and then moved to the emergency stairs in Lucretia's wing; he'd take the same route as before, only this time the bellhop was holding more than a suitcase.

Frank ducked through the fire door into the stairwell. He drew his automatic and took the safety catch off. Failing to prevent the creaks on the stairs he swore never made a sound before, he carefully ascended to the fourth floor.

Hesitating by the fire door that opened into the corridor outside Lucretia's apartment, he attempted a remote viewing. First, he tried to get a fix on the location of the guards but drew a blank. Then he concentrated his inner vision on Crow and Lucretia. Same again: no connection. Frustrated, Frank raised his pistol to shoulder level and gripped the door handle with his free hand.

And pulled the door open. Arms numb and his legs feeling like they had come loose at the ball joints, he stumbled into the corridor. Sighting his pistol in the direction of Lucretia's front door, he dropped into a firing squat. When his eyes refocused from the blur that comes with too much adrenaline, he saw the area was clear. Exhaling with relief, Frank trotted back and put his ear near the elevator doors to prevent being surprised from behind. The shaft was quiet. He did the same thing to the front door of Lucretia's apartment, but heard nothing. Besides the humming of the overhead lights, the building was silent.

Maybe Crow had called the guards inside to assist him. Right now they could be taping garbage bags around her ... No! He shook the thought away. Standing to the side of the spyhole, Frank carefully inserted the spare key into the lock. It turned with a click. Frank pushed the door open.

Nothing moved. The hallway stretched before him. Lit by a table lamp, it was clear as far as he could see. And silent. Leaving the door ajar, he edged along one wall towards the mirrored bedroom. As he strained his hearing for sound and held his breath, the tension seemed to inflate inside him until he could no longer bear it. If anything moved, he was sure he'd shoot.

He peeked around the edge of every doorway, his automatic following the sweep of his eyes. But one room after another was empty of life. The entire apartment appeared disused. Not neglected, but too clean and orderly, like it was a show home unaccustomed to occupation. No scratches or discarded cups; no books on armrests, or open magazines; not even a coat inside the front door.

Increasingly troubled by this aspect of vacancy, he stood outside the mirrored bedroom; the place where everything began – his viewings, the affair – and where he'd seen her last. If there were to be an ambush, it would be here, in the centre of her world. Frank stepped inside.

In the mirrors nothing save Frank and the furniture was reflected. The bed had been made. Frantic, Frank rushed forwards and opened the wardrobe doors. Empty but for the coathangers. Caution gone, he ran through the remaining rooms – kitchen, living room, bathrooms – until he arrived at the equipment room, where Crow stored the tools and apparatus of his manipulation. But the wooden rack had gone and there was no sign that the upright frame with the chains and cuffs had ever existed.

'No,' Frank whispered; it was all he had the strength to utter. Finally, he lowered his automatic. It was as if Crow and Lucretia had never lived there. Disoriented with confusion and the sudden onset of grief, Frank wandered back into the central concourse of the penthouse.

'Drop the gun, Frank.'

He looked up. Agent Ally Kram tensed. She stood inside the front door and pointed a handgun at the middle of his chest. Slowly, she began to walk towards him. 'I said drop it.' Frank looked down at the gun in his hand, but never released the grip or trigger. 'Damn it, Frank. Drop it!'

Frank shook his head. 'You let her get away.' He heard his voice outside of his body like someone had spoken near him.

Kram's pretty features tightened and she blanched with fury at this mention of his preference for Lucretia. 'You have three seconds to surrender your weapon.' Her voice was too full of emotion.

Excitement had long drained from him. There was nothing inside now but a morbid sense of loss. Instinctively, his inner voice told him Lucretia was gone, for ever. Risking everything for the girl his whole life had been preparation for, he could not allow the agency to take him in. It would be better if he died right where he stood; he was certain they'd cancel him for ruining the investigation and endangering their strict anonymity.

'One,' Kram said.

Frank looked up. She had tears in her eyes.

'Two.'

He began to walk towards her.

'Hold your fire, agent!' Behind Kram two men appeared. Frank stopped moving.

Guns drawn, they circled behind Kram, making swift but silent progress towards her back. Instantly, Frank recognised them as Crow's two guards. 'Agent Kram, hold your fire,' the older man said. 'That is an order. We'll take it from here.'

She gritted her teeth and squinted her eyes. 'No! He's ruined everything, sir. He's not getting away with it.' Frank knew she was about to shoot. So did the men behind her. She fired the moment the younger man thrust his shoulder into the middle of her back. A bullet zipped past Frank's ear and embedded itself with a *thock* in the wall behind him. The older guard walked past the struggle, smiling, with his sidearm trained on Frank's chest. 'We're all friends here, Frank. On the same side. It's over. Relax. Take it easy. It's over.'

Frank felt dazed. 'You're agency?'

The man approached him slowly. Over his shoulder, Frank saw the younger man wrestle the gun from Kram's hand and then subdue her against a wall. Her face was red and now damp with tears.

Frank took a step back when the man reached for his weapon. 'Where is she?'

'Lucretia?' the guard said. 'Safe. She's safe.'

'Take me to her.'

The man smiled. 'Sure, buddy. Right after you give me the weapon.'

'Get back!' Frank roared and the man paused, his smile gone. 'You're with Crow,' Frank accused. 'You took her back to him.'

'Steady. Just cool it, Frank. We're going to explain it all, but I need your gun first.'

'Fuck you!'

'Frank! Listen to me.' As a show of faith the man holstered his weapon. 'See. No one wants to do it this way. You want answers. You'll get them all. But not here. It's not safe. We have to move out.'

Frank aimed his gun at the man's face. 'Where is she?'

The man held his arms out wide. 'She's on our side, Frank. Crow too. And Lucretia's in charge of the operation.'

Frank shook his head. He felt dizzy. It was as if the walls were moving back and forth at the periphery of his vision. The agent came closer. Frank could smell his aftershave as he said, 'She set you up, Frank. It was never a real assignment. Just an exercise. We had to see if you were right.'

A clash of disbelief and the horror of real belief immobilised Frank's mind and his body. The man took the automatic from his hand and he never felt him do it. 'Just a precaution,' the agent said, and slipped cuffs around Frank's wrists.

Outside the building, two black Sedans with dark windows were waiting. Kram was eased into the first car, Frank escorted to the rear. In the back of the car they gave Frank an injection. They said it would make him relax, but in seconds he lost consciousness.

Twenty

Still dozy from sedation, Frank gained enough consciousness to realise he sat cuffed to a chair, in a vast space with a concrete floor and walls half lost in shadow. He looked up. Above his head he could see the vague outlines of steel struts and corrugated metal. Looking down, Frank closed his eyes, blinked and then reopened them. On the table before him was a bottle of water, a sandwich on a paper plate and a packet of cigarettes. It could have been a warehouse or aircraft hangar. And he was no longer in the city. Sunlight and air of the distinctive freshness and clarity he recognised from the countryside seeped under the giant roller doors in the distance ahead of him. Two cars were parked inside the facility near the doors. Parts of the area were strongly lit by overhead lights, suspended from the ceiling on lengths of cable. There was a ring of whitish light in the centre where he sat and a dim glow behind him.

'He's waking up,' someone said. In shirts and black ties – sleeves rolled up – the two agents he'd once thought were Crow's guards appeared from behind his chair. Both men looked pleased with themselves. 'The greatest piece of surveillance equipment known to man looks like a piece of shit right about now,' the younger agent said.

'I'm Hooper,' the older man said as he pulled a chair out from under the table and sat down. The younger guard remained standing. 'This is Starr. Guess you hate the sight of us. But don't worry, after this briefing you'll never see us again. So how you feeling, champ?'

Frank swallowed the saliva that had pooled in his mouth and started to dribble from his bottom lip. 'Tired. You drugged me.'

Hooper nodded. 'Had no choice, buddy. It'll wear off. Enjoy it while it lasts.'

The younger agent sniggered. He filled a paper cup with water and offered it to Frank's lips. He drank greedily. 'Wanna eat something?' Starr said.

Frank shook his head. 'Where am I?'

'Safe,' Hooper said.

Frank began to recall the events prior to his sleep. 'Why am I still cuffed if we're on the same side?'

Hooper smiled. 'Good question. A safety precaution. We have a lot of information for you, Frank. Some of it may offend. Most will challenge all of your beliefs. And as we can't have you freaking out so they have to stay on. But not for ever. Just until you complete the operation.'

'You said it was over.'

'That was only the first stage. There's another task you have to fulfil.'

'Fuck you. The whole thing was a scam.'

Hooper smiled.

'Where's Lucretia? I want to see her.'

'Not here. But you will see her, for the final debriefing.'

Closing his eyes, Frank searched with the tatters of his hope and remaining strength for the belief that he would see her again. Hooper spoke: 'But if you're up to it, champ, I'd like to make a start. Are you ready to have your world turned inside out?'

* * *

Burning; his buttocks felt like they were burning against the wooden seat of his chair. He guessed he must have been there for about five hours. Outside, it was getting cooler and the light was fading. Inside his clothes the sweat had dried to grit on his skin. The drug had left him restless but apathetic. A powerful inertia made him feel sleepy but edgy too. Hooper and Starr had left him alone to 'think it over'. And what he had to think over was the true story behind his departure from air force intelligence. All the time he'd been looking for downed aircraft and prisoners of war, it seemed the agency had been watching him. That, Frank could believe; his entire experience of the agency so far had involved deception and manipulation. Back in intelligence, his journal falling into the wrong hands had been their doing too, and the order for his discharge had been issued by something carrying more weight than the military hierarchy. The agency was not an organisation that accepted volunteers. Nor did it issue invitations. It just took who it required and gave them no chance of ever going back.

Hooper returned to his chair. He took a cigarette from the packet on the table and lit it with a silver Zippo. 'Ready for some more, champ?'

Frank kept quiet.

'I take that as a "yes", so where was I? Yeah, we fuck up your life and disgrace you. It's obvious, ain't it? You got something we want. The insights, Frank. The remote viewings the air force were so kind to nurture. Only they didn't. Not really. The remote-viewing project is ours. The military is just a cover. We used the forces to uncover and extract psionic-sensitives like yourself. In return they get all that scrap metal and the locations of the GIs getting rubber-hosed that you find for them. Only we had a problem with all the other gifted individuals that

229

came before you. None of them worked out for what we had in mind. They never made it.' Hooper paused and Frank wondered if the agent wanted him to believe that the other psionics were dead. 'Moral issues. Ethics. Shit like that got in the way. We needed someone who, let's say, liked the upskirt view. You know, the hidden-camera action. Would look anywhere, at anything, for his own satisfaction. Unscrupulous. Young and good-looking would help too. We wanted a ladies' man, Frank. And look what we landed. A regular Lothario. Lucretia, then this widow, your supervising agent, a chick out buying groceries – bang, bang, bang, bang. You don't mess around, Frank. I mean, me and Starr were jealous. We had to sit through it all. But we liked your style.'

Frank remained mute. Let them take his silence for compliance. He sat through it to get to Lucretia. She was at the end of Hooper's wild stories. Agent Hooper leaned on the table. 'But did you notice any changes, buddy? After you met Lucretia?'

'What do you mean?'

'The viewings were easier, weren't they?' Frank stayed quiet. 'Go on, Frank, admit it. They became clearer. Your range improved. All the hard work to facilitate your second sight disappeared, didn't it?'

Frank knew it was true but wouldn't give Hooper the satisfaction of a reaction.

'And all that jogging too. Man, just as well me and Starr had the car. That was like marathon training. And all that food you shovelled. Not to mention the action with the chickadees. Man, where did you get so much energy?'

'What are you saying?'

'Well, it wasn't a second wind, Frank. Not a diet or the city air. It happened for a reason. I think you know that. There's something inside you, Frank.

Money can't buy it. Science can't clone it. We don't know how the fuck it really works. But we do know how you got it. And so do you. Lucretia gave it to you.' Hooper leaned back in his chair and lit another cigarette. 'Bet you'll never forget the first time she kissed you. Huh?'

They fed him again at the table and watched him pee in the bathroom, situated at the opposite end of the building to the roller doors. There were offices back there, and other rooms. Frank wondered what they were hiding. He tried to find Lucretia with his senses: she was not in the building. Starr took him back to the table and then disappeared through one of the doors at the back of the hangar.

'How old would you say Lucretia is?' Hooper asked when he was seated.

'When do I get to see her? She's not here. You said I would see her.'

Hooper smiled. 'Man, you're good at this. No, you're right she's not here. But if you co-operate, she'll be on her way.' Hooper stopped smiling. 'Now answer my question. How old is she?'

'Twenty-five. Maybe younger.'

Thoughtful, Hooper nodded. 'Reasonable. But way out. You know, she lived through both World Wars.'

Stunned for a while, Frank then began to laugh.

Hooper joined in. 'She joined us in the fifties. Knew the Kennedys. Fucked one of them.'

Frank stopped laughing.

With both elbows on the table, Hooper leaned forwards. 'Long time, Frank. She's been around for a long time. And now you're like her. You know it too. She'll tell you the same.'

His wrists hurt from where they strained against the metal cuffs. 'What do you want me to do?'

231

'Soon. We'll let you know soon enough.'

'I'm sick.'

'I know. Feverish, stomach cramps coming on, then cold sweats, the delirium that's getting worse every hour. And we both know how to make things easier, don't we?'

Frank thought of a woman's skin and of the wine beneath.

He'd been asleep for a few hours when Starr woke him up with a cup of coffee. 'Ready for some more, buddy?'

Frank stood up and followed Starr back to the table. Hooper was waiting for him. 'Lot to take in, Frank. Hope you got some rest.'

'Something bothers me.'

'Shoot.'

'About this virus. I have no scruples, that's why I got the job. That's what you're saying. But I don't believe other men failed to fall for her. She could turn a priest into a satanist. Why didn't they work out?'

'They fell for her all right. Fell hard and got themselves all fucked up. That's for sure. But it's tricky. She can tell you better than me. But people of Lucretia's type can't just give it away. You have to be halfway there already. You know, compatible. Most people wouldn't be able to deal with it. You were the first we put before them that they took.'

'They?'

'Uh-huh. There are others. Most of them came on board at the end of the Second World War. That's when we found out about them. From German files. Nazis had been after them for years. Chasing them and rounding them up. That's where they're from, Europe. You see, Lucretia and Crow maybe pass this gift about once every fifty years or so. It's an exceptional thing for them to take someone. You see, you have to be like the one that gave it to them in the first place. Lucretia picked up Crow in England, when Queen Victoria was on the throne. And only because he reminded her of the guy that turned her.'

'But Crow ... I don't believe it. They're not in love. He's the one who ...'

'Who wears the pants? Think again. All a role, Frank. Weird set-up. Lucretia's idea. She's creative. Fucked up, if you ask me, but what would I know? I'm not like you.'

'What do you mean?'

'You've been turned, Frank. They call it the bond. And there is no going back for you. You're one of them now. One of the chosen few. More people get chosen by NASA to fly around the moon, Frank. Don't look so pale. Whoever they take never really gets a choice. And think of it: immortality, man. Or near enough. Some of the really old ones are, like, a thousand years old. Not many of them left, and we only get access to the young ones, but if you're careful, you're gonna be around for a long time, Frank. Long time.'

Frank shook his head, his disbelief no longer suspended. 'I don't believe you. I can't believe this.' Sweat dripped from his nose.

'Took me ages to swallow it myself. But it's a fact. In time you'll find out for sure. You know you've changed in a way that can't be explained by conventional science. Take this sudden appeal you have to women. You couldn't fuck your way out of a paper bag when we first spotted you. Remember? When you used to spend your weekends looking at grid references on air force maps? But now the chicks are fighting over you. That's one of the good things. You get to live for ages and fuck who you like. Think of it. Plus you'll have remote viewings like never before. You'll be able to read people's minds too, Frank. You get glimpses now, but to do it continually? That takes a while, but it will come. Sooner for you than most, I heard. Because you were so good to start with. You were perfect. Maybe even the best yet. And you know she and Crow were looking into your head the whole time. Keeping tabs. It's how they were able to play you so well. And they made you see things too. See what they wanted you to see. It was amazing. But don't sweat it, Frank. You never had a chance. And with your new strength, charisma, stamina, you're a super being, Frank. That's what you are. Fuckin' Superman.'

'Then why do I feel like shit? Tell me that, Hooper. And I'm not talking about the withdrawal. Why can't I shake off this mood? I'm all black inside. I thought it was the sedative, but it's not.'

Hooper looked at his hands. 'You can't have everything, Frank. There just had to be a downside. There always is. As I understand it, one part of you will always be broken.'

'My heart.'

Hooper nodded and lit another cigarette. 'You'll learn to live with it. Even though the pain stays fresh.'

Frank was no longer listening. And he didn't care who saw him weep.

'You have to be careful, Frank. You know, careful how much you take. Because you always will take from whoever you fuck. It's the appetite you have. It's why you've not eaten in three days and why you feel like shit. You're hungry for something else. You need a special nourishment. It must be just eating you now, boy. Eating you inside out.'

Across the table from Agent Hooper, Frank sweated and ground his teeth. He could taste dog shit and ran an ever-rising fever. Inside, he felt queasy and cold.

'Last time you had some pussy was that chick in the supermarket. Alice. That was about three days back. About as long as you can live without the sex and the feeding when you're new. In time, it gets less. You can go for longer. But with Alice, you did just fine. Did what you needed and then took off. You knew not to take too much because it made you so high and you had to stay alert. That was good. Real progress. We knew it was nearly over around then. You were hunting by yourself and being discreet. You learned with Barnes-Dubois and Ally Kram that you over-indulged and got yourself in a whole heap of shit. Well, you weren't to know. There are problems there.'

'What will happen to them?'

'I can only speak for Mrs Barnes-Dubois. You put her about halfway to being what you are. And that's bad news. But what were we to do? Lucretia let you hang around until you learned to hunt for yourself. To obey your instincts and so forth. And you did. Well done. She knew you were right for this. For us it was a big break, since we lost three bonded agents last year. Down in the south. They retired. One was the best we ever had. But Barnes-Dubois, she's not agency material. We can't use her, Frank. If you follow.'

'She was a nuisance, but I never meant any harm. I couldn't help it.'

Hooper gave Frank a paternal smile. 'We know that. Casualty of war, buddy, she's a casualty of war.'

Frank's feverish skin stiffened with cold. He swallowed.

'Relax. Physically, she's fine. And will stay fine. But she got enough of it to be changed. An advanced case of nymphomania is the worst she'll suffer. Oh, and a lifelong addiction to your memory. She'll be looking for you everywhere. Anyone who reminds her of you will get the time of his life. At least until her looks fade. Then, well. She'll get cruel, Frank. Be a real handful.'

Frank shook his head emphatically. 'No.'

'Afraid so. Already she's put four of the best private dicks on your tail. They won't find you. We'll see to that. People can get awfully discouraged when they go up against us, Frank. And there's nothing any lawyer or policeman can do for them. Not even the president or the supreme court can help. You see, not even they really know who we are. Who you are. No one does. You remember all that shit about the secret world government? All that shit them ufologists spun a while back? Well, you're it, buddy.'

'And Agent Kram, what about her?'

Hooper smiled. Leaning back in his chair, he threaded his fingers together behind his head. 'Now I'm real glad you brought that up, Frank. It suggests to me a growing sense of responsibility about your potential. And you're gonna need that.'

'Cut the crap, Hooper. She's here. I know it. She's in restraints in one of those back rooms. Every hour, Starr goes and checks on her. She's refusing food.'

'You people never cease to amaze me. You sniffed her out. Just like she smelled you, Frank. Man, you are good.' Hooper clapped his hands and whooped. The sound disturbed a pigeon from the roof. Frank heard it flap its wings in a confined space.

'Tell me, damn it!'

'Well, you took her way past the halfway mark, Frank. She's in trouble. Got what you can literally and truthfully call a fatal attraction. It's no good to be stuck in between like she is. No going back. Only forward. If not, she dies.'

The insidious truth made Frank want to puke. 'You set her up to get two for the price of one. Lucretia turned me and then I turned another agent. Someone already on the roster. So you get two out of the operation. You chose her because you knew I was susceptible to women like her. Clever girls I was never able to get. Smart and sexy girls. Tough girls. You profiled me. From the girls I watched on the bases. You knew the type to put near me after Lucretia tried me out. You bastards. You sick, scheming fucks. I'll never work for you. Never.'

Hooper grinned. 'Now I knew those cuffs would come in handy. You pull any more and they'll go right through your wrists. But first-class work, Frank. First class. And finally you're thinking like agency. Second guessing. If you weren't so single-minded in your pursuit of ass, you could have worked it all out a long time ago. But you pussy hounds are all the same. Just don't think.'

'But Agent Kram is innocent. She's –'

'Not like you? Think again, Frank. Know how we found her? Your partner? She went after one of our own when she was Bureau. And she showed all the right credentials for this line of work. Like you, Frank, she had appetite. Wouldn't let no oath of allegiance stop her from getting some of what she wanted from a truly special man.'

The man in the boarding room who imprisoned, loved and transformed Ally Kram was agency then. Someone the FBI wanted caught: a criminal. They employed criminals. Never had Frank felt so insignificant. He experienced a childlike terror of everything around him. What had he become mixed up in? Bonded immortals who preyed on the vulnerable for sexual gratification and worse; the agency above every law, accountable to no one; and now the wildest and most perverse side of his nature would become his only purpose in a very long life. If there had been a gun within reach, Frank wondered whether he would have put the barrel in his mouth and pulled the trigger to stop the panic attack.

'You got to finish her, Frank.' Hooper was no longer smiling. 'This ain't over until you deal with what you started. And you better get used to it. Kill or complete, Frank. Kill her or complete her. That's the rule with the bond. When you fuck up and take too much, you got to kill or complete.'

'And if I complete her?' His voice shook because his throat felt it had closed down.

'Then she's going to be with you always.'

'This is impossible.'

Hooper's hideous grin returned. 'Come on, it's not so bad. You saw something in her you liked. Admit it. And she's perfect for you. She's so like you, Frank. And real pretty too. Most men would do anything to have a sweet little thing like that chasing them all over town, for ever.'

'But I'm not like most men.'

Hooper smiled. 'You're learning fast, Frank. Real fast. But it'll be like an arranged marriage, Frank. For both of you guys. You see, that's why we need you. You got to fuck your way into people's heads. That Watergate shit is old school. This is the new age of state security, Frank. It's all psychic now.'

'I don't want to hear another word until I've seen Lucretia.'

Hooper nodded his ascent. 'Guess you about ready, boy. Reckon so.'

238

Twenty One

'Hello, Frank.'

So she had come back to him, but for how long? A new agony introduced itself to Frank's existing pain and uncertainty. Sitting up on the bed in the bare room, where Starr had finally taken him so he could rest, Frank tried to fill his face with all the emotion of a victim so Lucretia would feel guilt, and then sympathy.

Such a reaction was expected by her: she recognised it because she had seen it before, many times. Beside the cot – an old hospital bed with an iron frame painted white – a solitary chair completed the furnishings of his cell. Her body was hidden within a long woollen overcoat, the dark colour making her hair disappear where it fell across her shoulders. Lucretia sat down on the chair and crossed her legs. Frank moved his hands into his lap so she would see his cuffs.

'They will come off soon and you will be free again.'

'Free?' he said. 'You call this freedom? My body and mind have been irreversibly altered without my consent. I'll live an unnaturally long life cursed with the pain and longing of a broken heart. And I'm to serve these evil sons of bitches for every second of that sentence. Freedom doesn't come into it. You did this to me. You said you would be with me for ever. Said you loved me and now I'm frightened and sick and alone with my hands chained together. You bitch. You fucking bitch.'

Lucretia smiled. 'Like me, Frank, part of you enjoys this pain. No? In self-pity we are tragic figures but also heroic. It absolves us of greater responsibility to anyone or anything but our pain and the temporary relief of it. Our pain is a kind of freedom. It is the way of the bond. And you were right for it.'

'Bitch!'

'Tell me this, Frank: if I gave you the choice to be free of it now, would you have me take it away?'

Outraged at her assumptions, Frank could not speak. His face shook with emotion. Then he felt himself washed through by a grief that made him feel sick: the despair of the sentenced. She was right. 'What about us?' he asked, but his voice had weakened to a whisper and he had to swallow a lump in his throat to get even that out.

'We will always be together, Frank. Always touching in the deepest part of ourselves. I told you this once. It was no lie.'

'A memory? That's not what I want. I'd rather be dead if that's all you can give.'

'You have become me. It is all you are allowed. I cannot be with the one who bonded me, because he is bonded to another in turn. But I feel him inside me. Every day I feel him. This is the way.'

Tears welled in Frank's eyes. 'Damn you! Pretending to love me so you could recruit for them –' He shook his cuffed hands, pointing them at the door. 'So don't say you had any feelings for me. Nothing was real.' His voice failed and he could not continue.

Until he stopped sobbing, Lucretia remained silent. 'I loved you as much as I was able. You are the first I have bonded with since Eldrin. And it is especially difficult for us to bond in this way, with a sacrifice. Chance must be involved. It must come from the hunt. But you . . . With you it was different.'

'What about Crow? You telling me you love that piece of shit?'

'He reminds me of the first one who bonded with me. As do you. He played a role to engage your sympathy with me. He has another side. A wonderful side. There is nothing more to say.'

Frank shook his head in disbelief at her candour and composure. 'And Kram? You got her mixed up in this, too. And I don't love her, so how do I bond with her. She'll be killed if I don't. It'll be on your hands.'

Lucretia smiled. 'She is more like me than you can imagine. In time you will find me in her.'

Frank's voice rose and became more shrill the more he recognised her effortless acknowledgment of his plight. 'How do you know that?'

'Because you once dreamed of a man who gave her the taste for this life. In a room in a boarding house. He kept her for a week. That man was Eldrin Crow.'

'No.'

Lucretia nodded, her face solemn. 'She has fallen in love with you because you remind her of Crow, the fugitive who made her faint from the pleasure he gave. It is why she hated you at first, because you made her remember Crow and his betrayal of her, and his destruction of her life. But she could not help herself. Eventually she became your lover – she had no choice. None of us do. We are prey to something far deeper.' Lucretia paused and lit a cigarette. 'Your betrayal of her for me was too much. It's why she tried to kill you in the apartment. At that moment, I knew she was right for you. And Crow only took her in that boarding house because he too looks for me in other women. In Ally Kram, he found part of me. Frank, we are all connected. You and Ally are shadows of the love Eldrin and I share. And we are the futures you will discover.'

Clutching his face, unable to speak as he fully comprehended the extent of Lucretia's manipulation, Frank rocked back and forth on the bed. She had even chosen a replacement for herself. 'Is this not an act of love?' Lucretia asked him, her voice gentle. 'To replace the one you mourn? You talk of your pain, Frank. I lived through mine for seventy years until I found Eldrin. Heartache like that you will never know if you take this girl for your own.'

'But why the agency? Why?'

Lucretia looked at her gloved hands, folded in her lap. 'It is a regrettable connection. But we have only survived for so long because of secrecy. Our secret is not one we can easily keep. Not now. It became a nomadic life. A hunted life. But the agency offered protection. Shall I say, they were preferable to our former masters. Now we can travel anywhere and never worry about security. In return, we must serve their needs.'

'But they are evil, Lucretia. We are evil.'

She inhaled deeply from her cigarette. Her eyes narrowed behind the white smoke. 'Evil? The idea of what is wrong changes, Frank. And this life is long.'

'Will I ever see you again?'

'It is unwise to seek the one who gave the bond. At times it will feel impossible not to do so, and sometimes this happens. But it will lead to the greatest misery of all. The search brings despair, then madness and finally death.'

242

'I cannot accept that.'

'It is your choice. I think you will make the right one.'

Slowly, the expression on her face changed. Frank could feel her eyes inside him. His resolve to fight her and this life began to falter. She moistened her top lip with the tip of her tongue. Even now, after all she had done and said, he could not resist her. Never had he felt such a loathing for himself. 'All I can offer of myself is this last time together,' she added.

Immediately, Frank rose to his knees on the bed, fighting the desire to succumb to her, determined to curse and then banish her. But Lucretia removed her coat and let it fall to the floor of his cell. Inside his teeth, he could feel the thump of his heart. Before him, the eternal freshness of her beauty cast its spell. Resistance and anger and pain vanished.

As he reached for her with cuffed hands, she took a step towards him. One of her legs whispered between his fingers and palms. Sliding his hand upwards, from the top of her knee-boot to her thigh, he found the warmth of her natural flesh above the glass of nylon. Pantyless and ready, no opposition met his fingers when they touched her sex. Lucretia bit her bottom lip. Frank slipped one finger and then another inside her. He swore her eyes grew from blue to black. Moaning, Lucretia rotated her hips so the ends of his fingers tickled her deep inside, while the width of his knuckles began to stretch the mouth of her sex.

Welcoming the return of the wild blood inside his head, Frank felt his whole body, no longer tired and sick, pull towards her. 'Have you missed the feel of me inside you?'

'Yes. With you it was always good. You can be gentle, but also hard. You can both submit and

243

assert.' Frank removed his fingers from inside her. Holding her hips, he guided her forwards. When she stepped out of her skirt, he put his mouth on her sex. Giddy with anticipation, Frank swore to himself he would always remember this taste of her in his mouth. And as he moved his lips through her wet floss, she spoke to him.

'Sometimes they will surrender. You will just take them. You know how it is done. In your eyes there is power. But there will be times when you must fall under their heels.' Frank circled his tongue around her spot. Her voice sounded breathless. 'As you have seen me in life and dream, so you must be.' Dropping her head back, she stripped her blouse from her chest. Reaching behind her back, she unhooked her black silk bra and let it drop to the floor. Glancing up her body as his mouth played with her sex, Frank saw her begin to tease her own nipples. Moving her hands in circles, she applied pressure to the pinky centre of her breasts with just the tip of her middle fingers.

'On the bed. Now,' she then said, her movements quick, her face on the verge of tears. Squashing his back against the wall, she put her feet near his head and stretched her body down the bed. Frank sucked the sharp tips of her boots with tears in his eyes: burning tears of remorse and grief and sweet relief. Her fingers unbuckled and unzipped. Breathing hard, she scooped his balls and cock from out of their hammock and into the cool air. The warmth of her mouth then covered his shaft to the root.

One leg straight, the other bent at the knee, she opened her sex to him. Needing no encouragement, Frank sank his mouth into her lips. They rocked back and forth on the bed, each of their faces lit with rapture. Their mouths became greedy for the taste of the other. Lavishing his mouth on her sex, Frank slid

244

his hands up and down the back of her thighs until her stockings felt hot. Forming a ring at the base of his cock with her thumb and finger, still tight in leather, Lucretia moved her head up and down so her mouth traversed every contour of his shaft. Around his sex, her lips appeared thicker and her lipstick developed a matt finish as the gloss was massaged into the skin of his cock. Occasionally, she would break from her meal and pant encouragement to the head busy between her thighs. 'Make me come, Frank. Make me come on your face.' To which he pressed at her clit with a stiffer tongue.

And they sucked at each other until their jaws began to ache, and to the point when Frank was forced to clench the muscles in his sex to prevent a flood inside her mouth. Only when Lucretia began to shake and groan – her smudgy mouth poised above the head of his phallus – did Frank allow the dam to break. His back arching, a cry escaping, he watched his seed pump over her chin and string between her lips. And finally, he felt it dollop inside her mouth.

Face flushed and eyes half-lidded, her own climax overwhelmed her with a brief palsy that made her body shudder. When it passed, she kissed his cock. The sight of her intensely sexual face, still sticky with his cream, initiated the stirring of his second erection. His mind gained some independence from the wretched intoxication it suffered at the sight of her. Part of him now wanted to use her with a vengeance – to exalt in her salaciousness and inconstancy, but also to feel a mastery before his mistress was lost again to another's bed.

Sensing the irrational in her lover, and knowing how it boiled into his mouth so he could taste it, Lucretia smiled and relaxed her long body against the mattress. It was an invitation and challenge for Frank to do with her as he wished. 'You slut,' he whispered, rising to his knees.

Spreading her arms and rolling her head about until strands of hair streaked her face, Lucretia basked in the display of his jealousy and desire – an ecstasy in men she adored and felt adored by. It brought her closer to something savage and sometimes dangerous in her lovers. Before her, Frank could only feel himself as innocent and insignificant – her life had been long. Could he comprehend the scope of her experience and the reach of her desire? But this sense of her power fuelled his lust and nearly made him blind. He'd always dreamed of finding and then succumbing to a sensuality of such an intensity it would border on self-destruction. In Lucretia, he had found the opportunity. Instinctively, he had always known her desertion would be the inevitable conclusion of such an affair. Frank held her by the hips and dragged her down the bed towards his cock.

'Yesss,' she cried out – the word lasting as long as the passage of his cock through her. 'Hard Frank. Fuck me hard. With your beautiful cock you must be hard.'

She placed her ankles, still bound in the tight leather of her boots, on his shoulders so the side of her heels touched his cheeks. He leant over her body, his hands tight on her kneecaps, her legs resting on his shoulders and so her calves rested against his back. Using all the power in his hips, Frank thrust through her. His energy was infinite, breathlessness an impossibility, the sight of her pleasure-stricken face and freed breasts a lure to prevent a cessation in his fast, continuous, grinding occupation of her sex. Mastering her, mating with her, making her his own. From this moment forward, so many others would be seduced and then handled by him: that was her legacy, now alive inside him. Dozens of faces assembled in his imagination, each distorted in pleasure and sweet discomfort. Scores of breasts would leave their taste in his mouth. Hundreds of legs would be caressed by his hands. Wrists would be held down and buttocks would be spanked. He could see it all: his future. His new life: an eternity of respite from Lucretia through them. 'Yes,' Frank cried out, momentarily but finally alive to his destiny.

Lucretia became wordless. The cock took control of her. Penetrated, she was pushed and pulled around the bed, then hung off the bed, and was finally thrust to the floor. Finding her breasts, Frank's hands became firm but never clumsy. Their mouths formed a seal so tongues could freely lash. 'Use me,' she croaked. 'Be rough.'

Frank bit her neck. 'Come in me,' she pleaded.

'Now. Coming in you now,' he cried out.

Ten claws sank into the back of his arms. Her face was lost beneath her hair. Just the glint of an eye and the profile of her jaw could be seen. Around his buttocks her legs clamped, to hold him in place until his seed was delivered. 'Harder,' she yelled, so she would feel the ghostly impression of his thickness rifling through her for a few days yet. Legs locking, her mouth opened but not even a shallow breath escaped.

'Is it all inside?' she asked after catching her breath.

'Every drop.'

Their recovery was unnatural: she had not finished her cigarette before Frank was peeling the leather gloves from her hands and sucking her fingers. An erection was poised between his legs. As he unzipped her boots and kissed her hot legs, he began to wonder if his virility was due to Lucretia's almost supernatural beauty or the miraculous changes in his physiology that both she and the agency claimed he had undergone. He felt no fatigue in his muscles or shortness of breath.

'I caught you in time, Frank. You will never lack this vigour,' she said.

'What, you can read my mind now?' he said, derisively.

'Yes. You want to push your cock in my ass.'

Frank eyed her from around the ankle he kissed.

'Am I right?'

Frank pulled her on to all fours and kissed her buttocks. The very thought of tracing his tongue around an anus would ordinarily have made him wince. Now, he was unable to stop himself performing the act. 'You are right.'

Biting her fingers, Lucretia groaned. 'Slow. Go slow at first.'

'Can't stop getting hard for you. It could never be the same with others.' The idea fired a pang through his chest.

'It will be. In time it will be. The intensity of your life will be everything to you. Now, a little more. Go deeper.'

'You ask too much of me when I love you.'

Lucretia screwed her eyes shut. 'One of us even broke his original bond for the love of another. It had never been known before. Do not underestimate the bond, Frank. Oh ... That is good ... More.'

Half of his shaft was now packed into her rectum. Leaning on an elbow, she slipped her other hand between her legs and began to rub her sex. Sliding his fingers through her hair, Frank made a fist. Gently, he pulled her head back. 'Tell me you'll miss this.'

'Maybe, for a while.'

'No! Always.'

Lucretia showed him a sly and smiling face. 'No. There will be others in your place soon enough.'

Suddenly chilled by the horror of her confession, but feeling curiously dizzy at the same time, Frank remembered the sweet pain Eldrin enjoyed over her betrayals.

'See. You love the idea already. I can feel your pain. Think of me with all the others until you go crazy. Then you will hunt to relive the embrace of my ass.'

Seizing her hips, until the chain between his cuffs became taut, Frank slipped the rest of his erection inside her. She squealed and then began to laugh. 'Tell me, Frank. Tell me there will be others. So many others.'

'There will.'

'Take just enough. Listen to me inside you. Obey the instinct. Only take more when you know it's right. Like you will with Ally. Bury your cock inside her soon. Then feed. Where there is love there must be food. Forget this and you die.' Frank began to withdraw from the stranglehold of her anus, before a slow push back inside her. Lucretia gasped and spoke with increasing difficulty. 'Remember what you saw of Eldrin's suffering. He played the role well. What you saw is what you will be if you do not feed. And Ally will lose her mind soon if you do not go to her.'

As he thrust between Lucretia's buttocks with a greater vigour, he thought of Ally Kram: her need for restraints and torment before the intense surrender of prolonged penetration. 'She is wonderful,' he said before he could check himself.

'Fucking her is good, no? Oh, she likes it rough. And that beautiful red hair. You would be a fool not to take her.'

At Lucretia's bidding, visions of pantyhose bindings and of Kram's mouth sucking on a ball gag spilled into Frank's head. 'Yes!' he cried out, and as his thrusts became harder Lucretia's questions shortened.

'You will take her like this.'

'This hard. Yes. Harder?'

'Yes! Frank, yes!' The sides of the bed banged against the painted brickwork. It felt like the whole world was moving under Frank's knees.

'I'll take her in this place. Like this. After a cane has been put across her buttocks.'

Lucretia made a chesty groan and then began to gulp for air as she came. Together they shared a vision – the binding and bonding of Agent Ally Kram. Frank felt the sap begin to rise through him. In less than a second it was boiling inside his shaft.

'Love her hard, Frank. Fuck me. Fuck her. Make her your own. Make her love you always.'

Falling across her back, Frank flattened Lucretia's body against the bed. Muscles contracted inside his sex. Unstoppable, the pump began and soon the very last of his vitality cooled inside Lucretia.

'Love you,' he murmured. Half asleep, he became lulled into a deeper state of rest by the lapping of a giant cat's tongue. Lucretia had disentangled herself from under his body and now she fed. Purring, she engorged herself on her progeny for the last time. From him, she drained the last of his innocence, and the last of his resistance to her legacy. It tasted good.

Hours later, the chill of her absence woke Frank.

Twenty Two

When he entered the room, she wouldn't look at him.
There was something deliberate in the way she stared
at the floor. Her eyes were too fixed and she smoked
the cigarette far too quickly: she knew it was Frank
who had come in and closed the door. Sitting on the
edge of the bed, near the pillows at the end furthest
away from the door, Agent Ally Kram wore the same
pistachio suit she had worn the day the investigation
ended. Frank remembered how she looked – legs
apart, face frozen in hate, arms forward, white fists
squeezing the gun – but no longer thought of her with
repulsion. Back then, she was keeping him from the
one he loved. Now, her heart was broken in the same
way as his, because of the one he loved. Sympathy
filled him, a sense of responsibility was there too. The
latter he had refused to acknowledge before now
because it got in the way. But most of all, Frank was
hungry. It seemed an age since he fed from sweet
Alice. The interrogation followed by Lucretia's fare-
well visit drained him further. Sleep deprived,
anxious, strung out, he now looked at Ally Kram in
a different light.

Her sulk suited him; it gave Frank time to stare at
her legs, so slender, the skin beneath her sheer hose
lightly freckled. With her jacket removed, the white

shirt she wore appeared especially tight over her milky breasts. And beneath the long red tresses, her pale throat he knew to be warm, soft as a lamb, nothing but a thin shield to a sweetness that would slake his sensual thirst.

'You know?' he asked, angling his head to steal a better look at her shapely feet.

She nodded.

Frank tried to chuckle, but the effort exhausted him. Sustenance: where there is love there is food. 'Played us for a couple of human mice.'

Ally sniffed and drew on her cigarette.

Frank approached the bed. Carefully, he sat down at the other end. Her body tensed. Now he could smell her fully. The perfume of vulnerability filled his lungs and head. He thought of her bound in that boarding house and then thought of the first night he visited her hotel room; how she arched into his body, pushing her sex over his cock, like it was she who penetrated him, or at least seemed to want to. Excessive sensation, totally alive to all feeling, abandoning self and responsibility through submission; an extraordinary woman. Between his legs, Frank began to feel heavy. His face felt hot and his skin became so sensitive he swore he could feel each air molecule jostling against his body. Anything for this woman; he would promise anything for just a taste.

'You look good,' he said. Wrong thing. Ally shook her head and then stared at the wall. 'I'm sorry,' he added. 'I mean it. It's all been so crazy. I've been crazy. They were too good for me. I walked right into the whole thing.'

'Tell me about it.' Her voice was quiet, but Frank sensed a reconciliatory tone.

'It became our destiny long before we had a clue. Everything felt like chance, but we were just being directed all along.'

She nodded and then wiped an eye.

'But you know, it's so good to know I'm not alone in this,' he said.

Ally let her hair fall across her face so he could not see her reaction, but the attempt at concealment said it all.

'We have a big decision to make, Ally. It's pretty fucked up now. Will be for a long time yet, I guess. But ultimately, I think we have a real chance at something here. It's a journey so few have travelled. I have to try it. Are you coming?'

She moved quickly and was in his arms before he could flinch. For a while she sobbed against his chest. Defeated by her most intimate self, she could not help loving someone she wanted dead for loving another. Frank sensed the frustration and the anger. The poison needed to come out; she needed to be broken down before she could rebuild anything of herself. And he had to take a lover, had to bond with Ally Kram. It was a trap and they were still working their way through the agency's labyrinth of deceit.

Massaging her neck with his fingers, Frank then slipped his hand into her hair. He turned her face upwards so he could see those fierce green eyes. With a cry, Ally pushed her mouth into his. Tightly, they gripped each other's bodies and fell back on the bed. Letting go of the bewilderment and guilt and self-loathing, they worked quickly. Untucking, unbuttoning, unzipping, tearing, tugging, yanking: she reduced him to a naked man driven by a thick cock and he stripped her to a pretty girl in white lingerie.

Rolling her pantyhose down her legs, he then spanked her backside until she moved on to her front and into position. Down came her panties and after snapping them off her toes he threw them against the wall. Around her wrists he bound her hosiery, until her hands were rendered useless. Seizing her hips he pulled her up to her knees. 'You're so wet. Ready for me?' Frank asked with two of his fingers moving deep inside her.

'Bastard. Fuck me. Finish this. Just get inside me,' she answered, panting with emotion. 'Oh yes. Oh yes. Force it. Force it, damn you.' Holding her by the waist, so his spread fingers felt imbued with the power to pass completely around her middle, Frank pushed his cock inside Kram. Widening her quickly and then pushing to a depth, the suddenness and volume of his penetration made her whimper. Her elbows gave way and her face fell into the pillows. Over her back he climbed and with all the power in his hips he dug inside her. When all of his sex was buried, he pushed on and ground his groin against her buttocks. 'You're going to be mine,' he said, carried away by the danger of encouraging her passions. 'All mine. I'm taking you as my own. Going to bond with you.'

Her eyes filled black with pupil and her mouth chewed and then spat pillowcase. Thumping his body against her, Frank felt his cock engorge her until she became weightless and strengthless; her slender white body allowed itself to be used and shaken and twisted to accommodate the positions he exploited to enjoy her body. On her side with one leg in the air, his hand behind her knee, he was able to inhale her hair and bite her neck while rifling through her. Feet on his shoulders, her knees bent, he plunged to the back of her womb and watched her suffocate with excitement. Legs around his waist, his mouth pulling at her nipples, he nudged her up the bed until she had to press her bound hands against the wall to prevent herself from being squashed. Blind with the single desire to drive himself to a paralysing ecstasy, Frank took her body across every square inch of bed. Then to the floor, then up in the air so she bounced off his stomach while he walked her around the room.

'Bastard. I should have killed you,' she swore, with hair plastered across her face and the skin of his shoulders squeezed between her red nails.

'You should have done. Every day I'm going to make you hurt for me.'

She tried to club his face, but Frank caught her hands and then thrust into her so hard she became wordless, pulling her own hair with hands tied together.

'There are so many things we can do,' he whispered into her hair, when his body pinned her to the bed once more. 'You'll dress for me.'

'Yes.' She spoke but her eyes were closed.

'Restraints will be used, often.'

This time she never answered but clawed at his chest as if she wanted more restraints brought to her at once.

'You'll suck me on your knees and accept me in your ass.'

Legs locking, head twisting in the sheets, nails drawing blood on his neck, Ally Kram lost herself in climax. Pumping wave after wave of his seed inside her, Frank put his mouth to her throat and suckled until she passed out. Power surged back through his body, fired out from the heart into the blood vessels, to the muscles and to the cells. Exhaustion and despair became euphoria and peace. They were together, for ever. But he'd think about that later.

Ally was asleep when Frank left her room and took a shower in the washroom further down the corridor from where they had been confined. When he ventured into the hangar, Hooper was waiting for him. Seated as usual at the same table, and smoking.

Agent Starr was nowhere to be seen, but one of the black Sedans was idling before the roller doors. They had been opened a fraction to allow the exhaust fumes to escape.

'Don't look so pleased with yourself,' Frank said. 'Could it have gone any other way?'

Hooper smiled. 'I believe congratulations are in order. You two will make a fine couple. We got all kinds of plans for you.'

'There's a fuckin' surprise.'

'One day you might even look back fondly on our association.'

Ignoring the offer of informality, Frank sat in the chair opposite Agent Hooper. 'So what's next?'

'We're leaving you the second car. Everything you need for the next couple of weeks is in the trunk. Clothes and shit.' Hooper pushed a leather flight bag across the table. 'Passports and new driving licences inside. Plus credit cards and cash. You and the wife get some R'n'R for a couple of weeks and then you start earning. Your itinerary is in the car. All the arrangements have been taken care of. We sending you on a honeymoon to Vegas. We got some old friends there who gonna look after you.'

'She's not my wife.'

'Whatever you say,' Hooper said, smiling. 'Details for the new assignment will be posted to your hotel in Vegas.'

'Who we going after, the Russians?'

Hooper laughed. 'Get out of the eighties, man. You think we'd trust you with any of that James Bond shit? We gonna break you in real easy. And then you're gonna meet a lot of successful women, Frank. Plenty of them are calling the shots now and we can't get to them through the old methods. They're too smart. Was a time we could get a guy in a motel room with a hooker, or make him lose big at the tables and then he was working for us. But these career girls? Whoa. They're something else. It's where you come in. Find out what they're missing. What they want. Then you step up to the plate and get them hooked. A challenge for you, Frank. Your speciality.'

Frank looked away from the agent and into the dark. 'She gone?'

'Lucretia?'

'You know who.'

'Long gone. But don't you go foolin' over her, boy. That's a whole world of hurt you don't want. Between me and you, she's poison. Now, little Ally? She's a fine young thing.'

Frank stared at Hooper with all the loathing he could muster into his face. 'Did I ask you for your opinion?'

Hooper smiled and held his hands up. 'Easy, champ. Just looking on the sunny side.' He stood up. 'That's all I got to say. Lucretia filled in any gaps and I got to fly, Frank. You take care now.'

Sitting still and silent, Frank watched the agent walk away from him and towards the idling car. He swallowed; it was as if his last living link with Lucretia had been broken. In the distance, he heard Ally call out to him in her sleep.

NEXUS NEW BOOKS

To be published in December

VELVET SKIN
Aishling Morgan
£5.99

Henry Truscott, hero of *The Rake* and *Purity*, returns in *Velvet Skin* to continue his habits of indulgence and dissipation. There are ample opportunities in eighteenth-century Devon for an imaginative aristocrat to pursue his perversions. Even so, Henry manages to find himself in trouble – like being caught pony-carting by the local vicar, for example. But the fiendish, rapacious Lewis Stukely, a neighbouring landowner, makes Truscott look like a monk – and Stukely has designs on Suki, Truscott's beguiling servant-girl.

ISBN 0 352 33660 9

THE BLACK FLAME
Lisette Ashton
£5.99

For private investigator Jo Valentine it is a surveillance operation unlike any other: a coven of witches practising orgiastic pagan ritual; a sadistic preacher intent on extracting penance from every nubile young sinner who falls beneath his cane; and an ongoing feud with her submissive partner. Caught in the midst of this volatile situation, alone, bound and helpless, Jo is subjected to a dark revelation in the pleasures of pain. Tied, teased and tormented, she is immersed in so many sexual excesses that it borders on being a religious experience. The next volume in Lisette Ashton's series of bestselling erotica.

ISBN 0 352 33668 4

BAD PENNY
Penny Birch
£5.99

Penny Birch is a very naughty girl, and this collection of stories shows just how far she'll go to prove it. It begins with her sexual awakening and goes on to cover the most erotic episodes of her life as her love of sexual submission develops and becomes increasingly complex. Always enthusiastic, she delights in the strange and imaginative, often finding herself tied up or having her bottom spanked. As these accounts of her perverse pleasures unfold, you'll come to realise just how bad she really is. A Nexus Classic.

ISBN 0 352 33661 7

To be published in January

REGIME
Penny Birch
£5.99

Anabelle is the perfect Mistress, and determined to prove it, claiming she can make a submissive woman yearn to be not just her plaything, but her property. Penny is talked into taking up the challenge, to be put through Anabelle's regime of elaborate sadism and to try to resist the pain, the pleasure and the mind games. At the farm purchased by Anabelle and her boyfriend, Penny is systematically brought low, made into a servant, stripped of her volition and her liberty, treated as a wild animal, and at last made into Anabelle's pet. By the end she is close to breaking point, and needs only to make the final act of submission.

ISBN 0 352 33666 8

SLAVE ACTS
Jennifer Jane Pope
£5.99

The fourth book in Jennifer Jane Pope's *Slave* series continues the story of the bizarre establishment devoted to the satisfaction of specialist tastes, hidden from prying eyes on a remote Scottish Island. Here, the rich can indulge their every desire, from SM power games to pony-girl carting, assured of the utmost discretion. But why do so many of the slaves look the same?

ISBN 0 352 33665 X

DARK DELIGHTS
Maria del Rey
£5.99

In this anthology of short stories Maria del Rey once more demonstrates her love of the bizarre and the power of her erotic imagination. Superbly written, original and highly arousing, this collection revels in the forbidden, taking the reader on an intimate journey through the world of dominance and submission. Recalcitrant secretaries, naughty girls, fetishists and submissives come face to face with the bitch mistresses and strict masters of their darkest and deepest desires.

ISBN 0 352 33648 X

If you would like more information about Nexus titles, please visit our website at www.nexus-books.co.uk, or send a stamped addressed envelope to:

Nexus, Thames Wharf Studios,
Rainville Road, London W6 9HA

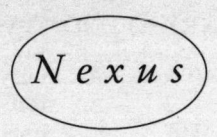

NEXUS BACKLIST

This information is correct at time of printing. For up-to-date information, please visit our website at www.nexus-books.co.uk

All books are priced at £5.99 unless another price is given.

Nexus books with a contemporary setting

ACCIDENTS WILL HAPPEN	Lucy Golden ISBN 0 352 33596 3	☐
ANGEL	Lindsay Gordon ISBN 0 352 33590 4	☐
THE BLACK MASQUE	Lisette Ashton ISBN 0 352 33372 3	☐
THE BLACK WIDOW	Lisette Ashton ISBN 0 352 33338 3	☐
THE BOND	Lindsay Gordon ISBN 0 352 33480 0	☐
BROUGHT TO HEEL	Arabella Knight ISBN 0 352 33508 4	☐
CANDY IN CAPTIVITY	Arabella Knight ISBN 0 352 33495 9	☐
CAPTIVES OF THE PRIVATE HOUSE	Esme Ombreux ISBN 0 352 33619 6	☐
DANCE OF SUBMISSION	Lisette Ashton ISBN 0 352 33450 9	☐
DARK DELIGHTS	Maria del Rey ISBN 0 352 33276 X	☐
DARK DESIRES	Maria del Rey ISBN 0 352 33072 4	☐
DISCIPLES OF SHAME	Stephanie Calvin ISBN 0 352 33343 X	☐
DISCIPLINE OF THE PRIVATE HOUSE	Esme Ombreux ISBN 0 352 33459 2	☐

MAIDEN	Aishling Morgan ISBN 0 352 33466 5	☐
NYMPHS OF DIONYSUS £4.99	Susan Tinoff ISBN 0 352 33150 X	☐
THE SLAVE OF LIDIR	Aran Ashe ISBN 0 352 33504 1	☐
TIGER, TIGER	Aishling Morgan ISBN 0 352 33455 X	☐
THE WARRIOR QUEEN	Kendal Grahame ISBN 0 352 33294 8	☐

Edwardian, Victorian and older erotica

BEATRICE	Anonymous ISBN 0 352 31326 9	☐
CONFESSION OF AN ENGLISH SLAVE	Yolanda Celbridge ISBN 0 352 33433 9	☐
DEVON CREAM	Aishling Morgan ISBN 0 352 33488 6	☐
THE GOVERNESS AT ST AGATHA'S	Yolanda Celbridge ISBN 0 352 32986 6	☐
PURITY	Aishling Morgan ISBN 0 352 33510 6	☐
THE TRAINING OF AN ENGLISH GENTLEMAN	Yolanda Celbridge ISBN 0 352 33348 0	☐

Samplers and collections

NEW EROTICA 4	Various ISBN 0 352 33290 5	☐
NEW EROTICA 5	Various ISBN 0 352 33540 8	☐
EROTICON 1	Various ISBN 0 352 33593 9	☐
EROTICON 2	Various ISBN 0 352 33594 7	☐
EROTICON 3	Various ISBN 0 352 33597 1	☐
EROTICON 4	Various ISBN 0 352 33602 1	☐

Nexus Classics

A new imprint dedicated to putting the finest works of erotic fiction back in print.

AGONY AUNT	G.C. Scott	☐
	ISBN 0 352 33353 7	
BOUND TO SERVE	Amanda Ware	☐
	ISBN 0 352 34457 6	
BOUND TO SUBMIT	Amanda Ware	☐
	ISBN 0 352 34451 7	
CHOOSING LOVERS FOR JUSTINE	Aran Ashe	☐
	ISBN 0 352 33351 0	
DIFFERENT STROKES	Sarah Veitch	☐
	ISBN 0 352 33531 9	
EDEN UNVEILED	Maria del Rey	☐
	ISBN 0 352 33542 4	
THE HANDMAIDENS	Aran Ashe	☐
	ISBN 0 352 33282 4	
HIS MISTRESS'S VOICE	G. C. Scott	☐
	ISBN 0 352 33425 8	
THE IMAGE	Jean de Berg	☐
	ISBN 0 352 33350 2	
THE INSTITUTE	Maria del Rey	☐
	ISBN 0 352 33352 9	
LINGERING LESSONS	Sarah Veitch	☐
	ISBN 0 352 33539 4	
A MATTER OF POSSESSION	G. C. Scott	☐
	ISBN 0 352 33468 1	
OBSESSION	Maria del Rey	☐
	ISBN 0 352 33375 8	
THE PLEASURE PRINCIPLE	Maria del Rey	☐
	ISBN 0 352 33482 7	
SERVING TIME	Sarah Veitch	☐
	ISBN 0 352 33509 2	
SISTERHOOD OF THE INSTITUTE	Maria del Rey	☐
	ISBN 0 352 33456 8	
THE TRAINING GROUNDS	Sarah Veitch	☐
	ISBN 0 352 33526 2	
UNDERWORLD	Maria del Rey	☐
	ISBN 0 352 33552 1	

------- ✂ ---------------------------

Please send me the books I have ticked above.

Name   ....

Address   ....

          ....

          ....

          .... Post code ....

Send to: **Cash Sales, Nexus Books, Thames Wharf Studios, Rainville Road, London W6 9HA**

US customers: for prices and details of how to order books for delivery by mail, call 1-800-805-1083.

Please enclose a cheque or postal order, made payable to **Nexus Books Ltd**, to the value of the books you have ordered plus postage and packing costs as follows:

UK and BFPO – £1.00 for the first book, 50p for each subsequent book.

Overseas (including Republic of Ireland) – £2.00 for the first book, £1.00 for each subsequent book.

If you would prefer to pay by VISA, ACCESS/MASTER-CARD, AMEX, DINERS CLUB or SWITCH, please write your card number and expiry date here:

....

Please allow up to 28 days for delivery.

Signature ....

------- ✂ ---------------------------